Praise for *Next of Kin*:

Breaking new ground, be it cultural, locational or relational, is fraught with challenge. Add vulnerability and danger to the mix and you have the makings of a thrilling story. The characters and situations Carol Preston explores in Next of Kin provide a terrific story about overcoming prejudice, adversity and tribulation, all within the context of a blossoming, realistic, love story. It's a fabulous read. I highly recommend this book.

Mazzy Adams on Goodreads

I always find the context of Carol Preston's books very interesting and this is likewise the case with Next of Kin. The story reveals the many of the problems that were prevalent at this time in history, some of which are still with us. The book also deals with the age old problem of overcoming bitterness through forgiveness.

Sue Barnes (Australian Christian Readers Blog Alliance)

Beyond the Fight

Copyright © Carol Preston 2016

Published by Rhiza Press
www.rhizapress.com.au
PO Box 1519,
Capalaba Qld 4157

National Library of Australia Cataloguing-in-Publication entry :
(paperback)
Creator: Preston, Carol, 1948- author.
Title: Beyond the fight / Carol Preston.
ISBN: 9781925139365 (paperback)
Subjects: Australian fiction.
Dewey Number: A823.4

Beyond

THE

Fight

CHAPTER ONE

Baker's Gully, South Australia, August 1914

Something tightened around Mabel's throat like a vice and she sensed a huge weight on her chest. She threw her head back as hard as she could, but no matter how hard she tried to take a breath, nothing happened. Cold crept over her; voices spoke to her. They seemed a long way away. Moving, blurred images hovered above her. *Are they angels? Am I dying?* Although panic throbbed through her body and she sensed she might be close to death, the figures around her were comforting. She'd been to this place before. *Please God, let it end soon. Please don't let me die.*

'Through your nose, dear, remember? Breathe through your nose. Try not to gulp air through your mouth. That's it. Much better.' The doctor's voice became clearer in her hazed mind.

'Mabel, can you hear me?' Mother was mopping her face. 'We're here, Mabel. It's over, now, dear. Can you hear me?'

Mabel nodded as she felt air flowing into her nose and down into her chest. Her body sank into the mattress and gradually relaxed. She opened her eyes and her mother's face came into focus. The doctor was nodding. Father hovered in the background while Mother continued to mop her face and arms. It was all familiar. Tediously familiar.

She sighed loudly. 'I'm fine, Mother.' That and a thin smile were all she could manage.

'You're very pale.' The doctor moved in closer and picked up her limp wrist. 'You'll be tired, as usual. You must rest.'

'Is there nothing more that can be done, Doctor?' Mother moved from where she'd been sitting on the bedside, while the doctor listened to Mabel's chest and put a thermometer in her mouth.

He turned to her parents and shook his head. 'You know we're doing all we can. This was a nasty turn, but generally I think she's managing the attacks better these days. She's eighteen now–a young woman. It's likely she'll have to deal with asthma all her life. She knows what to expect. It's unpleasant but the important thing is not to panic.'

'That's easier said than done.' Mother shook her head. 'It's terrifying to see her this way. Sometimes I think she's never going to get another breath.'

'You have the drops I've prepared. Give her twenty or so every half hour for the next couple of hours. Ginger in a cup of tea will also help.' He looked around the room.

'I have the room cleaned thoroughly, and very regularly, Doctor.' Mother's usual distress at the thought that there might be dust or mould in Mabel's room was evident.

'Yes, I'm sure you have, Mrs Smart. We can't be sure it's not some allergen from outside, in the garden, or maybe something in the fields … wheat or the wattles perhaps. Some things can't be avoided altogether. Not when you live on a farm.' The doctor patted her arm. 'And she needs to keep calm,' he added, raising his eyebrows.

Mabel saw the look that passed between her mother and the doctor. *They think I'm overly emotional. That's what they assume causes my asthma.* She turned to her father and caught his eye, pleading with her expression for him to take charge of Mother. *He's used to dealing with her constant worrying.*

Father smiled and gave her a quick wink, then moved up behind Mother and took her by the shoulders. 'Now, Emma, come away and let the doctor finish up. No point in going over the same old ground. The crisis has passed now and you heard the doctor. Mabel needs to rest.'

Mabel was grateful. She hated having her mother and the doctor discussing her condition in front of her as if she were a bystander.

'I'll make tea,' Mother said, drawing in her breath. 'I need a cup myself.'

Within minutes of the three leaving the room, Mabel felt herself drifting into sleep, her final thoughts fading. *If only Mother realised that it is she who causes the most emotional upheaval in me. If she's not fussing about my health she's planning my future.*

***

Mabel had no idea how long she'd slept when she roused to the faint sound of voices in the parlour downstairs. She rolled to the side of the bed and pulled herself up, letting her legs drop to the floor. They were always a bit shaky after she'd had an attack. When she felt she could put her weight on them she stood and turned to her reflection in the dresser mirror. She pinched her cheeks to bring a bit of colour into them and ran a brush through her long dark hair. After draping a ribbon around her head and tying it at the back of her neck, she felt more ready to face her family. Just as she opened her bedroom door she heard her name being mentioned in the conversation downstairs. She paused and listened to her parents' voices. *More of Mother's plans for me, no doubt.*

'I can't imagine what Richard Grimwood would think of these turns, Albert. I've been praying she'd grow out of them by now. I'm sure young men on the land like to think the women they marry will be robust.'

'You surely don't think he'd want Mabel to be working in the fields?' There was a hint of amusement in her father's voice.

'Don't be silly, dear. I'm concerned with how Mabel will manage childbirth. Having a large family—sons to carry on the farm—will be paramount in Richard's choice, I'm sure.'

'Are you now? Well, I'm not so sure of that. It's certainly not what I thought about when I proposed to you.'

There was the clink of cups and saucers and Mabel realised she'd fallen asleep before having the tea her mother had gone to prepare. Her mouth felt parched and she opened her bedroom door further. Stepping out onto the landing, she checked that her legs were not still wobbly. She was about to descend the stairs and join her parents but paused when her father spoke again.

'Anyway, I doubt if marriage is what's on the minds of young men like Richard at the moment.'

The rustle of paper suggested her father was reading the newspaper, which meant it was likely four-thirty in the afternoon: his usual break from his business of overseeing their farm. Lately her mother had taken to joining him for a cup of tea and discussing what always seemed uppermost in her mind: the marriage of her children. The fact that Mabel's older sister, Clara, was still unmarried at the age of twenty-one was of great concern for Mother. Her brother, David, seemed less of a worry. He was just twenty and would one day inherit their substantial farm, so was considered a great catch. Mother clearly assumed she would soon be fighting off the girls who would set their caps at David, even though David showed not the slightest interest in marriage. Frederick was only thirteen, so his future had not yet been addressed, but plans were already being made for Mabel's young sister, Isabel, who was now sixteen.

Mabel's ruminations came to an abrupt halt when she heard her father's next words. 'This talk of war is uppermost in most people's minds and certainly in that of young men Richard's age. Everyone has their opinion on whether Australians should be involved in a dispute between Belgium and Germany.'

'Well, I think it's preposterous. No sensible young man here will give it too much thought. They have farms to run, families to provide for. What have we to do with what's happening in Europe?' Mother's voice trembled as she spoke. Mabel imagined she was gripping her teacup fiercely.

'Regardless of what you think, Emma, it seems young men are rushing to enlist.'

There was a gasp and Mabel wondered if her mother had fainted. She moved to the railing at the top of the stairs and peered over. She could see that the parlour door was partly open. *Perhaps now isn't the best time to go down.* Still, the idea of a war, in which young men Mabel knew might be involved, was a dreadful thought. She started down the stairs again, hoping her father would say more.

'What seems almost worse is this ridiculous notion that German folk here might be involved in some kind of espionage.' Father's voice faded away as if he were reading further.

There was a long silence before Mother spoke again. 'What if they were, Albert?'

'Pardon, dear?' Father sounded preoccupied.

'I said, what if they were? What if there were German people amongst us … spying?'

'Are you thinking of anyone in particular, Emma, dear?' There was a little sarcasm in Father's tone.

Mother coughed and cleared her throat. 'Not directly, but we do know families who have German connections. There are so many Lutheran churches here. That suggests that their background was German, doesn't it?'

'Possibly, but most of those families have been here for a number of generations. The idea of such people becoming spies for Germany the minute war is declared on the other side of the world is ludicrous.'

'What about the Hoffmans and the Wagners? Both families have stores in town.' There was another gasp from Mother and Mabel could tell by her tone that she was going to become dramatic. *If asthma was caused by not staying calm, then I don't understand why Mother doesn't have it.*

'Mabel was in school with Sophie Wagner and they're still close friends. Do you think there'll be trouble, Albert?'

Another long silence followed and Mabel assumed Father was ignoring Mother's foolish remarks when he spoke again with a very serious tone.

'I hope not, dear, but if this report is anything to go by, it seems there are plans afoot to round up German folk in the community and have them interned. It's outrageous, I say.'

'Interned? What does that mean?'

Mabel was at the bottom of the staircase, gripping the handrail. She began to tiptoe towards the parlour door before realising how foolish it was to be acting like a spy herself. She pushed open the door and entered the room, anxious to hear her father's explanation. Sophie Wagner was her dearest friend and the idea that her family might be affected by a war thousands of miles away, was unthinkable.

'Yes, Father, what does "interned" mean?' She slid onto a chair beside her mother.

'Mabel!' Mother spun towards her and grabbed her arm. 'What are you doing up? You're supposed to be resting. And why haven't you put on a dressing gown? You'll catch your death … I mean, you need to be rugged up. Your chest is– '

'Please, Mother. I'm fine. I want to hear what Father's talking about. I couldn't help but overhear when I woke.' She turned to her father. 'What does the paper say about the German people?'

Albert glanced at Emma and rolled his eyes. 'Well, I'm not sure if anything will come of it but apparently there is some worry about those here in Australia with German ties. Some silly notion that they might be co-opted in some way by the Germans to assist in the war.'

'But the Wagners wouldn't have anything to do with that,' Mabel said. 'Sophie's grandparents came here many years ago and they're both dead now. I don't think Sophie's mother had any German relatives.'

'Please stay calm, Mabel.' Emma gripped her arm tighter. 'You know what the doctor said. You mustn't get agitated.'

'I'm not agitated, Mother. I'm simply trying to understand.'

'Why don't you make Mabel that cup of tea, dear?' Albert said. 'With some ginger in it, as the doctor suggested.'

Emma nodded. 'She hasn't had her drops yet, either. I'll see to it.' She rose from her chair, patting Mabel on the shoulder. 'Clara should be back from the store soon.' She glanced at the clock on the sideboard and shook her head. 'The milliner's shop is not far from the Wagner's bakery. Clara took Isabel with her today as well. Why the girls insist on learning to make hats is quite beyond me. If my sister hadn't set up that business and put ideas into the girls' heads … Really, Albert, do you think–'

'I think Mabel could die of thirst before you get that tea if you don't go now.' He waved her away, then turned to Mabel and winked. His eyes were a soft blue and, though his fair hair was becoming streaked with grey, it was hardly noticeable.

Mabel thought her father looked much younger than his fifty-five years, unlike her mother, whose features were pixie-like and creased with worry lines. Her dark hair was now sprinkled with noticeable grey and although she was just a year older than Father, she was beginning to look aged.

'I'm sure there's nothing to worry about in regard to your friend, Sophie,' her father continued. 'It seems like a gross overreaction to me. Let's pray that those in power come to their senses.'

Mabel nodded. 'I hope so, Father, but what does "interned" mean?'

'Well, it seems there are some camps being set up so that German people can be housed there until this war business is dealt with. A bit like house arrest, I suppose. It appears some businesses in Adelaide have already been raided and searched, and some stores closed down. A few people have been … rounded up, is the term they use.' He shook the paper and huffed. 'I've never heard such nonsense.'

Mabel drew in her breath. 'But that's terrible, Father. Surely they won't do that here? The city is twenty miles away. The authorities can't possibly be worried about the few shopkeepers we have. And what about the farmers? They wouldn't be taken from their farms, would they?'

Albert shrugged. 'I imagine it will only be the men they intern, though I'm not sure how women and children could be expected to manage without their men. Let's wait and see what comes of it before we worry about people like the Wagners. As you say, anyone who came from Germany in that family passed away a long time ago.'

Mabel nodded and took a deep breath. A shiver ran up her arm. 'I am a little chilly, Father. I'll get my dressing gown while I'm waiting for my tea.'

When Mabel returned to the parlour, feeling snug in her dressing gown, her mother was laying a tray of tea and scones on the table.

'That's better, dear.' Emma smiled her approval. 'We don't want a repeat of this morning, do we?'

'So you think I have asthma from getting cold, Mother?' Mabel slid back onto her chair and cradled a cup of tea in her hands.

'I don't know, dear.' Emma sighed and sat down. 'It's not clear but we must take every precaution. A few drops of ginger in your tea and then take these drops the doctor left. Most of all, you must stay calm.'

'Of course,' Mabel said, glancing at the grin on her father's face. It was clear he agreed that the person in the family most likely to become agitated wasn't Mabel. Mabel didn't believe her asthma attacks were connected to her emotional state. She was sure it was something in the air, which was a disconcerting idea. She could control her emotions. There was no way to control the air.

If anything was going to test Mabel's theory it would be this news of war and the possible implications for people she cared about, like Sophie Wagner. The notion that Sophie or any of her family might be spies was laughable, but the idea that they might be taken off to some internment camp made Mabel feel sick in the stomach.

'I think I'll visit Sophie after church on Sunday, Father. I'd like to see if she's worried about any of this.'

Emma gasped. 'No, dear, I don't think that's a good idea at all.' She looked at Father pointedly, as if expecting support. 'Who knows what might be going on in their home? The authorities might be checking up on them. I think you'd best stay away for a bit and let things settle down. I'm sure people around here will be disturbed by all of this business.'

'Emma.' Father spoke sternly, and just as well. Mabel was about to interrupt her mother with her own objections to such a silly idea. Of course she would go and see if her friend needed support.

'There's no need for hysterics, Emma,' Albert continued. 'I'll make enquiries on Monday about what might or might not be happening for those in our community who are of German descent. We'll see what's to be done then. I believe there will be some community backlash over the suggestions that these people need any kind of internment. Most of the families who would fall in the category the authorities seem worried about, are upstanding and well-respected people who can be vouched for by many of us. It might be more difficult to establish credibility in the city but here in the country we all know each other well.'

'Exactly.' Mabel was quick to back up her father's sentiments. 'Sophie's family needs to know they have friends who will stand by them even if there are some who jump on the band wagon and get suspicious.' She brought her cup to her mouth and drew in a long drink.

Albert cleared his throat. 'However, until such times as I can find out if anything untoward is happening, it would be best if you held off visiting Sophie, Mabel. We don't want to make more of this than needs be. We may stir up suspicion by our concern when there may well be none.'

'But, Father–'

'Your father has spoken, Mabel,' Emma said. 'Let that be an end to it. Besides, I believe we've been invited to the Grimwoods for lunch after church on Sunday.'

Mabel sank back in her seat. Father continued reading and didn't look up at her again. Mother sipped her tea with a look of dreamy satisfaction on her face.

Please God, don't let my life be limited to worrying about asthma attacks and a future with the likes of Richard Grimwood.

CHAPTER TWO

Mororo, New South Wales, September 1914

A sting to his ear caused Percy to lurch sideways. A blow to his shoulder followed. A small rock glanced his arm and fell to the ground in front of him. *Someone is throwing stones at me!*

His first inclination was to turn and face his attacker but he knew that could well result in a blow to his face. He pulled his hat lower over his forehead and peered ahead. He was glad that his brother and sisters, whom he'd come to walk home from school, were well ahead of him. He could see that Connie was holding court as usual. At fourteen, and the eldest of his siblings still at school, she seemed to feel it her responsibility to instruct her younger brother and sisters about the importance of learning. He could just hear the tinkle of her voice in the distance. Fortunately, they would be unaware of what was happening behind them.

The next stone almost took off Percy's hat. He could hear others falling short of his body and ricocheting off the track. He hurried forward. *Surely they'll give up soon. It must be youngsters walking home, probably thinking it a lark to annoy a man on the road. They must have had a bad day at school.* His thoughts raced, his ire rising. He'd have liked to turn and give them a piece of his mind, but considered it wiser to ignore the prank.

'Pie, pie,' he heard behind him in a childish voice, which was carried away on a gust of wind.

Pie? Why on earth would they be yelling about a pie?

'Spy, spy.' The words were clearer this time.

Spy! He shook his head and almost chuckled. He wondered what they were being taught at school that would have them playing spy games. Unfortunately, his musings caused him to lose concentration and he turned his head just enough for a small rock to catch his cheek, close to his eye.

'Now that's enough!' He spun on his heels and called to the three boys who were about twenty paces behind him.

No sooner had he yelled when they ducked sideways down a track leading to properties by the river. He watched them scuttle away for a moment before his attention was taken by the grassy river bank down in the valley. A few cows meandered in the fenced fields. Two rough log cottages could be seen amongst the trees. He'd have considered making his way after the boys, who were still jostling each other and guffawing as they kicked up dust and stones along the track, but his thoughts had already moved to a comparison between their farmland and his own parents' holding.

Whatever possessed Dad to buy land two miles away from the river and on the side of the hill? The rain water is gone before it nourishes the land enough to produce good grass, so the few cattle it can sustain are barely worth the trouble. The crops we've tried are equally paltry. No wonder he has to supplement his income with wood cutting and work in the saw mill.

Percy's thoughts were interrupted by the sensation of blood trickling down his cheek. As he wiped it away he could feel swelling around his cheek bone and smarted at the pain his touch caused. He shook his head and headed for home, reassuring himself that his future was not in farming. He would not be a slave to the land, not even good land.

He'd spent time woodcutting with his father since the age

of twelve, keen at first to make some extra money and help his mother out, but the work was spasmodic and dwindling now with big companies taking over most of the forests and hiring permanent workers. Percy had resented having his schooling cut short because he was the oldest son, and now did everything he could to continue his education. *A man must surely do better at making a living if he uses his head.*

His mother was folding a mountain of washing on the table when he pushed open the front door. Two-year-old Laura and three-year-old Winnie were playing with wooden blocks in the corner of the room. He tousled the dark curls on the tops of his young sisters' heads before taking off his coat and hat.

'What kept you?' his mother said as he moved towards her and planted a kiss on her cheek. She looked up and gasped, dropping the shirt she'd been shaking out. 'What on earth happened to your face?'

Pushing the pile of clothes to the far end of the table, she banged her palm on the cleared end and pulled out a chair. 'Come here and sit down.' She turned towards the kitchen from which the clatter of crockery and the sound of Connie's voice could be heard. 'Connie,' she called. 'Please bring me a cloth and some hot water.'

'Don't fuss, Mum.' Percy hung his coat on the back of the door and wiped at his cheek. 'Ah.' He couldn't help grimacing as he touched the tender spot. 'It's just a scratch.'

When Connie appeared beside him with a bowl of steaming water he took the cloth from her hands and dabbed at his face. Connie grimaced at the sight of him and her mouth dropped open as if she were searching for something to say.

'Sit down and let me do that properly.' His mother spoke in a tone that said she didn't care if Percy was twenty-two years old, he was still her boy and she'd not be denied caring for him. 'You can get yourself back to peeling those vegetables for tea, Miss.' She waved a hand at Connie. 'Get Clarrie and Rita to help you when they've finished feeding the chickens. And make sure Dottie comes back in with them. She's likely to wander off.'

When Percy dropped onto the chair his mother plunged the cloth into the hot water and squeezed it out. He pulled back as she began her ministrations, but she persisted.

'Now tell me what happened. Did you fall?'

'Of course not. It was some silly boys throwing stones.'

'Why on earth would boys throw stones at you?' She dipped the cloth back into the water and squeezed it again.

He braced himself for more pain and closed his eyes. 'I don't know, Mum. I'm sure it was just a prank. They were yelling something about spies. Probably making up a game.'

Percy realised his mother had stopped sponging his face. He opened his eyes. The colour had drained from her face. She was a tiny woman, in some ways still childlike in her demeanor, but her face was too thin and lined, making her look drawn and older than her forty-two years. She worked too hard in Percy's estimation, trying to coax vegetables from hardened ground and milk from a cow that looked as weary and thin as she did. No matter how much work went into preparing the land, what it produced was never enough. They had to resort to trapping possums and rabbits, which made lean pickings at the best of times.

No wonder Mum has to save every penny, so she can buy decent vegetables from our neighbour's farm. Percy was thankful Mrs Lange was such a kind soul. Even though she was his father's cousin, there was no call for her to fill his mother's basket quite so full as she did, and charge so little for the food. Still, along with his gratitude to the Lange family, Percy also felt annoyed that his mother had to resort to what amounted to charity in order to feed the family.

'What is it, Mum? You look like you've seen a ghost.'

'You haven't heard the news, have you?' Her voice was almost a whisper.

'What news?'

'You're too busy reading about telephones and cars and other contraptions to keep up with what's happening in the real world.' She shook her head.

'Telephones and cars are the real world, Mum. They're the future. You know that the first automatic telephone exchange opened in Sydney a few months ago. Thousands of people now have their own telephone. You can talk to someone in Sydney or Melbourne or anywhere in between on one of those contraptions, as you call them. This year there'll be extensions into Adelaide, too. Just think what that means for the future.'

'I'll tell you what it means for my future, son. Absolutely nothing. Even if I knew someone in Sydney or Melbourne or Adelaide, I certainly wouldn't be talking to them through a wire. I've never even sent a telegraph and why would I when I'm perfectly capable of writing a letter? If I have something to say to someone whose face I can't see, I'll be using pen and paper for the foreseeable future, which may well be shorter than we all think.'

Percy huffed. He was relieved his mother had put down her cloth and dropped into the chair next to him, but disturbed by her last words. 'Don't talk like that, Mum. You'll be with us for a very long time. You may be weary but you're not nearly ready for the scrap heap.'

'I'm not talking about my future, Percy, but the future of us all.' Her eyes glazed over as she stared at the wall behind him. 'I imagine they've been discussing it with the children at school,' she said, as if talking to herself.

'What are you talking about?'

She reached for his hand and held it tightly in her own. 'Australia is at war, son.'

'People have been talking about war for three or four years.' He waved his arm, rejecting the news. 'All this nonsense about Australia supporting Britain in a war on the other side of the world. It's just politicians postulating, surely.'

'Not any more, love. Prime Minister Cook has given an undertaking that Australia will defend Great Britain. Young men are enlisting and training to go overseas. You see, even with your wonderful telephones, you're still slower to get news than I am.' She stood and picked up the newspaper from the sideboard. As she sat back down she spread it out on the table. 'Fred Lange gave me this when I picked up some vegetables this morning. He's worried and he thought your father would want to read it, even if it is a month old.'

'I didn't think Dad would be home until the end of next week.' Percy leaned over to better see the news article and read out loud. '"Prime Minister, Joseph Cook, pledges full support to the mother country. Britain declared war after Germany invaded Belgium on the fourth of August, breaking its 1839 agreement with Britain and France to respect Belgium's neutrality."' He squinted, then pulled the paper closer and smoothed it out. '"He presumed to speak for all when he added, *Our duty is quite clear—to gird up our loins and remember that we are Britons.*"' Percy shook his head as he read about the Prime Minister's plan to send 20,000 troops and to place Australian ships under the control of the British Admiralty.

'This is crazy.' He pushed the newspaper away. 'But you shouldn't worry, Mum. I'm sure it won't affect us here.' He huffed loudly. 'Remember we're Britons, indeed!'

'It's not being British that I'm concerned about, Percy.' She spoke now in hushed tones. 'Fred Lange says that we'll be considered Germans.'

'What?'

'You see here.' She tapped a passage further down the page. 'Germany declared war on Russia on the second of August and then on France on the third, and now Britain is involved. The whole world will be against Germany. And see here.' She pointed to a passage towards the bottom of the page. 'Before the first day was over, shots were fired at a German steamer in Melbourne.' She sat back and rubbed her eyes.

'This is awful, Mum, but I still don't see how it will affect us. You can't seriously believe we'll be considered Germans. Father was born here. Just because his father and grandfather came out from Germany over fifty years ago, no-one thinks of us as German.'

'I'm surprised Mr Lange is worried about all this,' he went on. 'He was born here, too, and his father died years ago. Besides, hardly anyone in the cities would even know Mororo exists. This is all happening a long way away from us, Mum.' He patted her arm. The distress on her face tugged at his heart. It was enough for her to worry about day-to-day survival. He hated to think she would worry herself about a war on the other side of the world.

'It's not so far away as you'd like to think, Percy.' Tears welled in the corner of her eyes. 'Fred told me that people are already being questioned. Shops are being raided. People who have German ties are being taken away to some kind of camp. There's been a rush of German people wanting to be naturalised. They want to become Australian citizens now, but it may be too late. People will be suspicious, even of those they've lived alongside for many years.'

'That's ridiculous. No-one could suspect us of being spies.' His voice faded as he remembered his ordeal on the way home from the school. *Surely not ...*

'This talk of Australians having to consider themselves British and fight for Britain shows just how deeply people consider their roots, Percy. When I was young ...' She paused and took a deep breath. Percy wondered if she was going to continue. 'When I was young discrimination against German people was very strong around the Clarence River. There was a large community of German immigrants who came out in the fifties to work around Grafton. There was trouble ...' Her voice faded.

'Mum, please don't cry. It's a long time ago. We're forty miles from Grafton now and over four hundred miles from Sydney where there might be any authorities looking for Germans.' He put his arm around her shoulder and squeezed it. 'Who around here would even know my grandfather was German? He died many years ago as a young man and we haven't been called Schmidt since then. No one would associate a name like Smith with the Germans.'

She reached out and touched his cheek. 'Apparently someone does,' she said, looking into his eyes. 'If what happened today is anything to go by, some people have long memories.'

'I'm sure those boys were throwing stones and calling out "spy", because they've heard these silly reports and I happened to be going by. Now, enough of this talk.' He pushed back from the table. 'You put that paper away and forget about this. No-one is going to round me up for being a German spy, I promise.'

'I hope not, Percy. Dear God, I hope not.'

***

The night Percy's father returned home, the talk around the table was dominated by his sisters, Ida, Vera and Connie, who, as usual, seemed to speak of nothing but getting married. Percy loved his sisters dearly but such talk soon bored him. He kept the younger ones entertained with stories while they ate their soup, and once they'd left the table to play in the fading light, his mind drifted to his own future. When the discussion turned to Germans and the war he tuned back to what his father was saying.

'The Langes have always held onto their pride in their German heritage. They wear it like a badge. It's one thing to work for them as a domestic, Ida, but the idea of engagement to anyone in that family at the moment is out of the question.' His features were wiry and angular, and when he frowned he looked quite fierce. Percy saw his sister shrink away and he wished his father wasn't so harshly spoken.

'Didn't I say it wasn't a good idea, Fanny, her going to work for Anna Dora?' He continued, turning to his wife with the same frown.

'Jack, please,' she responded with a pleading look. 'Don't start that again. Your cousin has been very good to us. I don't know how we'd have survived without her and Fred.' She turned back to Ida. 'You're only seventeen, dear. There's plenty of time to think about marriage. You've only worked for Anna Dora a short time. Do you think you know young John well enough to be thinking about a future with him?'

'Of course I do, Mum.' Ida flared up. 'They're a wonderful family. How could you doubt it?'

'Yes, they are,' Vera and Connie chorused, glaring at their father.

'No-one's questioning the goodness of the family.' Jack spoke sternly. 'Anna Dora and Fred have made a good life here. No family should take greater pride in being Australian. But they've never hidden the fact that they come from German stock and right now, I don't think that will do them any good. Until all this business about war settles down, I want you to be careful.'

'Do you really think there's going to be that much trouble, Dad?' Percy asked.

Jack nodded. 'Possibly. I've heard there's been an internment camp set up at the Holsworthy Military Camp down south and one at Berrima Gaol, near Sydney. Now there's talk of one at Trial Bay. That's too close for comfort.'

'But, like I said to Mum, most of those who came here from Germany are dead. Surely those born here won't be considered a risk.'

Jack shrugged. 'I've heard it doesn't matter if you were born here or not, whether you were naturalised or not. Those who have fathers or grandfathers from Germany are also suspected of being "enemy aliens" by some. There's a call for us all to notify the government of our addresses.'

19

'Jack, you can't.' Fanny's eyes flew open.

Percy reached across the table and took her hand. 'Don't fret, Mum. They say the war will be over by Christmas anyway, so they'll hardly have found most people with German heritage by then.'

Ida, Connie and Vera had gone quiet, their eyes almost popping from their heads as the conversation proceeded. Percy noticed tears rolling down Ida's face as she leaned into their mother's shoulder. 'It's not fair,' she said, her voice shaking. 'John and I are in love. We've talked about getting married next year. It's just not fair.' With this she pushed back from the table and ran from the room.

Vera and Connie followed on her heels and Fanny moved as if to go after them.

'Leave them,' Jack said firmly. 'Ida will have to adjust to the idea of waiting. By next year this could all be behind us, but right now I don't want her caught up in it. She might plan to marry and then find her fiancé taken off to prison.'

Fanny sighed as she settled back in her chair. 'I thought all the discrimination against German people was behind us. I can't believe it's coming back to haunt us now.'

'At the moment they're talking about selective internment,' Jack continued. 'They can't fit everyone in these camps, so they're targeting community leaders. Those who could have influence over others, I suppose. That might help us to avoid trouble, but people like the Langes stand out in the community. They've been involved in all sorts of politics and community projects over the years. Much like Wilhelm Fischer, Anna Dora's father, who got involved in council affairs right from when he and my father arrived here nearly fifty years ago. Made quite a name for himself, he did.'

'It's frightening, Jack.' Fanny looked at Jack with such pleading in her face that Percy sensed there was more to her fears than had been spoken of. He took her hand across the table again and when he squeezed it she turned to him, tears spilling from her eyes.

'It'll be all right, Mum. Won't it, Dad? Like you said, we're not prominent in the community, even if the authorities come looking around here. Mororo is hardly on the map.'

Jack nodded. 'If we keep our heads down this could pass us by without any trouble.' He looked into Percy's eyes. 'You've no inclination to sign up, then?'

'Sign up?' Percy was taken aback and felt his mother's grip on his hand tighten. 'You mean enlist to fight?' He shook his head. 'Not likely. I can't think of anything I've less inclination for.'

'Good.' Jack grinned. 'I've raised you to avoid fighting, not to go looking for it. The best thing a person can do at a time like this is mind their own business and that's just what I intend for us.'

Percy saw a look pass between his mother and father that again suggested something unsaid. He didn't want to worry them further but decided the time had come for him to voice his own plans.

'I've been thinking about my future as it happens.' He released his mother's hand and sat back in his chair.

'Oh?' She glanced at Jack's face, the furrows above her eyes deepening.

Percy went on, despite his father's apparent distraction. 'You both know I've been interested in the possibility of work in Sydney in the telephone business. Positions are opening up in installations and repairs, and now with so many young men opting to enlist, it would be a good time to make enquiries about–'

'The telephone business?' Jack cut in abruptly. 'You can't be serious. It's one thing to be interested in tinkering with such things–if they ever really take on–but to consider it as a job! You can't imagine you could ever support a family with an invention most people will never use.' His eyes darkened as he fixed Percy with a look of disapproval.

Percy drew in a deep breath. 'Better than with a farm that

barely feeds the crows!'

He regretted his words the moment they were out of his mouth. He'd always tried to respect his father even though he questioned some of his choices. There was no denying that Jack was hard working and above all, loyal to his family. Percy knew he'd always be able to count on his father to stand by him if he were ever in need. But he also knew, along with everyone else in the community, that Jack Smith was not a man who would accept being ridiculed or looked down on.

'I'm sorry, Dad.' He reached across the table to touch his father's arm but saw it jerked away. When he looked up into blazing eyes, he knew he'd wounded his father deeply. 'I didn't mean that. I know how hard you work. I understand that making a living from the land is what you've known and it's a fine occupation … if you're cut out for it. But I'm not made that way.'

'No-one's made that way.' Jack's tone was cold and hard. 'It's what you set your mind to. It's what you do because you have to.'

Percy nodded, watching for a softening in his father's expression. 'I see that's how it was for you, Dad, but it doesn't have to be that way for the future. There are other options now. Times have changed and will change more now with this war. People will turn their hands to other things, new inventions, different ways of doing things. Please, Dad. I want to do something other than farming. I want to use my head, my knowledge.'

'You think it takes no thought to run a farm?' Jack raised his eyes to the ceiling and slumped back in his chair. There was sadness in his voice now, as if he felt beaten, not by Percy's ideas, but by his own ideals. It was clear he hadn't made a success of farming and he was honest enough in his better self to admit it. It was a cruel truth and Percy felt grief for his father. He hadn't meant to shame him.

The moment passed as Percy watched his father pull himself

from his slump and sit upright again. 'Whatever you think of my efforts to support this family, it's going to be up to you in the future. You're the eldest. There's only you and Clarrie to carry on here, and he's only eleven. Your mother and sisters need you, especially when I have to be away. Running off to Sydney is not an option. It's your responsibility to be here.' He thumped his fist on the table, avoiding eye contact with Percy.

As his father rose and picked up his dirty plate, Percy's heart sank. He caught his mother's eye and saw her struggle. He knew she felt Jack's shame. She'd defended his decisions before, even though Percy knew she'd talked with Fred Lange about a better property and had been saving money in hopes of convincing Jack to move. Percy was sure his mother would find a way to do this without hurting her husband's pride. It was the kind of woman she was, and Percy loved her for her kindness and faithfulness. He also knew that she sympathised with his own desire to make a life of his own. He hated seeing her torn between the two of them.

Fanny stood and took the dirty dish from Jack's hands. She gestured for him to sit in his arm chair. 'I'll do this, love. You rest. I know your back is playing up. I'll get the girls to help me. I'm sure they've commiserated enough over Ida's disappointment. And don't worry about her. She can wait a while to make marriage plans. She has her whole life ahead of her.'

Jack nodded as he handed over the plates before heading for his arm chair. Percy noted that his father's shoulders were stooped and wondered if it was because of the two weeks of logging or his worry about the future of their farm.

'There's a chance I might get the job of running the ferry across the river at Harwood,' Jack said, taking up his pipe and tapping it on the ledge over the fire. 'It seems the man doing it now has taken ill.' He eased himself into his armchair. 'That would make a good change.'

'It would, Jack.' Fanny smiled 'That would be much easier on your back. I'm sure there are good changes coming. We just have to get through this war business and then we can get on with the future.' She turned to Percy, her face full of love and pleading for understanding. 'All will be well, son,' she said. 'You'll see.'

Percy nodded. 'I'll call the girls to help you. And I'll round up the young ones. It's almost dark outside. We'll need some more wood for the boiler so they can have baths.'

As he headed for the bedroom, Percy shook his head, annoyed with himself. *My timing wasn't good to bring that up, but there's a new world coming and I'm going to make the most of it.*

CHAPTER THREE

Baker's Gully, South Australia, December 1914

Mabel threaded her arm through her aunt's and waved over her shoulder at her mother and father before climbing into the carriage and settling herself on the bench seat.

'Thank you for inviting me, Aunt Sarah. You can't imagine how happy I am to be coming to your house today.'

'The pleasure is mine, my dear.' Sarah grinned at her and patted her knee. 'I've so many things to sort through and you'll be a great help. George was such a hoarder and most of his things I put in the back room, thinking the boys might want something later, but they've all gone from home now and I'm left with it.'

She sighed and shook her head as she clicked the reins and urged her horse forward. 'I hardly know where to start. I'm nearly sixty and the house is too much for me. I should have packed it up and moved to something smaller years ago. Your help is just what I need to get me going.'

'It's so sad that you lost Uncle George so young, Aunt Sarah. Thanks for asking me to help you pack up. We can help each other. I doubt Mother would have let me out of her sight without such a good reason. She hardly stops fussing these days. It's all this talk of war.'

'Lost him.' Sarah sniggered. 'It rather sounds like I misplaced my husband. In fact it was a relief to see him out of pain, dear. It was very bad at the end. Such a cruel disease. No, I think the good Lord was kind to take him, even though I've had to manage on my own these past twenty-five years. Just as well I was a good milliner.'

'You're a wonderful milliner, but you're also very brave. I can't imagine Mother managing without Father at all.'

Mabel studied her aunt's profile and noted the sharpness of her features, the strong forehead and determined set of her jaw. Greying hair escaped in wisps from the edges of her bonnet and she blew them away as if chasing naughty children. Her appearance was definitely more robust than Mabel's mother's fragile one, and it seemed Aunt Sarah's approach to life was more practical by far.

'Well, my dear sister feels the burden of living greatly,' Sarah said, confirming Mabel's own assessment. 'Any extra pressure on her would likely bring her undone. Now, tell me why you were so keen to come to my place today? Beyond wanting to help me, of course.'

'I do want to be helpful, Aunt Sarah. I wasn't just saying that to avoid going to the Grimwood's for lunch again. But truly, I'm so tired of Mother's constant plans to throw Richard and me together. He really is a boring young man.'

'I see.' There was another giggle from Sarah. 'I believe he fits his family quite well, but with two of our sisters already married to Grimwoods, I should think Emma would be satisfied. However, they're a very influential family in this area, you know, dear, and I'm sure your mother only wants the best for you.'

'So she says, Aunt Sarah, but how can it be the best for me to marry someone I don't even like, let alone love?'

'Love! That's a novel idea, getting married for love. It wasn't something our people considered a high priority, I'm afraid, Mabel. Marrying well, securing land, mixing with the right people, these were the values of my day.'

'You don't think I should marry for love?'

'Of course I do, dear, but don't tell your mother I said so. She'd never forgive me.'

'Didn't you love Uncle George?' Mabel asked.

'I grew to care for him. He was a kind man. But my father made it clear to me from an early age that he'd not approve of me marrying anyone with less land than he had.'

'That's a dreadful reason to marry.' Mabel twisted on the bench seat to better see her aunt's face. She couldn't imagine her own father saying such an awful thing to her about marriage. 'Did Grandfather Golder choose Father, too?'

'Let's just say your mother made it easy for our father by choosing well. There were fifteen of us children. We all knew Father's intention to make a good name for himself in the community. He wasn't a man to be crossed, so mostly we did as he expected. It made for a peaceful life.'

'He was very well respected in the church, wasn't he? Mother always tells me that he was a "pillar of society", and that we must carry on his legacy.'

'Dear Emma.' Sarah shook her head. 'She certainly was her father's daughter.'

'What do you mean?'

'Enough said, I think. Speaking of your Grandfather, do you mind if we stop in at the cemetery on the way home. I try to keep the flowers fresh on Mother and Father's graves. I suppose it's the least I can do as I live the closest of all the children.'

'Of course I don't mind, Aunt Sarah. I can't remember the last time I went to the cemetery. Mother doesn't like to visit the graves very often.'

'No, she prefers to think of Father and Mother as she remembers them: alive. Emma finds death even harder to cope with than life.'

Mabel wondered what had brought about such sharp differences in her mother's and aunt's dispositions and what had caused her aunt's obvious disapproval of her mother. She thought it presumptuous to ask such a question and decided not to for the moment.

'My other grandparents are buried at Clarendon and Kangarilla Cemetery, too. Perhaps we could visit those graves.'

After collecting flowers, they drove up Kangarilla Road and through the gates of the cemetery. Sarah was quiet and seemed to be thinking deeply about something. As they got down from the carriage and approached the graves, Mabel's thoughts turned to her Grandfather Golder, of whom she'd only ever heard good things from her mother. Now she wondered if there was another side to him.

'*Thomas Golder, died October 10, 1880, aged 75 years.*' Mabel read from the headstone. '*Thou shalt come to thy grave in a full age like as a shock of corn cometh in in his season (Job Ch.5 V.26).*' The words were scratched and a little hard to read.

'I know that's from the Bible, Aunt Sarah, but it's rather a strange thing to put on a grave stone, don't you think?'

Sarah nodded. 'Father chose it. He was ill for a long time before he died. There was little he could do physically, but he did plan his funeral down to the last detail, even the words that were to go in the newspaper. "*Died at Wayside Farm after a long illness born with Christian fortitude.*" His exact words.' She pulled wilting flowers from the small vase at the base of the headstone and began to arrange the fresh ones.

Mabel looked across at her grandmother's grave and read, '"*Lydia Golder ... died 1905.*" I was nine when she died. I don't remember much about her, except that she never seemed much bigger than me and she always wore that little blue hat to church, with the big bow tied under her chin. She lived for a long time after Grandfather, didn't she? Twenty-five years.'

Sarah chuckled. 'Yes, it seems to be the lot of many a woman to outlive her husband. Mother was nearly twenty years younger than Father. Just as well, I suppose, with all of us kids to care for. They were married in the mid-forties and Father was back and forth from the goldfields during the fifties. She had to manage on her own quite a bit. She was tiny, but also very strong in her own way.'

'Did Grandfather find much gold?'

'Enough to buy three sections of farmland. Much like your Grandfather Smart did. They both did pretty well at gold mining and both spent their takings on land, which is why they were so well established by the late fifties.'

Mabel moved towards her other grandparents' graves with a handful of flowers. 'Grandfather Smart died in 1874 and Grandmother lived another seventeen years. Just as well my grandmothers had lots of children to help them when they lost their husbands.'

Sarah nodded. 'They were tough women in those days. They had to help on the farm as well as raise the children, and they had none of the modern conveniences we have in our homes now. Just a daub and wattle hut with a few out buildings. The women had to help clear the land and plant, at least until their sons came along and could work with their fathers.'

'They all came out from England, didn't they?'

Sarah nodded. 'The Smarts came in 1840 from Somerset.'

'Did Grandfather and Grandmother Golder come at the same time?'

Sarah hesitated and fiddled with the flowers she'd just put into the vase on her mother's grave.

'Mother's parents, James and Sarah Dix, also arrived around 1840 when Mother was about twelve. They were well established when Father arrived in Kangarilla in '42. He married Mother in '46 and began farming wheat and potatoes, gradually building up his holdings. So you can be very proud of your grandparents, Mabel. Landed gentry they all became–despite their beginnings.'

Sarah's last words were almost a whisper, but Mabel didn't miss them. 'What do you mean, "their beginnings"?'

Again, Sarah hesitated as if choosing her words. 'Just that they began with very little and worked hard.' She pushed herself up from her mother's grave.

'Do you miss your mother, Aunt Sarah?' Mabel moved to give her aunt a hand up and was surprised at the agility with which she pulled herself upright.

'It'll be ten years next June since Mother passed. She was nearly eighty and a great companion and help to me after George died. She was an amazing woman, and yes, I do miss her. She didn't have an easy life. I tried to make it a little easier for her after Father died.'

'Why was it so hard when Grandfather was alive?' Mabel was sure there was more to her Grandfather Golder than she already knew.

Sarah shrugged. 'Having fifteen children meant she was almost always unwell or exhausted.' Sarah's face dropped and Mabel wondered if she was going to cry.

'I'm sorry, Aunt Sarah. I didn't mean to make you sad.'

'It's fine, dear. I don't get maudlin about the past. Mother survived and that's to be commended. My memories of our last few years together are very pleasant. I'm rather pleased she's not here to be witnessing so many young men going off to war, though. That would have broken her heart.'

'Yes, it's hard to believe it's happening, isn't it?'

'I can't imagine how awful it is over there on the front lines. It's bad enough here, what with young men racing off as if it's a picnic they're attending, leaving their fathers and mothers to tend the farms. Shopkeepers are profiting from it by raising prices and people are squabbling over their parentage. It's absurd if you ask me.' Sarah gathered up the spent flowers and threw them into the back of the cart.

Mabel nodded. 'I'm very worried about my friend, Sophie. Her father's been taken away to a camp on Torrens Island because his parents were German. He's lived here in Australia for years and he's a good man. He owns the bakery in Clarendon, or he did. It's closed up now and the rest of Sophie's family have moved to Adelaide. It's horrible that she's had to move. I miss her and I worry about her.'

'I'm sorry to hear all that, Mabel. It's terribly sad. Come on now, let's head for home and we'll have some lunch. You can tell me all about Sophie, but you mustn't worry too much. Everyone's saying the war should be over by Christmas, so perhaps she and her family will be home before too long.'

***

'Sadly, it doesn't seem like the war will be over soon at all. Not by the look of this report,' Sarah said as she read the newspaper over lunch.

Mabel looked up from her plate, her sandwich hovering in the air below her chin. 'What does it say?'

'That Australian troops have occupied another German possession in the South Pacific, the Island of Bougainville. It seems they previously took control of the German-owned island of Nauru.' Sarah shook her head. 'Sounds like the fighting is much closer to us than I imagined.'

'I thought it was all happening in Europe.' Mabel put her sandwich back on the plate. It seemed a dreadful thing to go about normal activities when so many young men were shooting at each other on the other side of the world. Or perhaps not so far away at all.

Sarah folded the newspaper and put it on the end of the table. 'Do you know if any of the Grimwood boys have enlisted?'

Mabel shrugged. 'I don't know. Father says a few of your young cousins may go and also Father's nephews. Father was one of thirteen so there are plenty of nephews to worry about. It's all they talk about at home. Mother is frantic that they'll all be killed, and she's especially worried that Richard Grimwood will go. I think she'd like me to marry him before that happens, so she doesn't have to worry about me being left on the shelf.'

'That's ridiculous.' Sarah huffed. 'You'd be risking becoming a widow before you bore a child. I can't believe even Emma would want that for you.'

'I don't want to marry Richard, not even if he goes to war and comes home a hero.'

'I'm not sure coming home a hero would make up for the horror of war, love. I feel sorry for any young men being pressured to go. Fighting Britain's battles doesn't make any sense, especially when so many of our forebears left there to come here and make a new life.'

Sarah's voice dropped and her next sentiments faded into a whisper. 'And some of them didn't even leave Britain willingly. The dreadful irony of history is sometimes beyond comprehension.'

Mabel sensed again that there was something her aunt was thinking but not saying.

'You do believe Mother wants the best for me, don't you, Aunt Sarah? I don't mean to imply that she doesn't care about me when I complain. I do love her, but I get frustrated when she presumes to know what I need or want. She's always so worried about me having an asthma attack. It's like my whole life revolves around it and I can't bear to think that will be so.'

Sarah took a long sip of tea from her cup and looked up at Mabel, her eyes repentant. 'Of course Emma wants the best for you, love. She worries about you too much, but that's what mothers are like. If you sense my disapproval of her, I'm sorry. I love her too, but we are very different people. We were so right from our earliest days, I'm afraid. I was the eldest girl in the family, and having four older brothers, I guess I became a bit of a tom boy. I had to, in order to survive their rough and tumble.' She laughed lightly.

'There were four more girls after you, weren't there? So it evened up in the end.'

'Yes it did, but I felt the girls coming along behind me were more and more fragile, and I got caught in the middle. I wasn't girlie like them and they liked to tease me. Especially Emma. She was a little princess and I always felt she was Father's favourite. Not that he had much time for any of us, really. He was always so busy with the farm. Emma seemed to be able to get his attention when no-one else could. I suppose I was a bit jealous.'

'But not now, surely. He's been gone for so many years.'

Nodding, Sarah went on. 'Don't get me wrong. He was a good man, well respected and a good provider. Pious even, at the end. But I think people should be remembered for who they were, not some fairy tale version.' She dropped her eyes away from Mabel and began to clear dishes from the table.

'You think Mother holds Grandfather Golder up as some kind of prince?' Mabel grinned.

Sarah returned the grin. 'And sometimes she still behaves like a princess. I guess I'd prefer it if she were a little more realistic.'

'I see.' Mabel pushed back her chair and helped clean away the lunch dishes. 'Well, I can't argue with you there. I think Father struggles with the same thing. Poor Mother. I feel a bit sorry for her. She finds it hard to face troubles. I don't want to be like that. I want to be more independent and work things out for myself. Perhaps this war will make us all a bit tougher. We're likely to have to face some dreadful things, don't you think?'

'I do, dear. But not today. Let's attack the wardrobes and chests of drawers in the spare room and get rid of some things. Perhaps it will be a good way to deal with our frustrations.' They both giggled as they headed for the back room of the house.

***

Mabel passed her aunt's telephone numerous times during the afternoon. While she'd never used one, she'd heard people talking

33

on the one at the Post Office in Baker's Gully. She remembered Sophie saying that her grandmother had one in their home in Adelaide, and that maybe they'd be able to talk together some time while she was away. It had seemed an unlikely prospect to Mabel at the time, but now …

'Aunt Sarah,' she said later. 'Do you use your telephone much?'

'Not a lot now, dear. Not too many people here have them in their homes yet, but I do believe they will become more common soon. I had a few customers who suggested it would be helpful if they could ring me up about their orders. "When I think of what kind of hat I'd like to go with my new coat, I need to call you and let you know right away, just in case I forget",' Sarah mimicked one of her well-to-do customers.

Mabel's tea went down the wrong way as she laughed and a coughing fit followed.

'Oh, dear. You're not going to have an attack, are you?' Sarah rushed to the other side of the table and began to rub Mabel's back.

'Of course not,' Mabel spluttered, clearing her throat. 'I'm fine. I haven't had an asthma attack for a couple of months.' She grabbed a napkin from the table and wiped her mouth. 'You're just so funny and my tea caught in my throat.'

Sarah smiled and moved back to her seat. 'Now, where were we? Oh, yes, the telephone. As I said, I haven't had a lot of use for it now that I'm not working in the shop.'

'But you think more people will have them soon?' Mabel turned in her chair and cast her eyes over the contraption hanging on the wall.

'I certainly do. There have been thousands of telephones in Sydney and Melbourne for a few years now and since the trunk line between Melbourne and Adelaide came last year, I believe there have been quite a few home installations. I feel chuffed to be one of the few. Do you know anyone else who has one?'

'Well, actually, that's what I've been just thinking about. My friend, Sophie–'

'The one whose father has been interned?'

'Yes. She told me her grandmother in Adelaide, where she's staying, has a telephone, and I was wondering …' her voice faded away.

'You'd like to call your friend?' Sarah asked. 'It's perfectly all right, dear. If you know the address I can call the exchange and get the number. I'm sure your friend would love to hear from you.'

Mabel's heart fluttered. 'I'd feel so much better if I could talk to her. We write letters but it's not the same, and I know she's missing everyone here. I don't have the address with me but it's at home. Maybe I could come over next weekend and bring it with me. I think in one of her letters Sophie even wrote the number, just in case I had an opportunity to ring.'

'You could call from the Post Office, you know, dear. There are public phones available.'

'I know, but when I'm there Mother is always with me, and I know she wouldn't want me to use the telephone, especially to call Sophie. She even worries about my letters. I'm sure she believes the authorities are listening in on everything, even reading people's mail, and I might be arrested as a spy or something.' Mabel couldn't help but grin as she spoke. Her mother's worries were really beyond believable and she knew Aunt Sarah would be amused by what she was saying.

'Good grief,' said Sarah predictably as a smile spread across her face. 'Dear Emma. How typical of her to turn this into a personal drama.' She shook her head. 'Never mind. You bring the number or the address next week and we'll call Sophie to see how she's getting on. It will be our little secret. We don't want your mother getting her knickers in a knot, do we?'

CHAPTER FOUR

Mororo, New South Wales, February 1915

Percy headed for the front door. He'd been trying to read most of the afternoon and could hardly concentrate with the chatter amongst his sisters. Ida was insisting she was going to marry John Lange, whether the war was over or not. Connie considered Freddie Lange the most handsome of the brothers and would choose him, even though he was ten years older than her. She was worried that he mightn't wait for her. Rita was only ten, but thought it all terribly romantic and couldn't wait for her sisters' weddings. She tried to involve Percy in the conversation, obviously hoping he'd reveal a secret romance of his own. It had all become too much for him.

'Where are you off to?' his mother asked as he strode across the floor and pulled his hat from the back of the door.

'I'm going for a walk,' Percy said. 'I'm feeling restless.'

'Well, be careful, dear. You don't know who's about these days.' She looked up from her mending and smiled at him, but he could see the fear in her eyes.

'Mum, please. It's been months now and nothing's happened. You must stop worrying.'

'They said the war would be over by now, but that's not looking likely, so the authorities might become more vigilant. I'm simply asking you to be careful.'

'I will be, I promise. I thought I'd walk down to the lower paddocks and check the cattle. You go back to your wedding talk with the girls. It seems that's more likely to happen than me being carted off.'

'I heard that,' called Ida from the other side of the room. 'You could at least be a bit excited for me.'

'I'll be excited if you are, Sis. Whatever makes you happy.' Percy chuckled as he left the house and wandered down the back path. *I must work out what will make me happy. I think I've waited long enough.*

It seemed that his father was not too worried. He'd taken off to do some more woodcutting as soon as the Christmas gatherings were over. Percy decided that he'd talk to his parents again as soon as his father came home. Surely they'd agree with his decision to move to Sydney. The Telephone Exchange was still advertising for workers. If the family could be happy about Ida getting engaged, they could surely be happy for him.

When he returned to the house he felt the fresh air had cleared his mind and the smell of roasting vegetables was a pleasant welcome. The conversation amongst his mother and sisters, however, was disturbing.

Vera was in tears. It seemed she'd not been home long from the Wiblen's where she worked as a domestic. 'The Wiblen boys are talking about signing up. They reckon it's their duty as there's a call for more enlistments. The Australians are still in training, it seems, in some God-forsaken place in Egypt, but they'll be heading for the front soon and they'll need reinforcements.'

'Please calm down, dear.' Fanny was rubbing Vera's arm.

'It's terrible that they feel this pressure to go, Mum. A lot of young men around here have already packed up and headed to Sydney to enlist.'

'There must be a lot leaving their jobs,' Ida said. 'I saw in the paper that some women have formed an Australian Women's National League and are offering to take up industrial jobs to free men for the fighting. What are they thinking? We don't want men to feel it's right to go off to the other side of the world and fight. It's horrible. What if John decides to go? I'll just die!' She dropped her head into her hands and began to weep. Connie put an arm around her sister's shoulder and patted her.

'Goodness me,' Percy said, rolling his eyes. 'When I left here a while ago you were all excited about weddings and now you're fretting over who's going off to the war.'

'You won't go, will you, Percy?' Vera moved towards him and held out her arms.

He took hold of her hands and squeezed them. 'Certainly not, Sis. I can't think of anything I'm less likely to do than enlist in a war.' He pulled off his hat and hung it up. 'I'll put the kettle on, Mum. It sounds like you could all do with a cup of tea.'

'Thank you, dear,' his mother said. He could hear her trying to calm his sisters as he headed for the kitchen.

'When will Dad be home?' Percy asked when he returned to the room, determined to change the subject.

'Early next week,' his mother replied. 'He didn't plan to be away long, in case–'

'Don't start that again, Mum, please.' Percy dropped into a chair. 'How about you girls go and make the tea and bring us some of Mum's rock cakes?' He grinned at his sisters. 'I've put the kettle on, but you're much better at the rest.'

Vera wiped her eyes and smiled weakly. 'What a poor excuse.' She cuffed Percy's shoulder as she passed him. 'Come on, girls,' she said over her shoulder. 'Obviously Percy wants to tell Mum something he doesn't want us to hear.'

'But I want to hear,' Connie whined. 'You promise you're not thinking of going to war, Percy?'

'I told you I'm not. Now go.' He shooed his sister into the kitchen.

'What's this about, Percy?' Fanny sat at the table and pushed wisps of hair behind her ears.

Percy sat beside her. 'I've decided I want to leave for Sydney soon, Mum. I can't do what I want to do here. I'm hoping you'll back me when Father gets home. He'll accept it if you do.'

'I don't know what to think, Percy.' The wrinkles in her forehead deepened and she grabbed his hand. 'We don't know what's going to happen here, and goodness knows what's going on in Sydney. I read this morning that the Australian and New Zealand troops are fighting the Turks now, over something to do with the Suez Canal. I don't understand any of it but the report said that the Turkish troops are led by German officers. The more we hear about Australians and Germans fighting each other, the more worrying it is.'

'Mum, you're getting yourself in a state about something happening on the other side of the world, something we can do nothing about. It does seem the war is not going to be over any time soon but we have to get on with our lives here.'

'It's not just on the other side of the world, Percy. Some men shot at a picnickers' train in Broken Hill. Two men, flying a Turkish flag. They killed four people before being shot dead themselves.'

'People like that are obviously madmen, Mum, no matter who they think they're fighting for.' Percy shook his head. 'I don't think it's a good idea for you to be reading all this news. It only upsets you.'

'We can't bury our heads in the sand, Percy.' A tear welled in the corner of her eye and rolled down her cheek. 'You heard what the girls said. There are young men all around who feel it's their duty to go and fight. Some even seem to be looking forward to it, like it's an adventure.'

'Well, you don't have to worry about me in that regard. I have other plans.'

'But we don't know how dangerous it will be in Sydney. At least here, there are fewer people, perhaps fewer dangers.'

'I thought you were worried I'd be picked up here for being German. In Sydney I'd not be known at all. With a name like Smith no-one's going to suspect me of being a spy. I can get a job and do my bit for the country while the war is going on. And I'd be helping you, too. I can send money home. Dad could stay here more and work the farm instead of being away so much. I can make a lot more than he can, if I get a good job.'

'I don't know, love.' She wiped her eyes. 'I'll see what your father says when he gets home. You know how stubborn he is. He likes to think he's the breadwinner.'

'Well, I can be stubborn, too. I am his son, remember. I'm just as ready to be a breadwinner as he is.'

Percy stopped when his mother's eyes flew open. She seemed about to say something, but then dropped her eyes away from him. She looked torn and frightened.

'What is it, Mum? You don't think I can get a job in Sydney?'

'Of course I know you can, love.' She patted his arm. 'I know you'll do very well at whatever you decide. It's just that …' She hesitated before going on. 'I'd miss you, that's all.'

The chatter of the girls returning to the room halted their conversation. Percy had the distinct impression that his mother was hiding something from him. *Perhaps she's really ill and isn't telling me.* He studied her face as she rose and helped the girls set out teacups, milk and sugar. She looked drawn and tired, but that was not unusual. He determined to have an honest discussion with her about her real reservations as soon as he could. As the younger children burst through the back door, the chatter rose to such a pitch he couldn't think any more and so pushed aside his concerns.

The day after his father returned, Percy was in the post office in Harwood. He'd not raised the issue of going to Sydney yet. He was waiting until he got a letter back from the Postmaster General. Percy had written asking for information about what training and work would be available in Sydney if he moved there.

'Interesting,' the man behind the counter said as he passed Percy's letter across to him. 'Postmaster General, Sydney.' He read the insignia on the top of the envelope. 'You interested in postal services, communications, things of that nature?'

Percy couldn't miss the suspicion in the man's tone. 'I'm interested in working in that field, yes.' He took the letter and turned to go. Numerous people were standing behind him, waiting to collect their mail. It seemed every eye was on him.

'The services will be looking for young men with those kinds of skills. Is that your aim?' The voice came from behind Percy.

He turned back to the man behind the counter. 'Am I looking to go to war? Is that what you're asking? If so, the answer's no.' Percy spoke firmly. 'I reckon skills in communications will be just as important here at home while the war is on.'

This time when he turned back to the door he saw disapproval in the eyes of a number of women.

'My son's just enlisted, young man. You should be ashamed, hiding behind the postal service to avoid fighting. The government will not put up with cowardice, you know. There's talk of conscription, so you'll not escape doing your duty soon.'

Several other women nodded and pursed their lips as if they found looking at Percy distasteful.

Percy attempted to walk past them. He had no intention of getting into an argument about enlistment with these people, especially women whose sons had gone, perhaps never to return.

'You're from over at Mororo, aren't you?' A man close to the door asked. 'Part of the Lange family, I reckon.'

'The Langes are related to my father, yes.' Percy was not going to lie. He could feel his heart beating strongly.

'Is that why you don't want to go to the war?' It was the postmaster again. 'Afraid you'd be fighting against your own?'

'That's ridiculous.' Percy swung on his heels. 'I've no desire to fight anyone. I don't agree with war. It's senseless.'

'Senseless, is it?' another of the women said. 'You think our sons are going over there for no good reason? Ready to give their lives for nothing!' Her voice rose to a sharp pitch.

'And they'll be takin' a lot of Huns with 'em,' another called. 'So don't be thinkin' your type won't suffer, too.'

Percy sighed, wondering how he was going to get out of the post office without a struggle. 'Look, everyone's entitled to their own opinion about this. I admire the courage of men who stand for what they believe, and if they think this is a war worth fighting, then it's up to them to go.' Again he attempted to move past the small crowd.

'I heard they'll be rounding up Germans in this area soon.' A woman turned to another beside her and nudged her. 'He'll not be so smug then.'

'Yes,' the postmaster said. 'I've had word the addresses of all German residents in the area are to go to the Government. Any who haven't sent theirs in will be in trouble. So you'll have to make up your mind whose side you're on soon. You'd be better to enlist than end up in the internment camp at Trial Bay, even if half your relatives will be there.' There was a snigger amongst a few in the group.

'Perhaps he'd rather sit the war out in prison,' a woman called from the back of the group.

'I'd be on the front lines in a shot if I were younger,' the postmaster said, raising his chin. There was a collective hum of approval.

Percy had had enough. He pushed through the huddle of customers. As he reached the door a woman poked him with her umbrella. 'Coward,' she hissed.

'Hun, more likely,' said an elderly man, spitting towards Percy as he opened the door.

Outside Percy hurried away and when he felt at a safe distance, he stopped and took a deep breath. *Have these people gone completely insane? Does no-one see the madness of this war?*

***

It was a long walk back to Mororo and Percy took his time, deep in thought. He'd read his letter before he moved on and was relieved to know that there was work available in Sydney. Mostly the exchange was being manned with women now, but there was a need for maintenance and repairmen, as well as telephone installation personnel. For anyone with a basic knowledge of the technology of telephones training was available.

There was no doubt in his mind that he wanted to apply. He was determined to post a letter back right away, saying that he'd kept abreast of telephone technology from its inception and was interested in any training or positions available. He'd send it from the general store in Mororo, where a minimal postal service was available. He certainly wasn't going to put himself through anything like he'd experienced in Harwood again, if he could avoid it.

He wondered how things would be in Sydney. *Surely in a big city individuals won't be targeted about the war. This idea of conscription that's being discussed by the government is a worry, but I'll face that if and when it happens.*

When he reached home his mother and father were in the parlour. They looked like they'd been having a very serious talk.

'Your letter came, then,' Fanny said, glancing at the envelope in his hand.

'Yes.' Percy put the letter on the table, took off his hat and sat down, facing his parents.

'There are positions available,' he said, watching their faces. Fanny seemed agitated. She kept glancing at Jack as if she were expecting him to say something. As usual, Jack was hard to read and remained quiet.

'We've had a notification from the Postmaster General, ourselves,' Fanny said. 'Your father picked it up this morning in town.'

'What about?' Percy asked, though he had a good idea what was coming.

'It's a directive from the government to give information about addresses and circumstances of all those who are of German descent.'

'It seems it's gone to everyone.' Jack spoke for the first time. 'So it's likely neighbours will be dobbing in neighbours. No point in trying to avoid this.'

Percy slumped in his chair. 'So what does this mean? Will they cart us all off to an internment camp for the duration of the war?'

Jack shrugged. 'I don't know, son. Perhaps they'll pick and choose. They'd have to fill a lot of prisons if they took everyone with some German connection from the past around here. Maybe they'll assess who could be a risk.'

'And how would they do that?'

'I've no idea. We'll have to wait and see.' Jack raked his hands through his greying beard and sat back in his seat as if that were an end to the discussion.

'We don't all have to wait and see, though, do we?' Fanny glared at her husband and when he didn't respond, she turned to Percy.

'What did your letter say, dear?'

Percy unfolded it. His mind was in conflict. 'It says there's training available, as well as work. I could go to Sydney as soon as … well, as soon as I'm ready.' He hesitated, unsure of what had seemed so clear to him a short while ago. 'I don't know what to think now. I don't see how I can go until this business is sorted out. I hear it's only men they've been taking, but how will the women manage?'

Fanny shook her head. 'Most of the women around here would manage well enough. They have children to help and I'm sure neighbours who have no German connections will assist where they can.'

'I'm not so sure of that,' Percy said. 'Not judging by my experience in the post office this morning. I couldn't believe how vicious and prejudiced people were.'

'What people?' Jack sat upright.

'I didn't know any of them,' Percy said. 'And they didn't know me, though someone suspected I was connected to the Lange family. They seemed determined to condemn me, either for being German or for not enlisting to fight against the Germans. There's no winning, is there?' He threw up his arms and then slapped the letter down on his lap. 'Blasted war!'

'Jack.' Fanny's voice was pleading. Percy looked from one to the other, unable to interpret the signals between his parents.

'Don't "Jack" me,' his father said, his tone indicating a sense of defeat. 'It's up to you.'

'What's going on?' Percy said. 'What is it you're not telling me?'

'We think it would be a good idea for you to go to Sydney, after all, Percy,' Fanny said. 'It would be better if you're not here. Whatever happens, we want you to be safe.'

'You want me to run away, while uncles and cousins and perhaps my father, are rounded up and thrown in prison! You're suggesting I hide?' Percy was offended. 'That's just the kind of thing these people in the post office implied. I'm not a coward, Mum. Just because I don't agree with going to war, it doesn't mean I'll abandon you all.' He sprang up and paced the floor.

'Please sit down, dear,' Fanny said, wringing her hands together. 'And keep your voice down. I've asked Connie to keep the little ones outside for a while. I don't want her rushing in here thinking something's wrong.' She took a deep breath. 'Of course we don't think you're a coward. It's just that …' her words faded.

He moved to her chair and knelt in front of her. 'What is it, Mum? You've been acting strangely these past couple of months whenever this issue comes up. I know you're afraid for Dad and me, but this might not end up affecting us. We might not be seen as a threat at all.' He patted her hands, moved by the level of distress he could see in her face.

'It's not that simple, Percy,' she said. 'There's something we need to tell you. Something that affects the outcome of all this.' She looked up at her husband again, as if pleading for his support. 'Jack?'

Percy turned to his father, whose face remained passive, his eyes withdrawn.

'I don't see how his being in Sydney will make any difference,' Jack eventually said. 'There'll be pressure there for men to enlist. Would you rather that?'

'That's not the point, Jack, and you know it.' Fanny's tone was strong now. 'Percy can resist that pressure if he needs to. It's the other … it's not fair, Jack. We have to tell him.'

Jack huffed. 'You weren't always so ready to give into prejudice, my girl. Once you'd have fought for anyone of German descent to have a fair go.'

'Please Jack, that's not the point, either. I'll still fight for people of any background to have a fair go. But Percy deserves the truth so he can deal with what he has to and not something that doesn't concern him.'

'You were happy to keep that from him all these years … until now.'

'He was a child, Jack. He needed protection. He's a man now.'

'And isn't it protecting him that you're still trying to do?'

Percy listened to this interchange, astounded by the depth of feeling in his mother and father's tone and completely confused by their words.

'What on earth are you two talking about?' He stood up and looked from one to the other. 'I'm not a child anymore, so stop treating me like one and tell me what the dickens is going on.'

'All right, Percy. Please sit down.' Fanny took a deep breath and sat upright.

Percy sensed some dreadful agony in his mother. His heart beat wildly and his stomach lurched as he sat, waiting.

The moment lasted an age before she began, falteringly, tears rolling down her cheeks.

'If they come looking for men of German descent, Percy, then you have to know that it doesn't include you.' She looked into his eyes and sniffed. 'You are not of German descent.'

'What do you mean?' Percy interrupted.

She wiped her eyes, her face seeming to age before him. 'Jack is not your father. Not your natural father.'

There was a soft groan from the other chair and Percy looked at Jack, whose face had drained of colour. Percy's mind spun with questions, but he couldn't find his voice. He looked back to his mother and stared, waiting for her to go on.

'In every real sense, of course, Jack is your father, but you were nearly three when Jack and I married. He took us both on, loved us both. He's been a wonderful father, right from the start.' She was choking on her words. 'But Jack is not your birth father. You are not of German descent, so you should not be targeted for internment.' She sat back in her seat, looking exhausted and haunted.

Percy was speechless for minutes. He waited for further explanation, his mind racing. 'What are you saying?' he eventually asked. 'Are you telling me that you were married before, to someone else? My birth father?'

Fanny shook her head. 'No, Percy, I'm sorry. I wasn't married. Your birth father was … I didn't know him. He was …'

'You were unmarried? He …' Percy couldn't find words.

'He wasn't a good man, Percy.' She paused for a moment, the words too difficult. 'He took advantage of me.'

'But how …?' The words stuck in Percy's throat.

'The details are not important, love. What's important is that you know he wasn't German, nor of German descent. He was English.'

'So you did know him?' Percy stood. His knees felt like jelly but he forced himself to continue walking up and down the parlour. He felt like he'd start screaming if he didn't move. 'All these years, you've kept this from me? You've always taught me truth is important. Integrity, honesty.' He waved his arms about, drowning in a sea of confusion. 'You raised me to believe in these things. To respect my father.' He stopped suddenly and turned to Jack, accusingly. 'Why didn't you tell me the truth?'

'What good would it have done?' Jack looked up at him, his face drawn and pale. 'Your mother needed to put that behind her. You needed a normal life. We did what we thought was right for you. I would never have told you.'

'You don't think I have a right to know where I come from?' Percy felt an anger he'd never experienced.' He paced again. 'So who else knows? Who's been watching me all these years, feeling sorry for me, wondering if I'll ever find out who I really am?'

'Please, Percy.' Fanny was weeping loudly, her hands reaching out to him. 'Hardly anyone knew. Most people believe to this day that Jack is your natural father, even though I always denied it. There was prejudice against the German community then, too. I didn't want people to think badly of your … of Jack. I didn't want them to believe he was capable of such a thing, but

I'm sure some still did.'

'So you insisted he wasn't my father before you were married and then pretended he was afterwards.' He banged his fist onto his chest. 'So who knew the identity of my real father?' Percy demanded. 'Surely someone did.'

'No one who's still alive, Percy. I promise.'

'You promise! How can I know if you're telling me the truth now? So tell me who it was. What was my real father's name?' Each time he said 'real father', his mother flinched. Percy knew he was hurting them both with his words, but he couldn't hold back. His own pain was turning to fury. 'I have a right to know who my father is.'

'I don't know his name, Percy. He was a jockey from Sydney. He was staying at the hotel where I worked. He was English, well spoken, probably rich. I think his father had a property, raised thoroughbred horses. That's all we know. I never wanted to know any more.' Her voice faded away.

Percy dropped into a chair and hung his head into his hands. The room was deathly quiet. After a few moments he looked up. His parents appeared old and worn out, and very sad.

'I can't take this in right now. I have to think. One thing I do know. I'll be leaving for Sydney as soon as I can arrange it.'

CHAPTER FIVE

Kangarilla, South Australia, May 1915

Mabel replaced the phone in the cradle and turned to her aunt. 'Sophie's had a visit with her father. She's so upset. He's in a tent, crammed in with six other men. One of them is a Lutheran pastor. Can you believe it?'

Sarah tutted as she set out knives and forks on the table.

'Sophie said there were lines and lines of tents, and they could only visit her father for half an hour, sitting in a big shed with lots of other men having visits. It was horrible.'

'Are they eating well enough? Do they have sufficient clothes to keep warm? That's what I'd want to know. Poor things. It's going to be a cold winter. The government should be ashamed, locking good men away like that.' Sarah finished laying the table for lunch.

'It was the first visit Sophie and her mother have been able to have. They had to catch the train up to the port and then get a boat across to Torrens Island, and they were being watched all the time. Her mother cried all the way home in the train.'

'Dear, dear, and it doesn't sound like the war is nearly over yet. The news in the paper is not good. There's a dreadful battle going on at a place called Gallipoli. That's in Turkey, I think. There's an article all about what happened when the Australians and New Zealanders landed there a few weeks ago.

"A Day of Heroes and Slaughter" was the headline. Dreadful.'
She tutted again. 'So many of our young men were killed. Small
compensation that they were heroes if they come home to us as
corpses. And now it seems the troops are locked in battle there
and can't go forward or back.'

Mabel dropped into a chair at the end of the table. 'I can't bear
to hear about it. I can't imagine why so many people are encouraging
more men to go. Some with wives and little children have even
gone. I heard them talking about it after church this morning.'

Sarah nodded. 'Yes, some of the women are more militant
than the men. They seem to be followers of Eva Hughes, the Prime
Minister's wife. I've heard she's out on the streets haranguing
people to take up the cause. I feel very sorry for any young man
who isn't inclined to go.'

'I much prefer that other woman, Vida Goldstein. She's
campaigning against the war and she's formed a Women's Peace
Army. I heard her speaking on the radio last week. Mother made
me turn it off. She says it's too distressing for me to listen to, that
I'll bring on an asthma attack.'

'Have you had one recently?'

'Just one a couple of weeks ago, but it wasn't so bad. I'm sure
it was something in the garden. We'd been out for a picnic, which
Mother says is a good way for me to relax, but I think there's
something in the grass that makes my throat start to sting and then
it gets worse until I can hardly breathe.'

'That should have convinced Emma about the cause of the
attack, surely.'

'No, she thinks it was because we'd been arguing about
Richard Grimwood through the afternoon and she says I got
myself worked up.'

'And did you?'

'I did get annoyed. Apparently he and his cousins are talking

51

about enlisting, but they haven't done it yet. I think they're stalling because they don't really want to go, and I don't blame them for that. But mother thinks he's waiting because he wants to secure a promise from me that I'll wait for him.'

Sarah turned to the stove and lifted out a freshly baked loaf of bread.

'Now there's a smell that won't give me asthma,' Mabel said, enjoying the aroma. 'That looks yummy.'

'My own recipe.' Sarah grinned. She drew a large bread knife from the drawer, then looked up at Mabel. 'I didn't know there'd been talk of you waiting for Richard.'

'There hasn't. Mother reads all kinds of things into everything he says. We've been there for lunch after church a few times lately and I don't think he has an interest in me at all. Why would he? I'm sure he'd fine me too much of a liability to be a prospective wife.'

'Which is a great relief to me,' Mabel went on quickly when her aunt's eyes flew open. She hated to sound as if she were feeling sorry for herself. 'It's just that Mother takes his every comment to me to mean he's madly in love with me. It's so frustrating.'

'So you argue with her and get frustrated. You don't think that contributes to your attacks?' Sarah repositioned the loaf on the bread board and held the knife over it without looking up at Mabel.

'Not really, but I guess it doesn't help.' Mabel sighed.

'Well, just remember I have this mixture I've made up for you. Lobelia and cayenne pepper; twenty drops in water as soon as an attack starts and repeated every thirty minutes. One of my neighbours swears by it and I've seen it work for her. She says ginger and turmeric are also helpful.'

'Thank you, Aunt Sarah, but I'm sure I won't have an attack here. I feel very much at ease when I'm with you.'

'Oh, and I forgot. Avoid milk. That's the other thing my neighbour says. Seems a sad thing when we live in a farming community. Everyone drinks milk, don't they? I'll bet they have lots of that at the Grimwoods.'

Mabel nodded. 'Yes, I do know milk doesn't sit well with me, but I'd rather not talk about Richard or my asthma anymore, Aunt Sarah. It's all we ever seem to talk about at home. I'm glad to be here today and so pleased to be staying over.'

'Good. I'm pleased too, dear, but I want you to know that your asthma is manageable and having an attack now and then does not make you a liability. You mustn't think that it does.' Sarah's tone was firm and as she pushed the knife through the bread, Mabel sensed her aunt's frustration. 'So now there'll be no more talk about that here.'

After dusting her hands on her apron, Sarah moved to the cupboard and brought out a jar of jam and some cheese. 'I'll only be here a few more weeks. The buyers were back a few days ago, and they're very happy to go ahead. So with a bit more of a clean-up in the back room we'll be all done here. Now, let's eat while this bread is warm.'

'Are you excited about moving to your new place?' Mabel asked after she'd devoured two large slices of bread with cheese and jam.

'I am. It's not so far from here, so I'll be able to continue with the local ladies' guild, and doing the flowers at church, and I'm still close enough to the stores I'm used to.'

'And you won't have all this work to do in such a big house.'

'That's right. I'll be able to rest more. "Act my age", as your dear mother likes to say.'

'I can't imagine you resting too much, Aunt Sarah. You're too active and sociable for that.'

***

The following morning Mabel was in the back room taking down some old curtains when the doorbell rang. She could feel a sneeze coming on and dropped the bundle of curtains she had in her arms. She was holding her finger under her nose to stop the sneeze when she heard Aunt Sarah talking to someone.

'Please come in. It's right over here. It works fine most of the time but then occasionally it goes all crackly, so I'd like you to check it out. But mostly I want to know how I go about moving it to my new house. That will be in a few weeks.'

'I see,' came a male voice. 'Let me see now.'

Mabel blew her nose when her sneeze had subsided and pushed her hair back into place. She entered the parlour, curious as to what the man near the telephone was doing. She was immediately struck by his handsome face. He had black hair slicked back neatly and a small black moustache. When he looked up at her she was sure she blushed.

'Hello,' he said, a grin spreading across his face. 'I didn't see you there.'

Mabel straightened her apron and brushed a cobweb from her arm. 'I was in the back room taking down some curtains. I heard you come in.'

'This is the repairman, Mabel.' Sarah came into the room from the kitchen. 'He's here to do some maintenance on the telephone and help with moving it when I go.'

'I see,' Mabel said, nodding. She felt a little foolish standing there watching him work, but couldn't bring herself to leave.

'I'm going to make a cup of tea,' Sarah said. 'Would you like one when you're done there, young man?'

He smiled and nodded. 'Why, thank you. That would be wonderful. This is my third call out this way today and I could do with a break.'

'Tea and scones it will be, then.' Sarah spun on her heels and went back to the kitchen.

Mabel moved a little closer. 'Do you mind if I watch?'

'Of course not,' the man answered with a grin. 'Your mother is kind to offer me tea.' He continued to take the receiver apart and poked at the inner workings of it with a brush. 'Not many customers do that.'

'Oh, that's my Aunt Sarah. I'm visiting and helping her get her house ready for sale.'

'I see.' He looked up and flashed a wide smile. 'Mabel, is it?'

'Yes. What's your name?'

'Percy,' he said. 'Percy Smith. And is your surname Goble, same as your aunt's?' He glanced at her before looking back to the telephone and Mabel noticed his deep brown eyes.

'No, my surname is Smart. Aunt Sarah is my mother's sister.'

'Mabel Smart. I'm sure I'll remember that.' Percy nodded and turned back to the phone. He tapped the end of the receiver, then dialled some numbers and put the receiver to his ear. 'I think there might be some water in the line. It happens sometimes after rain. It'll dry out soon enough. There doesn't seem to be a lot of rain about now.'

'No, it's been very dry, actually. Father says the whole country is in drought. It's very hard on the farmers around here.'

'Do you live on a farm? Is that what your father does?'

Mabel nodded. 'We have wheat and fruit and some cattle. Father has tried his hand at a few things. Same as a lot of the farmers around here.'

'Your farm is close by then?'

'Not too far. A few miles, just over at Baker's Gully.'

'Baker's Gully. I don't think I know that. I'm new to the area, so I'm still finding my way around.'

'I see. Where do you come from?'

'At the moment I'm staying at the roadhouse at Chandler's Hill. I've come out to do a few repairs and some maintenance around here. Then I'll be back in Adelaide. I have a room in a guest house there.'

'You don't live at home then, with your parents?'

Percy hesitated. He put the receiver back in the cradle of the telephone and fiddled with some wires.

'I'm sorry. I didn't mean to pry?' Mabel felt her face colour.

'No, it's fine,' Percy said after a moment. He turned and flashed her another smile and his eyes lit up. 'I'm originally from New South Wales. My parents live north of Sydney.'

'My goodness, you are a long way from home.' Mabel sensed that her disappointment showed in her tone. 'Are you here for long?'

'Probably. I've been in Sydney the past couple of months, doing some training and working at the Telephone Exchange. When this job came up in Adelaide a few weeks ago, I applied and was accepted. I like it here. Not so busy as Sydney, not so crowded and noisy.' His grin broadened. 'I think I could get used to living here very easily.'

'How are things going here?' Sarah's voice interrupted their conversation.

Mabel found it hard to drag her eyes from Percy's. 'All fine, I think, Aunt Sarah,' she managed after a few moments.

'Just about done, Mrs Goble.' Percy wiped the telephone over with a cloth. 'I've checked it all and it seems to be working fine. There's a little moisture in the line, I think, but that should sort itself out with the dry weather.'

'And moving it to my new place?'

'That won't be any trouble at all. I'll be happy to come back and do that when you're ready. You just need to call the office in Adelaide and tell them when.'

'Good. Then let's have some tea and scones,' Sarah said, laying a plate of scones on the table.'

***

'So, Percy,' Sarah said when they'd drunk their tea and Percy had started on his fourth scone. 'I'll look forward to having you come back and set my telephone in the new place. It's not far from here, so I'm assuming the line is laid.'

'I think it's all good around here, Mrs Goble. If you give me the address I'll check all that out for you before I come.'

'Good. I'd rather not be without the telephone now. I've become used to having it if I need it and Mabel would miss it, wouldn't you, love, if you couldn't call your friend?'

'I would, Aunt Sarah,' Mabel said. She turned to Percy. 'My friend's father is in an internment camp on Torrens Island because his father was German and the government suspects him of being a spy.'

Percy looked about to choke on a piece of scone.

'Are you all right, Percy?' Sarah reached over and patted him on the back.

'Yes, I'm sorry,' he said, regaining his composure. 'It almost went down the wrong way.'

'Another cup of tea should fix that.' Sarah poured more tea into his cup.

'Thank you, I'm fine now.'

'Do they have internment camps in Sydney?' Mabel asked.

'Yes, there are a few around New South Wales.' He picked up the teacup and took a long drink. 'It's a dreadful business if you ask me.'

'Do you know anyone who has German relatives?'

Percy hesitated and took another bite of scone before he answered. 'My parents have acquaintances whose parents came from Germany a long time ago, but they're very much Australian now. This idea that they might be spies is quite ridiculous.'

'I suppose anything's possible in war,' Sarah said, pouring herself more tea. 'I can understand that hostilities between those of German and English descent could get a little out of hand.

Considering some of the reactions, even around here, I can see how some with German backgrounds might need protection, but certainly not imprisonment.'

'Yes, everything about the war is unreasonable,' Percy said, nodding. 'It's a terrible thing, when so many from Germany came here to make a new life for themselves as Australians.' He fidgeted in his chair and Mabel sensed he was uncomfortable with the conversation.

'Are your parents farmers?' she asked, hoping to change the subject.

Again Percy hesitated and she was sorry she'd asked. He seemed reluctant to say much about his family and she didn't want to make him regret his visit.

'No,' he said, after a few moments. 'They have a property north of Sydney. They raise thoroughbred horses and race them.'

'Oh.' Mabel was impressed. 'That sounds interesting. Do you ride?'

Percy coughed and wiped his mouth. 'Not really. I mean, I can ride, of course. I came out today on the horse. I left the cart with some of my tools and things at the roadhouse. I like to ride when I can manage without the cart. But I don't race,' he added, and Mabel wondered if she looked disappointed. A horse racer sounded so romantic.

'You're not interested in following in your father's footsteps then, Percy?' Sarah asked.

'No.' Percy's answer came quickly and Mabel sensed all was not well between Percy and his father.

'I mean, I'm not really one for working on the land,' he said more evenly. 'I prefer to work with machines and I'm very interested in the things of the future, like cars and telephones, even aeroplanes. I find such things fascinating.'

'I see.' Sarah nodded. 'Well, I suspect your father has other sons to carry on his property?'

Percy paled and nodded. 'Yes, we're a big family. Plenty of others.' He pushed back from the table and straightened his waistcoat. 'Now, I really must move on. I've two more calls to make before I head back to the roadhouse. Thank you so much for the tea and scones. It was delicious.'

'Perhaps I'll see you again, Percy.' Mabel stood and held out her hand. She wondered if something she'd said had caused Percy to make such a hasty departure. He'd seemed uncomfortable answering questions about his family and she hoped she'd have another chance to talk with him. 'When you come to install Aunt Sarah's telephone in the new place, I mean.' She swallowed and hoped she wasn't blushing. 'I'm likely to be there helping her settle in.'

'I'll look forward to that, then,' Percy said. He took her hand and bowed his head slightly. When he turned to Sarah and dropped her hand, Mabel let her arm fall to her side but could still feel the gentle pressure of his fingers on her skin.

***

'What a nice young man,' Sarah said when Mabel returned from the front door after seeing Percy off.

Mabel busied herself clearing the table. 'He was,' she said, sensing she was colouring up again.

Sarah grinned. 'You were quite taken with him, I think. And he with you. Just as well your mother is not here.'

'What do you mean?'

'A telephone repairman,' Sarah said with a chuckle. 'The very thought would be enough to send Emma into a tizz.'

'I think he's a very clever man.' Mabel felt the need to defend Percy.

'Indeed he is, dear, and if he were interested in following in his father's footsteps and taking up a large property, raising thoroughbred horses, then I think your mother would be very impressed with him.

But Percy made it clear he's not about to do that. In fact I suspect there's quite a story behind that young man's family.'

'I think that's entirely his own business, Aunt Sarah. Mother's a snob and I won't be influenced by her grand ideas about family connections.'

'I agree with you, dear. Especially since her own family is hardly the paragon of purity she likes to portray it as.' Sarah collected up some cups quickly, seeming to catch herself out with her words.

'What do you mean, Aunt Sarah? There's something quite odd about the way you skirt around memories of Grandfather Golder. There's something about him that everyone hides. I just know it. Please tell me. I'm not a child any longer. Surely I deserve to know about my family's past.' Mabel put down the plates she'd been carrying to the kitchen and stood directly in front of her aunt. 'He wasn't from Germany was he?'

Sarah laughed. 'No, dear, he certainly wasn't from Germany.' She chucked Mabel under the chin. 'Your mother would skin me alive for telling you the truth about our father. In fact she'd deny it to her dying breath.'

'Now you really have me intrigued. You must tell me.' Mabel pulled her aunt by the sleeve and led her into the parlour.

'I hope you won't be sorry about this, Mabel.' Sarah dropped into a chair and straightened her apron over her lap. 'I'm not sure it's right to tell you, but I do dislike snobbery. It's so tedious.'

Mabel backed into a chair and leaned forward, excited by the thought of learning more about her grandparents.

'Well, here goes.' Sarah settled into her chair. 'I've told you my father arrived here in Kangarilla in the early 1840s, and that's true. He came from Kent in England, and that's all anyone knew of him for quite a long time.' She twisted in her chair as if she were reconsidering what she was going to say.

'Please, Aunt Sarah.' Mabel couldn't bear not to know the truth now.

'Well, he obviously worked hard and won the approval of Mother's family. She was only a slip of a girl when he married her and he was a man of forty. I doubt he reckoned on her being so strong minded, so as time went on, there were a few run-ins between them. He was off to the gold fields the minute she was pregnant, which was hard on her, and when he was home he liked a tipple, as many men do. She was often chasing him out of bed in the mornings to get to work on the farm, and as often dragging him into bed at night when he couldn't walk a straight line.'

Mabel gasped. Her grandfather certainly didn't sound like the virtuous gentleman her mother had painted him to be.

'He settled down in his later life,' Sarah said, as if sensing Mabel's thoughts. 'He became well known for his Christian piety. But he hadn't always been like that. I found out the truth of his past quite by accident one night when I was about fifteen. Mother and Father were having a row in our parlour and I woke up. I sneaked out to the door of the parlour and listened.'

Mabel nodded and a giggle escaped her mouth. She could imagine herself doing the same thing.

'It was clear Mother had heard things about Father. I'm not sure where from, but he was in no state to deny it. He was quite under the weather and clearly in no mood to be lectured to. He acknowledged all she'd heard was true and even added a few details that obviously shocked her.'

'Go on,' Mabel encouraged, visualising the scene. Although her grandfather had died long before she was born, she'd seen photos of him in his later years with a shock of snow white hair and a wild beard. She could still remember her grandmother's small frame and dainty features, and now imagined her standing over her husband, hands on hips, and reprimanding him severely.

For what, Mabel was yet to hear, but she was sure it would be deliciously shocking.

'It seems Father hadn't just arrived in Australia when he landed in Kangarilla. In fact, he'd been here since around 1832 when he'd been transported to Van Diemen's Land.'

Mabel gasped. 'Transported! You mean he was a– '

'-a convict, yes. He was transported for breaking a threshing machine, which hardly seems worthy of a seven year sentence. Perhaps there was more to it than that. Maybe he did it in a fit of anger. He did have quite a temper. Anyway, that's what his actions earned him. He was assigned to a farmer and then two years later he was in trouble again and given six months hard labour for losing forty of his master's sheep.'

'Losing forty sheep.' Mabel laughed. 'How could anyone lose forty sheep?'

'Mother asked the same thing that night as they argued and from Father's answer, I'd say the truth is he tried to run off with them and they got lost in the bush. It sounded like he and the sheep were rounded up quite quickly.'

'Doesn't seem he was a very clever convict.' Mabel sniggered.

'No, it doesn't. When he arrived here in South Australia six or seven years after that, he may have served out his sentence, or he may have absconded. He wasn't too forthcoming about that.'

'Oh dear, he was quite a rogue then.'

'Not only that but he admitted to Mother that in Kent, where he'd been convicted, he'd had a wife and child.'

'No!' Mabel's hand flew to her mouth. 'Does that make him a bigamist?'

'It would if the woman was still alive. I didn't find out about that. She couldn't have divorced him because women couldn't do that in those days. But he clearly had no intention of going home to her.'

'So Grandmother Golder knew nothing of this for all those years?'

Sarah shook her head. 'No, her father would never have let her marry him if they'd known any of that. I'm glad my grandmother was dead before it came out. She was a very proper lady. It would have been the end of her. I remember Mother being very angry with Father at the time of this fight, but I never heard them mention it again. Mother seemed to go on as if nothing had changed. She was a strong woman, and proud, but I sensed she'd made it clear to Father that he had better not step out of line again.'

'Poor Grandmother. That's a terrible secret for her to have to keep.'

'Yes, but after that Father was well-behaved, and as I said, became quite a paragon in the community.'

'So that's all my mother remembers of him?'

'All she wants to remember. After Father died, I told Mother that I'd heard them arguing that night and knew about Father's past. I didn't feel it was fair for her to carry that all alone. We decided it was time the other children knew the truth, in case they ended up hearing it from someone else.'

'How did Mother receive that?'

'Not well at all. Emma refused to believe it, and refused to discuss it again or have it mentioned in her home. Some of the others were the same. They couldn't bear the idea of having a convict in the family. Others, like me, thought it was all so long ago that it didn't matter anymore. Father paid for his crimes and in the end made a good life for Mother and all of us. He left her well provided for and the boys had a large inheritance in land.'

Mabel nodded, her mind still spinning with the fascinating revelation.

'It's a story with a good ending,' Sarah went on. 'In fact, I think it shows that people can change, that good can come from bad, that life goes on in spite of hardship and disappointment. They're good things to know, don't you think?'

'I do, Aunt Sarah. I agree it's a story worth knowing. It makes me appreciate what a great woman Grandmother Golder was, too.'

'Then I'm glad I told you, but I think you need to keep it to yourself, at least for the time being. I don't want to upset your mother and I wouldn't like to think she'd stop you visiting me.'

'Neither would I, Aunt Sarah. I'm looking forward to helping you set up in your new home.'

CHAPTER SIX

Adelaide, South Australia, June 1915

'Letter for you, Percy.'

Percy was surprised by the postmaster's announcement. He approached the counter. 'For me? Are you sure?'

The postmaster nodded. 'It's addressed to you, lad. It's come through from the post office in Sydney. Somebody doesn't know you've moved down here.' He handed the letter across to Percy.

Percy read the sender's address and looked back to the postmaster. 'It's from my mother. I guess she hasn't got my note to say I'd taken this position.' He nodded and shoved the letter in his pocket.

'How are you going with the repairs around the city?'

'Just about done. One more this morning and I think that's it for this lot.'

'Good work. There's been a call from a Mrs Goble in Kangarilla about a reconnection, and there are a few maintenance jobs out that way that you can attend to next.'

Percy smiled. 'Fine. I'll head out to Chandlers Hill this afternoon. I can stay a couple of nights and see to those jobs.'

'Good lad.' The postmaster smiled and waved his finger at Percy. 'You're a good worker, Percy. We're glad to have you. I wondered if you'd stay on, with all the young lads rushing off to the war. You've no inclination then?'

Percy shook his head. 'No, Mr Johnstone. I reckon some of us need to stay home and keep things going here.'

'I agree, lad, but it's hard to find a young man who thinks like that these days. Even some of the young ladies are off to be nurses and such. I guess they're needed with all the injuries we're hearing about. Terrible business. Let's hope it's over soon.'

'I hope so, sir.'

'Before these pro-war activists get the referendum they're hoping for,' Mr Johnstone added, dragging his fingers through his beard as he began to sort mail on the desk.

'Referendum?' Percy looked up.

'Yeah, they're agitating for the government to have a vote on conscription. It'd be a sad day for the country if that happens.' He shook his head. 'There's too many who are ready to send the best of our nation off to fight England's battles, if you ask me. But I'm afraid the yes vote would win from what I'm hearing.'

Percy swallowed loudly. 'You think so?' The thought of being made to go to war caused his skin to crawl. 'I hope you're wrong, Mr Johnstone. 'There are a lot of men not suited to that kind of fighting.'

'And too many who think they are, I'm afraid. I doubt a lot of the young fellas heading off so excited have any idea what they're in for. I get the notices of death, and believe me, there'll be a lot of families already grieving the loss of their boys. I shudder every time I see the Department of Defence on a telegram. Terrible news to have to deliver.'

'I'm glad I don't have that job.' Percy finished packing his tools in his bag. 'I'll be off then. I'll head out to Kangarilla as soon as I finish the last job here, so I'll see you in a couple of days.'

Mr Johnstone nodded. 'And don't go down Main Street when you head out of the city. Stay well clear of there, won't you?'

'Why's that?'

'Haven't you heard? There's to be a protest march there today.

The ones against conscription are trying to make their message heard, but I reckon there'll be agitators down there making it hard for them. Could get nasty. I've not seen an issue divide this country as much as this war has.' He sighed deeply and pushed a pile of letters into a mail bag.

'Thanks for the warning, Mr Johnstone. I'll be careful.'

Percy loaded his cart outside the post office and headed to a Flinders Street store for the first repair job. It took a little longer than he'd expected and when he finished, he realised how hungry he was. In the cart outside the store he took out the sandwiches and flask of tea that he'd brought. While he was eating he remembered the letter from his mother and pulled it out of his pocket. He'd not let his family know that he'd come to Adelaide. They would still believe he was in Sydney. He chided himself for suggesting to Mr Johnstone that he'd sent a note to his mother. *I hardly know myself these days ... making up stories about my family!*

A further wave of regret washed over him as he gazed at his mother's handwriting. He knew she'd be upset by him being away, and not contacting her would be upsetting her. He wasn't ready to express his feelings in writing yet. In fact, he'd hardly let himself explore his feelings at all.

His arrival in Sydney still seemed a blur to him. He'd gone directly to the Postmaster General's Office and said he was ready to start work and training immediately. They'd been glad to have him. Everywhere seemed to be struggling for staff with the exodus to the war. He'd plunged right into the training and been given experience in maintenance almost straight away. Working on the telephones and machinery in the Exchange had fascinated him and helped keep his mind off the revelations he'd had from his mother, which he still found hard to believe.

Sydney had been abuzz with news of the war, crowded with people arriving to enlist. A camp had been set up at Randwick

Racecourse where men were training before being shipped overseas. Men and women in uniform were everywhere, bursting with excitement for adventure as soldiers and nurses. The war overshadowed any semblance of normal life in the city and Percy had trouble avoiding talking about it.

Everyone had asked if he was going to join up, and if not, why not? He felt he was constantly on trial, having to defend his decision not to enlist. When he'd found out there was work available in Adelaide, he'd volunteered immediately. He was glad to find Adelaide considerably quieter and much less frantic about the war, although protests and calls for recruitment were building up across the country with each week that passed.

Percy looked down at the letter in his hand. His heart thumped at the thought of reading it. *I wonder what's happening at home, if my cousins or uncles have been taken away to an internment camp? Or my father?* His hand shook as he thought of the man who was not his father at all. His head dropped, still in disbelief. Anger churned in his stomach again. He knew he'd have to come to terms with it eventually, but right now he could hardly swallow each time he was reminded.

His real father was not a good man. That's what his mother had said. And clearly, given the circumstances of his birth, this seemed to be the truth. But Percy found himself wondering what he was really like. 'A jockey, probably rich, a family property, thoroughbred horses.' His mother's words kept rolling around in his mind, haunting him, bringing a wave of both revulsion and curiosity.

Why on earth did I tell Mrs Goble and Mabel that my father owned a property in Sydney? He muttered to himself as he crushed the envelope in his hand. *I hate dishonesty. I don't know who I am anymore.* He resolved that he would not tell Mabel more lies. She had seemed such a sweet and innocent girl. He'd thought about her often over the past month and hoped she would be at Mrs

Goble's when he went back. He knew that giving her a wrong impression about his family would not endear him to her.

People hurried past on the footpath, looking flushed and excited, heading away from the demonstration in Victoria Square. A few women were talking animatedly and waving their arms about. Percy couldn't tell whether they were pro or anti-war. As the sound of their voices faded away, he took a deep breath and opened the letter.

Dear Percy,

I hope your training has gone as you'd hoped in Sydney. I worry about your safety and long to hear from you. The news we get here suggests that the city will be very divided about the war and I pray you are keeping out of harm's way. We have not had trouble here. No-one from the Lange family has been taken away, and no-one has contacted us about your father or you. Sadly we have had news that some of the Fischers have been interned. Willhelm Fischer was your grandfather's step-brother. He became a very prominent man in the Grafton area and some of his sons and grandchildren are well-known even to this day. It's sad that those who have made a positive contribution to the local community should now be punished for doing so. Some of your father's cousins have visited Trial Bay and say the men are reasonably treated and some are even glad to sit out the war without danger, even if they are not free to go about their lives.

As we are not expecting further internments, I wanted you to know that it would ease my worries to hear from you, and please me even more to have you home. I know that you are keen to work in the telephone business, but please know that your father and I are fretting about you and long to know you are safe. I understand that the information we gave you before you left was very distressing and I pray you can understand that we told you only out of concern for you.

We both love you dearly. Your father is very disturbed about the effect our news had on you. It was not his idea to tell you and I'm sure he regrets letting me do it. I hope you can forgive me and remember I only want what is best for you, as I always have.

Your loving mother.

Percy refolded the letter and pushed it back into the envelope. His heart felt dulled. The truth still sent him into a state of shock. Everything he'd known about himself seemed rocked to the core. He chided himself, arguing that this changed very little about him. Jack Smith had taken him on as a small child, loved him and his mother and raised him like his own son. He had been the only father Percy had ever known, and while he'd not identified greatly with him and had found him sometimes harsh and unbending, he had to admit that Jack was a decent and good man. He had always tried to do the best by his family. He'd been a good father, not only to his own children, but also to Percy, whom he'd never treated any differently from the others. Jack was surely to be admired for all that.

Yet for his mother to refer to Jack as his father, to speak of his grandfather as if nothing had changed, chafed at Percy's mind. How can she talk like that, given what she told me? He felt angry with his mother and at the same time unjustified. She'd been hurt and burdened with a trial that would have devastated most women. She'd been a strong and loving mother, one he admired greatly, so he could hardly hold her early misfortune against her.

Yet, his anger and confusion still haunted him. In Sydney

he'd found himself checking mailing lists for the names of property owners around the outskirts of the city, for families who raised horses, well-known identities in the racing world. They'd been numerous, and anyone he'd asked about these families had scant praise for them. Wealthy land owners were not known for their community spirit or their generosity. They kept to their own kind and often treated their employees badly. He'd been advised to steer clear of them all.

Percy had tried to convince himself that he'd not want to know these people and that he was glad to have escaped growing up in such an atmosphere. Families like that would not have taken kindly to an illegitimate child. Surely he'd been far better off in his modest, but loving, home.

These thoughts circled Percy's mind over and over until he was tired of them. He shook his head and checked the time, surprised to realise how late it was getting. He would need to hurry. It was eighteen miles to Chandler's Hill and he wanted to get to the roadhouse before dark. He had a few things to pick up from the guest house where he lived. He'd have to cross back through the centre of town. Hopefully, Victoria Square would be all quiet now.

***

As Percy approached he could see that there was a line of cars in Victoria Square. Four of them were halted; a man in the rear car was honking his horn and waving his arms at those in front of him. Percy had hoped he could cross Victoria Square at the lower end and then head out towards Chandler's Hill. It looked now as if he might have to go around another way, which would take longer. He pulled his horse to the side and got down from the cart to better assess the situation.

His attention was drawn for a few moments by the cars,

two black and two deep green in colour. They all had shiny horns attached to the windscreens and wooden trims around the seating. They looked very plush and attractive and it was unusual to see four cars all at once. There was a large crowd still gathered in the street, listening to a man on a soapbox on the footpath, not far from Percy.

'The leader of the opposition is right when he says the Hun must be punished and that the best instruments of punishment for these murderers is our brave boys, who have already shed their blood for the cause in Gallipoli.' The man punched the air as he spoke and there was a raucous round of applause and cheering from the crowd.

Then came a shout from a woman at the rear of the group. 'No, I say. It's a crime to send our innocent boys as cannon fodder for the Brits. Too many are lost to us already. No to war, I say.' While the woman's voice was no match for that of the man on the soap box, a chorus of 'hear, hear' went up around her.

Percy was horrified to see what followed. Two women waving banners with '*WHO WILL GO?*' printed in large black letters, turned on the one who had spoken and began to push her to the edge of the crowd, until she stumbled and fell among the boots of the agitated crowd. As a man bent to help her up, he too was pushed and shoved by the shouting, angry proponents of war.

Without thinking Percy ran along the street until he was amongst the group. He elbowed his way through to where the man and woman were still being jostled and taunted. Two or three others were helping them regain their footing, while almost losing their own in the crush of the onslaught against them.

'You've had your go, cowards that you are. We've listened to your bleating all morning. You should be ashamed. Where's your patriotism? Go home and cower.' The shouts came unrelentingly, as fists began to fly.

The smaller group, which was clearly part of the earlier protest against the war, was quickly isolated at the back of the crowd and surrounded by a mob of outraged pro-war advocates.

Unwittingly, Percy realised he was amongst the smaller group. He held one woman's arm to prevent her falling and almost tripped himself when a banner was poked into his side. As he straightened up, he felt a sharp sting as the wood of the banner came down on his arm.

'Your mother would be ashamed of you, young man. Why aren't you out there defending our country? The Hun could be on our doorstep any day now, and here's you, a strong and able-bodied man, leaving the fight to others.'

'Shame. Shame. Shame.' The taunting came from a group of women now advancing on the group and waving their banners.

Percy managed to manoeuvre himself to the back of the group and extricate himself, while others pushed forward toward the angry crowd and shouted back at them. He moved further and further from the furore until it seemed no-one's attention was on him and then scurried back down the street. He was shaking all over and by the time he climbed back onto his cart, he was sure he was about to throw up.

***

Later that evening Percy sat in his room in the roadhouse at Chandler's Hill. He still felt shaken and had not been able to eat a bite of dinner. He'd bought a newspaper at the general store and now had it spread on the small desk beside his bed.

In some states more than a thousand men a day have enlisted, it read. *Sporting clubs, community groups, local government and individuals are running daily recruiting programs. Women are stopping men in the street and begging them to enlist in the services. The Government has reduced enlistment height requirements and eased dental standards.*

It was a nightmare. Percy wondered how bad it would get, how anyone would be able to stand up to the pressure that was mounting to enlist. The thought appalled him. There were also reports of men coming home wounded. Some, still hardly more than boys, coming home maimed for life. Reports of horrific losses and feats of extraordinary bravery, side by side in the paper, reflected the division that was growing in every community across the nation. A scathing opposition to the war and the horror it was reaping, alongside a zealous drive to enlist more men for the forces at the front. Joseph Cook, now leader of the opposition, was firing the campaign with a call for the punishment of the '*maiming, murdering and poisoning Huns*'.

Percy's stomach churned as he read on. A man called Tom Barker was preaching against the war in Sydney, where he was editing *Direct Action*, a paper reporting weekly news from the front. He seemed to be the most determined opponent of what he called the '*capitalist war*'. He'd already served time in prison for his anti-conscription poster, which read '*TO ARMS! Capitalists, Parsons, Politicians, Landlords, Newspaper Editors, and Other Stay-at-home Patriots. Your Country Needs You in the Trenches! Workers, Follow Your Masters!*'

Percy shuddered. He wondered if it might be safer to be interned on an island somewhere. He could hardly imagine what a pro-war group of people might do to a person with German ties. It didn't bear thinking about. *Perhaps I should be grateful for Mum's revelations. Though that doesn't save me from those who would see me shipped off to the trenches.*

He drifted into a restless sleep that night, pushing away angry faces of irate women and allowing the sweet face of Mabel Smart to float through his dreams.

CHAPTER SEVEN

Kangarilla, June 1915

Mabel heard footsteps on the front path and edged towards the door. She took a deep breath and straightened her hair, then counted to ten, not wanting to appear too anxious to greet the visitor.

'Percy, how nice to see you again. I believe Aunt Sarah is expecting you this morning. She's in the kitchen packing up the last of her things.'

'Hello, Mabel.' Percy's smile was broad and warm. 'Yes, I can see the cart out front is packed up with quite a load. I hope you and your aunt haven't been lifting those heavy boxes.'

'They weren't so heavy, really. Mostly linen and clothes. The heavy things were taken across to the new place a couple of days ago. We had plenty of uncles and cousins to help.'

'Good. Well, I'll disconnect the telephone and then help you with the rest of the things.' He nodded as Mabel gestured for him to come inside and turned towards the telephone on the wall in the parlour.

'We'll be all ready by then to go over to McLaren Flat Road where her new home is. Perhaps you could follow us. It's only a mile or so.'

Percy shrugged. 'I have the new address here on the order so I'm sure I could find it if you have other things to do.'

'No, nothing else. Aunt Sarah is keen to get settled. She's been sleeping over there for the past few nights. We just wanted to make sure this place was spick and span. The new owners will be here in a couple of days.'

'Sounds fine. It shouldn't take me more than an hour or so to reconnect the telephone.'

'Perhaps you'd like to have some lunch with us when you're done? I could make us potato pie while you're working.'

'Potato pie! One of my favourites. My mother makes a great potato pie.' His voice dropped and the smile faded from his face at the mention of his mother. Mabel sensed he was missing her.

'I suppose it's a while since you had your mother's cooking, is it? You said you'd been training and working in Sydney. Was it too far to go back for a home-cooked meal every now and then?'

'Certainly was.' He busied himself with the telephone while he talked.

'I've never been to Sydney, so I've no idea how big it is and how far out the properties are. I imagine it's far bigger than Adelaide.' Mabel watched his face as he worked deftly with his tools and removed the telephone backboard. She saw his forehead crease into furrows and wondered if Percy found her too inquisitive. She was drawn to this young man and wanted to know all about him, but sensed it would be better to steer clear of questions about his family.

'Yes, Sydney's far larger than Adelaide, and not as well laid out,' he said. 'It seems to have grown without too much planning. I think the search for arable land in the early days meant it spread wherever there was water and good soil.'

'Were your parents early settlers?' The question was out before she could stop herself. 'I'm sorry. I should let you get your work done. I'll see how Aunt Sarah is going. She might need some help to wrap the last of her teacups.' Mabel grinned and hurried away to the kitchen.

***

Later, in the small cottage in McLaren Flats Road, as they finished eating potato pie, Mabel kept the conversation strictly to her own family.

'My cousin, Allan, has gone off to Adelaide to enlist. Mother's in such a tizz about it, but Father says he can understand young men wanting to go and fight. He doesn't agree with the war, but he says if he were young, he'd likely find the challenge of enlisting appealing. Young men do like to prove themselves, I suppose.'

'I imagine Emma almost faints at the thought.' Sarah rolled her eyes as she sipped her tea.

'She does.' Mabel nodded. 'You're not tempted, Percy?' She watched his face, hoping he'd not changed his mind about signing up.

He shook his head. 'Not at all, but with the ruckus going on in Adelaide about conscription, I might not have a choice in the end.'

'What ruckus?' Mabel leaned across the table towards him.

'There was a rally held yesterday in Victoria Square, protesting against conscription, and then a pro-war crowd set up their own meeting. The two groups got into quite a tussle. I was a bit caught up in it actually.' He lifted the edge of his shirt sleeve to reveal a dark bruise on his forearm.

Mabel gasped. 'You mean you were struck?'

He grinned and nodded. 'By a middle-aged woman with a banner, no less. It could have been worse, though. There were men throwing punches.'

'That's terrible.' Mabel was tempted to reach across and stroke his arm.

'I'm assuming you were with the group protesting against conscription?' Sarah's brow furrowed.

'Well, I wasn't with either group, really. I went to see what was holding up the traffic when I was heading out of the city, and when I saw a woman being knocked down, I went to help. Next thing, I was in the middle of some very angry people who seemed to have lost all sense of reason. I can't imagine what it's like on the front lines of the war when I see so-called peaceful people behaving like that.'

'Poor Allan.' Mabel's thoughts went back to her cousin. 'I doubt he's got any idea what he's getting into. He's hardly left Uncle Fred's farm at Koppia. It's very isolated over there. Perhaps when he gets to Adelaide and finds out what's going on, he'll change his mind.'

'He's in his early forties, dear,' Sarah said. 'Never married, and spent most of his life digging potatoes. He's probably dying for a bit of excitement.' She paused and looked remorseful about the word she'd used. 'I meant he's likely thinking it will be an adventure, travelling to the other side of the world.'

'It's not going to be a holiday, Mrs Goble,' Percy said, pushing back from the table. 'But I must be on my way. Thank you so much for the delicious lunch. It will keep me going well for the afternoon. I've another connection to complete over on Baker Gully Road.' Glancing at his watch he stood and picked up his plate.

'Please don't bother with those,' Sarah said. 'I've plenty of time to clear the dishes. Since I stepped back from my business I seem to have too much time on my hands altogether.'

'What kind of business did you have?' Percy seemed impressed.

'A millinery shop.' Sarah nodded. 'I had to support myself for many years after my husband died. I still own the business, but I have someone managing it for me now.'

Percy beamed. 'I think that's wonderful. I'd like to have a business one day.'

'You would?' Mabel was intrigued.

'Yes, I think I'd make a good businessman. I like working

with figures and I think I'd have good ideas about promoting a business. Perhaps a general store.' He nodded, looking pleased with the idea.

'Well, you're young, and I'm sure you could accomplish whatever you choose,' Sarah said, clapping her hands together. 'Perhaps you could manage a post office. I'm certainly pleased with the service you've given me. I'll commend you to your employer. All workers should be so pleasant and accommodating.'

'Thank you very much.' Percy smiled broadly and then looked down at Mabel. 'It's been lovely to meet you both. If there's anything else I can do to help, or if you have any further trouble with your telephone, I'd be glad to check it.'

Mabel searched for something to say, feeling dismayed at the thought of not seeing Percy again. 'Did you say you have another job on Baker Gully Road this afternoon?' She waited for Percy to nod. 'That's where I live. Our farm is just off Baker Gully Road. It's called Park Farm.'

'Yes, I think you mentioned last time that you lived that way.'

Mabel hesitated for a moment. 'Perhaps you could come to dinner?' she said. Once the words were out of her mouth her mind tried to picture Percy in her family home, meeting her mother. She wondered what her father would say to her inviting a stranger to dinner. She grinned at Percy, who seemed stuck for words. 'I'm sure it would be all right. After all, you are a stranger to these parts, and so far from home. Mother would want you to have a home-cooked meal, I'm sure.'

She glanced at her aunt, who was standing with a stack of plates in her hands and her mouth hanging slightly open. Sarah's eyebrows rose, crinkling her forehead. Mabel imagined she might be about to say that Emma never cooked and that she would actually be horrified at her daughter bringing a stranger to their home. But she merely shook her head as a grin spread across her face.

'Please say you'll come, Percy.' Mabel turned back to him and moved around the table to where he stood, still looking unsure.

'I don't think that would be appropriate, Mabel, although I appreciate the thought. I can't imagine what your parents would think and I would hardly be properly attired after I finish work.'

'That wouldn't matter at all.' Mabel rushed on. 'My brothers often come to the dinner table quite casually. Father only dresses because Mother prefers it, but they'll understand that you've come straight from work. I'm going home soon. I'll warn them. I mean, I'll tell them about you, how helpful you've been and how you're a long way from home. You shouldn't be going back to a roadhouse to eat alone. It's not right. Please, say you'll come.'

Percy's face flushed and he seemed to be in two minds. He looked to Sarah. 'What do you think, Mrs Goble? Would your sister mind?'

Sarah's grin faded and her brow creased deeply. 'I can't always predict what my sister will think, Percy, but I do imagine Albert will sympathise with a young man who's been badly treated in the city and needs a little home care. He's a very kind man.'

'Yes, yes,' Mabel said, seizing upon the idea. 'Of course Mother and Father will be concerned with you being set upon when you were only trying to help a poor woman. And they'll want to hear the news from Adelaide, I'm sure.'

'Well, I suppose I could come, if you really think it wouldn't be an imposition.' Percy's voice faltered. He still appeared reluctant.

'Good.' Mabel clapped her hands together. It was all settled in her mind. She would hurry home and prepare her parents. It suddenly seemed very important to her that they liked this young man, for she certainly liked him very much.

'And how on earth are you going to manage this?' Sarah said, when they'd given Percy instructions about how to find Park Farm and seen him off.

'I'm not sure,' Mabel admitted, dropping back into her chair at the table. 'I know Mother will get in a flap, but really Aunt Sarah, what's the harm? I'm merely inviting a lonely young man to dinner. He's such a long way from home. Didn't you say Sydney's over a thousand miles away? Goodness, it seems the hospitable thing to do, don't you think so?' She grinned up at her aunt. 'Surely what Grandfather Golder would have done … in his latter years.'

Sarah giggled. 'I agree, dear, but I still can't imagine what your mother will make of it. Even your father is likely to be suspicious of your involvement with Percy. After all, you've only met him twice.'

'It's been perfectly respectable.' Mabel arched up. 'We've been with you the entire time and Percy's been nothing but a gentleman.'

'I'm aware of that, Mabel.' Sarah held up her hands as if to defend her concerns. 'I'm merely suggesting that you might have to explain yourself and your intentions very clearly to your parents. Especially to your mother.' Sarah gathered the remaining dishes from the table. 'Now, I'm quite set up here and I think I could do with an afternoon nap, so I suggest you get along home and think carefully about what you're going to say when you get there.'

Mabel took her time going home in her cart. Aunt Sarah was right, of course. She'd need to be careful what she said to her mother or there'd be all kinds of misunderstandings and fuss. It would be terrible for Percy to turn up and feel unwelcome. She began to doubt her idea. *What if Mother starts going on about my asthma? What would Percy think of me then? I'm sure it would be the end of any interest he might have in me.*

By the time Mabel reached the house she was feeling very nervous about the evening ahead.

'I can't imagine what possessed you,' her mother exclaimed when Mabel said she'd invited a young man to dinner. 'A telephone repairman! He could be anybody.'

'Now, dear.' Albert patted Emma's arm across the table where they were having afternoon tea. 'I'm sure Mabel was trying to be kind. It sounds like the young man has been very helpful to your sister.'

'That's what he was being paid for.' Emma sniffed and lifted her cup to her lips. 'What on earth will we have to talk to him about?' She glanced around the lavish parlour. 'What if he's … not to be trusted. You don't invite perfect strangers into our home, Mabel. It's unheard of.'

'I was trying to be hospitable and kind, Mother.' Mabel was having trouble controlling her voice. She felt at once like crying at her mother's reaction and also reprimanding her. Aunt Sarah was right. Her mother was a snob. 'I would have thought it Christian charity to extend hospitality to a young man who's far from home and who's gone out of his way to be accommodating with one of our family.'

'It was kind of you, Mabel.' Albert nodded. 'Perhaps a little more warning might have helped. Nevertheless, it's done now. He's coming and we'll certainly show Christian charity. Won't we, dear?' He looked pointedly at Emma, who was still sniffing into her tea cup and holding it between her hands as if to stop them shaking.

Mabel was annoyed and disappointed. *What a fuss. As if we can't afford to extend kindness and share a meal.* But truth be known, she was mostly worried. It seemed an impossibility to hope that her parents would see Percy as anything but a passing tradesman, at best. Her father was right. She should have given her parents more warning, prepared them better. She should have got to know Percy a little more before inviting him to meet them. Though she couldn't imagine how that was going to happen unless Aunt Sarah's telephone needed attention.

Mabel put thoughts of the telephone from her mind. That was another thing she'd said very little about to her parents. Her mother would not approve of her keeping in touch with Sophie so regularly as she had. This war had made her mother even more anxious and suspicious than she usually was. It was truly cause for much angst, even here in their own country. What was happening across the sea, where men were armed with guns and intent on killing each other, was beyond Mabel's comprehension.

***

'So Percy, it must be difficult, being away from home.' Albert began the conversation once the family was settled around the dinner table. 'Tell us, what attracted you to working with telephones? Mabel said your parents have a property on the outskirts of Sydney.'

Mabel cringed. She'd hoped her parents wouldn't question Percy too much about his family, but of course that was naïve. What else would they talk to him about? She looked around at her brothers and sisters and wondered what they were thinking. David and Frederick appeared to be quite interested in their guest. David would say very little, she was sure, but he was watching Percy with an open face and his natural kindness was obvious. Frederick, at fourteen, would likely ask Percy about telephones if he were able to get a word in.

Isabel and Clara were watching their mother, whose lips were pursed in the usual manner when she was maintaining a strained dignity. Clearly Mabel's sisters could see, as she could herself, that their mother was not impressed with this young man.

Most eyes were on Percy as Albert concluded his question.

Mabel wished she'd not asked him to dinner. It had been impulsive and ill-conceived, and now it seemed any idea she'd had that Percy might be comfortable with her family, or them with him, was doomed.

'My parents are farmers,' Percy began, looking sheepish. 'But I've always been interested in machines, in the new technologies. I read a lot and I wanted to learn more about things like telephones. It seemed the best way was to train, to install and repair them. I'm learning more each day.' He swallowed loudly and looked to Albert as if seeking approval.

'I see.' Albert nodded and his smile suggested he didn't disapprove. He waited while Beattie, the kitchen maid, laid platters of food on the table. 'You'd probably be interested to know that in 1870 my three eldest brothers went by ship to Darwin to be part of the team that built the overland telegraph line from there south.'

Percy's face lit up. 'That's very interesting, Mr Smart. It must have been exciting.'

'Yes. I was only eleven at the time and the youngest in the family. I remember being quite jealous of my brothers.'

Percy nodded. 'We've come a long way since then but there's still so much to be learned about communications.'

'Well, for most of us these things remain confounding.' Emma sniffed. 'Why a person needs such a contraption is a mystery to me.' She indicated with a nod and a sharp look that her husband should begin to serve himself dinner. While he spooned vegetables onto his plate, she patted her mouth with her napkin. When everyone had a portion of dinner on their plates Emma spoke again without looking directly at Percy. 'Actually, I think telephones are rather mean spirited things.'

Percy looked up at her, clearly confused. Everyone else put their heads down and began to eat.

'Well, it's only between two people, isn't it, a conversation on one of those things?' Emma went on as if everyone was waiting to hear her explanation. 'News that otherwise might have come by letter and been shared around the table by everyone, is now secreted away between two people. And if such a private conversation is necessary, then surely the nature of it suggests it should be done face to face.'

She looked pleased with her assessment and picked up her knife and fork as if she'd summed up the invention soundly and everyone must surely agree with her.

'Aunt Sarah finds her telephone very useful, Mother.' Mabel was determined to defend Percy and dispute her mother's ideas, which were clearly meant as affront to their guest.

'Perhaps because she's had to engage in business she's found a use for it,' Emma said as if her sister were to be pitied. 'However, I doubt most of us on the land will ever need such a thing.' She turned to Percy with what could hardly be called a smile on her face. 'What of your parents' property, young man? Who will carry on your father's work? Mabel said he did something with horses.'

Percy swallowed loudly. 'Yes, my father was a jockey.' His eyes darted to Mabel.

'A jockey?' There was an audible gasp from Emma. David and Frederick leaned into the table towards Percy, clearly intrigued.

'Percy's father raises thoroughbred horses,' Mabel was quick to clarify. 'Isn't that what you said, Percy?' She looked across the table at him, her hopes dropping even further. This was not going well at all.

'Yes.' Percy paled but nodded. 'The family does have thoroughbred horses. But my father was a great jockey in his early days … before he was married. Mum has often told me about the races he won at Grafton each year. He and his brother were unbeatable, apparently.' He picked up the glass of water in front of him and took a long drink.

'Grafton?' Emma's voice held an obvious note of suspicion. 'I thought your property was in Sydney.'

Mabel would have liked to have thrown something at her mother. She looked to her father, her eyes pleading with him to contain Mother's interrogation.

'It is,' Percy said. 'But the races at Grafton were a great draw for jockeys all around New South Wales. My father liked to take horses up there to try them out. That's where my mother comes from. It's where they met.' His words seemed to rush out now.

Mabel could see how nervous her mother was making Percy and she was getting more annoyed.

'I see,' Emma went on. 'So you've no desire to carry on your father's work? I'm sure that must be a disappointment for him.'

Percy shook his head. 'I have a young brother. I imagine Clarrie might follow in Dad's footsteps. He's only twelve though, so it's hard to tell yet.'

'So you're the eldest son?' Emma went on.

'I am.' Percy's answer was a little curt and Mabel thought perhaps he was also getting annoyed with her mother's questions. He pushed a baked potato onto his fork and brought it to his mouth as if to indicate he needed a break from speaking.

'I think we should let the young man eat, Emma.' Albert tapped the side of his plate with his fork, taking Emma's attention away from Percy.

Mabel was grateful for her father's interjection. 'Yes, Beattie's gone to a lot of trouble with dinner, and I think she's made an apple pie for sweets. We all love her apple pie, don't we, Frederick?' She nudged her young brother's shoulder, causing him to break his stare across the table at Percy.

'We do. At least I do,' he said, grinning at her.

'Have you heard how cousin Allan is getting along, Father?' Mabel turned to her father, relieved to have the attention off Percy.

'With enlisting you mean?' Albert answered. 'I haven't heard any more beyond that he was heading to Adelaide to sign up. I imagine there's quite a procedure involved. Medical checks and some training in one of the local camps that have been set up for the purpose, no doubt.'

'Perhaps it's because Uncle Frederick was one of those who went to Darwin.' Isabel said. 'Allan might see it as an adventure and an opportunity to travel.'

'Perhaps.' Albert nodded. 'I'm still hoping that the war will end before too many end up overseas. History tells us that for most, war is a terrible thing.'

'I heard there was a march in Adelaide today.' Clara spoke for the first time. 'There's a lot of talk about a vote for conscription and some people are protesting about it. One of the customers today said there were riots in the streets.'

'You see why I disapprove of you being in town with all this going on, Clara.' Emma put her knife and fork down loudly. 'You could be in danger just walking down the street, even in Clarendon. Just hearing about all this is unseemly for a young woman. I do wish you'd give up this idea of millinery.' She said the last as if it were unsavoury. 'It's all Sarah's influence.' She huffed. 'A lady making a living in a shop is … well, it's quite unnecessary.'

'Really, Mother, that's unfair.' Mabel couldn't help herself. 'You know Aunt Sarah had to support herself for many years after Uncle George died. What else could she have done?'

'She could have remarried,' Emma said quickly. 'There were suitors. Most women who are widowed and still have small children would be more than pleased to accept an offer of marriage.'

'Perhaps she didn't love any of the suitors.' Mabel's retort was more fractious than she intended and she dropped her eyes from her mother's face. 'I mean, perhaps she preferred to concentrate on caring for her children herself. I think she was very courageous.'

'Or stubborn,' Emma continued. 'She could have accepted help from family. There was more than enough of that as well.' Her disapproval of her sister was obvious but it was not a new thing for Mabel to hear.

'I think that's enough of such talk,' Albert said, interrupting, just as Emma seemed about to continue. He turned to Clara. 'So, dear, did your customer say that there were people hurt in the riots?'

Mabel shrunk into her seat. She had decided not to say anything to her parents about Percy being caught up in the rally in the city. After her mother's initial response to the idea of having a stranger to dinner, Mabel had considered his misfortune in the city would have only added to his unsuitability in her mother's mind. Now it seemed it might come out after all, and she could only hope it might draw some compassion from her father, at least.

'Percy was there,' she said, looking along the table at him and smiling. 'You were trying to help a woman who'd been pushed over, weren't you, Percy?'

There was silence around the table. Percy's eyes rose from his dinner plate. 'Yes, I was there. It was quite a commotion.'

'What were you doing there?' Emma's voice emitted disapproval again.

Mabel sighed loudly. 'He wasn't rioting, if that's what you think, Mother.'

'Mabel.' Her father's tone held a warning. 'Perhaps you'd best let Percy speak for himself.'

'I was just passing through, actually,' Percy said. 'Heading out here for work. I was shocked by the degree of pushing and shoving, the obvious anger amongst the crowd–on both sides. It was probably naïve of me to think I could help.' Percy shrugged. 'It's sad to see so many people turning on each other.'

Albert nodded. 'The war is bringing out the worst of us in many ways.'

'It may yet bring out the best in some, though, Father.' David's statement drew every eye to him. 'I know the war makes people take sides but at least it's making them think about what they believe in. And there will be heroes on the front lines, I'm sure. I think some of the men who are going really believe they need to fight for their country, for our country. Perhaps they do.'

The only sound for a long minute was Emma's intake of breath. Mabel watched the colour drain from her mother's face and she looked as if she might be starting to sway.

'Don't get upset, Emma,' Albert said. 'I'm sure David wasn't saying that he's about to enlist?' He looked across the table at his son, his eyebrows raised into a question.

'No, I wasn't, Father,' David said. 'I don't have the strength of character that some of these boys have. I'm a coward, really. I've been called one right here in town and I'm not going to deny it. That doesn't mean I don't admire some of the men leaving their families and going to fight.'

'David, how could you say something so …?' Emma seemed lost for words. 'Of course you're not a coward. Going to war is foolish and I wouldn't hear of you going.' She took a deep breath and sat back in her seat.

'Someone has called you a coward?' Albert sat forward, his face creased with concern.

'Yes, Father. There's a growing number of people who are determined to see every young man in uniform. Women mostly. They're marching around with banners, calling for us all to go and support their sons and husbands who have already gone.'

Albert nodded. 'I'm sure it's their fear of losing their loved ones that makes them say such things. You mustn't take it too personally.'

'I'm trying, Father. I don't believe I'm called to fight but it's hard to maintain a sense of self-respect in the face of such criticism. Don't you agree, Percy?'

It seemed to Mabel to be an odd place for her brother to seek support. She turned to Percy, hoping he wasn't made all the more uncomfortable by this turn in the conversation.

'I agree with you, David.' Percy nodded and his expression towards David was warm. 'I've had criticism too, but as much as I hate the idea of war and all the horror it brings, I also can't help but have admiration for the men who go. I only hope that many can return reasonably whole and be able to live with the terror they've seen and experienced.'

'Well, I respect you both for your ideas,' Albert said. 'It's hard to know what to think about all this. I thought turning on those in our community who are of German descent was bad enough, but turning on our own young men because they choose not to fight, well, that's just appalling. I'm sorry you've had to suffer this, both of you. We'll all have to support each other through it and pray it ends soon. Now, I think this is getting a bit much for Emma, so we'd best turn our thoughts to other things.'

Mabel was saddened by what she'd been hearing from her brother and Percy. Young men were bearing the brunt of this war, whether at home or overseas, and she wasn't sure how to support them. One thing she knew for sure: her respect and admiration for Percy had only grown from this evening with him, despite the fact that her mother was clearly shaken and probably in no mind to think well of him at all.

CHAPTER EIGHT

Kangarilla, July 1915

Percy knocked tentatively on the door of the cottage in McLarens Flat Road. Mrs Goble's face broke into a broad smile when she saw him.

'Percy, what a surprise. Did I call about my telephone and then forget I'd done it?' She chuckled. 'Come in, come in. I'm joking. It's freezing out there.'

'Thank you, Mrs Goble. I was just passing actually and thought I'd check in to see all was well with your telephone. One of the lines came down in the wind and some of the servicemen have been out to check the poles. I've had to make some adjustments to a few of the domestic handsets.'

'I see.' Mrs Goble grinned at him and he suspected she could guess his real motive for dropping in. 'Well, now that you're here, you might like to have a cup of tea with me. I've made some fresh scones.'

'Yes, and they smell wonderful, Mrs Goble, but I don't want to put you to any trouble.'

'No trouble. You park yourself here in the parlour for a few minutes while I put the kettle on.' She gestured to one of the large lounge chairs and headed for the kitchen.

Percy sat down and cast his eyes around the neat, but

homely, parlour. There was a warm and welcoming feel to the room, in fact to the house, which he knew was down to Mrs Goble's genuine kindness. *So different to her sister*. His thoughts went back to the evening a month before when he'd sat with Mabel's family around the table.

He'd been so tense that night that he could barely get his food down, and he'd been left in no doubt that Mabel's mother had not liked him, nor approved of him being there. Then to top it off, he'd continued to lie about his own family, which had caused him to feel sick in the stomach. His head had spun with confusion for he'd almost forgotten what he'd previously said to Mabel. *I was such a fool to lie in the first place.*

'How did your dinner at my sister's home go after the last time you were here?' Mrs Goble came back into the room with a tray and laid it on the small table in the centre of the room.

Percy felt like she was reading his mind. 'Uh, not too badly,' he said, knowing he was lying again. 'Well, actually, it was difficult,' he confessed. 'I don't think your sister liked me much.'

'I wouldn't let that bother you. Emma doesn't take to people easily. I'm sure she'd like you fine if she wasn't worried that Mabel likes you too much.' She set out two cups on the table and poured tea into both. 'Just a moment and I'll bring the scones.'

Percy stared at the teacups, trying to take in what Mrs Goble had said.

'Here we are.' She came back into the room holding a plate piled high with light brown scones. 'The jam is right there by the sugar. You help yourself.' She handed him a small plate and sat down opposite him. 'So apart from Emma being put out, how did you find the rest of the family?'

'Mr Smart was very pleasant,' he said, piling jam onto a scone. 'And I liked David. He and I seemed to have some common ideas. It's difficult with the war issue, so many strong views. It's a bit tricky having a conversation without offending someone or being attacked. Verbally, I mean. I haven't been set upon physically … apart from my little run in with that banner in the city,' he added, anticipating her concern and trying to keep the mood light.

'I'm glad to hear that, at least.' She grinned and picked up her tea. 'All this talk of conscription is wearisome, really. It's all the women at the Home League talk about, and you're right, different views about it get people very upset. Women who've known and respected each other for as long as I can remember, now bicker like children.' She shuddered.

'Mabel's family were worried about her cousin, Allan.'

'That's Albert's nephew. It's a worry, but as I've said to them, he won't be the last. The longer the war goes on, the more pressure there is for men to enlist. And from all reports, this battle at Gallipoli is far from over. A place most of us had never heard of until a few months ago and now it's on everyone's tongue.' She sighed deeply. 'You haven't seen Mabel since, then?'

'No, I haven't. I trust she's well.' Percy felt his ears burn and sensed he was flushing. He'd thought often about Mabel over the past month and wondered how he was going to get to see her again. Her smile invaded his sleep and he'd found himself watching young women's faces in the street, as if she might magically appear before him one day.

'She's not, actually,' he heard Mrs Goble say. It jolted him from his thoughts.

'She's not well?' he asked, concern flooding his mind.

'She's had a rather nasty asthma attack. I think it's worse in the winter and she might have caught a bit of a cold. That always makes her breathing more difficult.'

'I'm so sorry to hear that,' Percy said. 'I didn't know she suffered with asthma.' *I really must see how she is now*. His heart began to thump and his thoughts ran to visiting Park

Farm. Mrs Smart's frown flashed before his eyes. *She'd likely not let me in.* 'Is she improving? It's hard to imagine her laid up. She's so full of life.'

'Yes, she hides her condition well. In fact, she'd hate to know I'd called it that. It sounds so permanent, but the fact is, it's something she's had to deal with since she was young and I'm afraid, unless medical science gets a wriggle on and finds a better treatment, she always will.'

'It sounds serious. Poor girl.' Percy felt his stomach knot. 'Do you think the cold weather affects her badly?'

'I'm sure it doesn't help, but really, there's a lot of speculation about what causes asthma. I suspect her mother is no help in that regard.' She rolled her eyes.

'Her mother? It's clear she's not an easy woman to please, but surely that wouldn't cause Mabel to have asthma?' Percy drew in some tea and felt it warm his throat. He wrapped his hands around the cup and was grateful for the heat. He realised he'd been very cold before coming into the house and the chill had seeped into his bones. *Mororo was never this cold. No wonder people become unwell here.*

'Not directly.' Mrs Goble addressed his question. 'But I do think the stress of having someone around who's forever anxious, really doesn't help.'

'I suppose not,' Percy said. 'I imagine when Mabel's unwell, her mother is even more anxious than usual.

'She certainly is, and she's quite convinced that the asthma comes from Mabel being anxious. It would be comical if it weren't so serious.'

'Oh dear, and with all that's going on in the world right now, I'm sure Mrs Smart has plenty to worry about.' Percy shifted uneasily in his chair. Seeing Mabel seemed like an impossibility. 'Do you think your sister would mind if I visited? If I went to the house and asked after Mabel, do you think she'd let me see her for a few moments?'

'I'm not sure, Percy.' Mrs Goble shook her head. 'She's very protective. No doubt the doctor's been a few times and Mabel will be under instructions to rest.' Mrs Goble picked up a scone and spread it with jam.

Percy watched her, his mind racing. 'So, she doesn't go out at all when she's got asthma?'

'Not until it's on the mend. However, I'd be surprised if she's not at church on Sunday. We all go to the Methodist Church in Kangarilla. Mabel often comes here afterwards. Emma doesn't approve of that, as I'm sure you're aware, but Mabel is determined when she wants something. She's not one to let her illness get the better of her. She likes to call her friend, Sophie, in Adelaide and she hasn't done that for nearly three weeks now, so I'm guessing she'll make every effort to be well enough to come Sunday.'

'I see. Well, would you please say hello to her for me? I hate to think of her being ill.'

'Why don't you come out here Sunday afternoon and see her for yourself? I'm sure she'd be glad of your visit.' Mrs Goble grinned at him and wiped crumbs from her mouth with a napkin. 'She's as taken with you as you are with her, Percy. Anyone with eyes can see that.'

Percy felt a hot wave of embarrassment rush up his neck and into his cheeks. 'Really? I didn't know I was that obvious. I do like Mabel. She's such a sweet girl. I can't imagine her parents, at least her mother, would be pleased to think Mabel had any feelings for me, though.'

'I'm sure you're right. Emma is set on marrying Mabel off to one of the landowner's sons around here, but like I said, Mabel can be very determined too, and I've no doubt she'd love to see you again.'

95

'I don't know what to say, Mrs Goble, but I must admit I feel very pleased about that.' Percy shifted in his seat and reached for another scone. 'May I?' He looked up into Mrs Goble's twinkling eyes.

'Of course.' She nodded. 'I'm glad to have someone to cook for. The creases around the corners of her eyes deepened and softened.

Percy could see that Mrs Goble approved of whatever was growing between her niece and himself. *If only her sister felt the same.* 'I'd like to come Sunday, as long as you think it would be all right. I don't want to upset your sister. That would do me no good at all, would it?' He grinned.

'Best not to think about what will and won't upset Emma, dear. Mabel will make up her own mind, I'm sure.'

***

For the second time in a week Percy approached the door of the cottage in McLaren Flat Road. This time his mind was on Mabel's health. He'd hardly been able to think straight since finding out she'd been unwell. He knew little about asthma but had asked a few people what they knew and he was worried by what he'd found out. It had made him realise just how she had touched his heart in the short time he'd known her. *If she's not here at her aunt's today, I'll have to go to her home. I can't bear not knowing how she is any longer.*

'Percy, I thought it would be you.' Mrs Goble smiled and held the door open.

Percy's heart sank and his face must have shown it.

'Don't worry, Mabel is here. She's in the parlour.' Mrs Goble waved towards the other room and gave his arm a nudge.

'How is she?'

'Why don't you go and see for yourself,' she said with a chuckle.

Percy walked into the parlour wondering if he was going to see Mabel laying on the lounge chair under a blanket and looking as pale as death, but instead she was arranging flowers in a vase on the small table in the middle of the room.

As he entered the room she turned and her face broke into a wide smile. Her cheeks were rosy, her dark hair glossy.

'Goodness,' he said, 'you appear to have recovered very well. You look lovely.' He stopped short, realising his feelings for her were obvious.

She blushed prettily, adding to the pink of her cheeks. 'Thank you, kind sir, I'm sure.' She curtsied slightly and gave him a cheeky smile as she rose from the floor. 'I'm feeling fine.'

'I'm so glad. I've been worried. Was it terrible?'

'The asthma, you mean? Or Mother's fussing? Really, it passes quite quickly and I'm a little weak for a day or two, that's all. A good sleep usually has me up and about. I had a bit of a head cold for a week after the attack, but I'm all better now.'

Percy nodded. 'That's good. I've heard some pretty awful accounts of asthma attacks in the past few days. I imagined you'd be in bed for weeks, especially since it's so cold.'

'Nonsense. My attacks aren't that bad. The wind is bad for me, but the cold doesn't bother me too much, as long as I rug up well. And that's why Mother agreed to my coming to Aunt Sarah's for a few days.'

'A few days?' Percy's spirits were rising by the minute.

'Yes, you see it's my birthday this week, the 19th of July. In fact it's my nineteenth birthday, so Mother could hardly refuse me what I asked for, could she?'

'Well, Happy Birthday for Thursday.' Percy made a mental note to remember the date. 'And what did you ask your mother for?' *I must find something pretty in town this week to give her.*

'A new coat.' Mabel clapped her hands together. 'But it wasn't so much the coat I wanted, as a few days with Aunt Sarah, because I knew she'd be happy to take me to Adelaide to the big stores.'

'I see. Well the coat sounds sensible, but are you sure you want to go into Adelaide?'

'Why ever not?'

'With so many protests and marches and banner waving women about the streets, it's not really safe these days, sadly. I'd hate to think of you getting caught up in one of those crowds.'

'What crowds?' Sarah came into the parlour with a tray of tea and scones. 'I could see how much you liked my scones earlier this week, Percy, so I made some more.'

'You're too kind.' Percy moved an ornament so she could lay the tray on the table.

'So, why are you two standing here in the middle of the room? For heaven's sake sit down and make yourselves comfortable. Mabel picked these flowers on the way back from church and she's been fiddling with them ever since. Anyone would think we were having royalty visit.' Sarah chuckled and dropped into one of the lounge chairs.

Percy and Mabel followed suit, glancing at each other and grinning.

'Now, what's all this about crowds?' Sarah began to pour tea.

'I was telling Percy that we're going into the city to buy a new coat for my birthday. He's concerned about the crowds.'

'It's not so much the crowds,' Percy explained. 'It's the protesters and marchers. When they get into these groups, people seem to go a little mad. They throw things about and yell out like banshees. It can be dangerous.'

'You haven't been attacked again, have you?' Mabel leaned forward, her eyes full of concern.

'No, but I stay well away from the rallies now.'

'Then we will too. Surely we can get to the stores without

encountering one of those mobs. We're going to stay in town overnight, so we can choose the best time to go shopping.'

'I see.' Percy nodded. 'Well, I'm sure you'll be sensible.' He looked to Mrs Goble, hoping for reassurance.

'We'll be careful, Percy,' she said. 'Mabel has rung her friend, Sophie, and she's suggested where we should stay. We can't fit in her grandmother's cottage but there's a guest house not far from where she lives and it's quite away from the centre of town, where I imagine all the ruckus goes on. We can still walk to the shops from there it seems.'

Mabel nodded. 'So you see, you've no need to worry.' She flashed him a smile as she sipped her tea. Percy's heart missed a beat.

'I know you can keep my secret,' she went on. 'I'm going to meet up with Sophie while I'm there. That's my other birthday wish. I haven't seen her for nine months now, and even though I've been able to talk to her on the telephone, I'm dying to see her in person.'

'And who is this a secret from?' Percy asked. 'Are you going to surprise her with your visit?'

'Goodness, no. She's looking forward to it just as much as me. It's Mother I haven't told. She'd only fuss and worry. She's sure that there are officials watching everyone who has any German relatives, ready to pounce on them at any minute, and terrified that I'd be carted off with them. Less said the better with Mother.'

'I see.' Percy nodded. 'Does she think your friend's father might be a spy?' He reached over and piled jam on a scone as he spoke, hoping to cover any sign that the issue of German heritage was difficult for him.

'No, I'm sure not, but she's always afraid something bad might happen. It's best not to worry her more than we have to, isn't it, Aunt Sarah?'

'It is, dear, but as I've said to you, I wonder if these little secrets of ours may not come back to bite us as far as your mother is concerned. She hardly has the best opinion of me as it is. If anything did happen, I'd be the worst in the world.' Sarah shook her head and frowned.

'You're not having second thoughts about taking me into the city, are you?' Mabel's face dropped and Percy wanted to reach out and take her hand.

'Would it help if I was about, sort of on hand, to look out for you?' The words were out of his mouth before he could consider them. He wanted to be with Mabel whenever he could, but didn't want to make things worse for her, or for Mrs Goble. He was sure Mrs Smart would not be reassured by his presence near her daughter, and if she knew that he also had German connections, be they now more tenuous than he'd once thought, that would make it even worse. *What a tangled web I've woven with my lies. How will I ever sort this out with Mabel, let alone Mrs Smart?* He shuddered at the thought.

'Would you?' Mabel's delight jolted him from his musing.

'Would I what? Oh, yes, of course. I'll be working in the city most of this week. I could work around your shopping outing and chaperone you, so to speak. I'd be happy to.'

'That's very kind,' Mrs Goble said with a knowing grin. 'I'm sure that would ease my mind considerably. I doubt any of those women with banners will be after me or Mabel, but it pays to be careful.'

'It does, indeed.' Percy nodded and bit into a scone, feeling excited about the prospect of the week ahead.

'When is your birthday, Percy?' Mabel asked after a few moments peace while they all enjoyed the fluffy golden scones and jam.

Percy thought for a moment. 'It's just passed actually,' he said between bites. 'June 27th.'

'And I'll bet you didn't celebrate at all.' Mrs Goble said. 'All alone in a big city like that.'

'I didn't,' he admitted. 'I forgot about it, actually, until you mentioned it just now.'

'That's terrible.' Mabel's forehead creased. 'Then we must have a celebration together in the city. A birthday tea for both of us. Please say yes.' Her face lit up and her eyes sparkled.

Percy's heart melted. 'I suppose that would be all right. I'm not used to celebrating birthdays beyond a cake from Mum and the family singing *Happy Birthday*.' His thoughts ran to an image of his family sitting around table; his sisters giggling as they sang and then placing fond kisses on his cheeks.

He was glad he'd replied to his mother's letter and sent some money home. He'd not mentioned his continuing struggle about her revelation, but had told her where he was staying and how he'd come to Adelaide. He hoped that his reassurance that he was doing well would ease her mind. A wave of guilt washed over him.

'Then a special tea is what we'll do.' Mrs Goble slapped her hands onto her lap, drawing him back to the present. 'How old are you, Percy?'

'Twenty-three.'

'Ah, both so young, and your whole lives ahead of you. Let's pray that this war is soon over and you can get on with things as you should.' Sarah leaned over and poured more tea into their cups. Holding her own up, she said, 'Here's to the beginning of a lovely new year for you both, with no mishaps.'

CHAPTER NINE

Adelaide, July 1915

Mabel sat wide-eyed as Sophie told her about her father's tiny quarters in the internment camp on Torrens Island.

'He's lost so much weight.' Tears welled in Sophie's eyes. 'We've only been able to see him twice in all these months and Mama hardly recognised him the second time.' She glanced quickly towards the kitchen door, presumably to check whether her mother could hear their conversation. 'Mama and Grandmama are always cooking. We've eaten so much since we've been here, even though there are rations. I'm sure they think we can somehow eat for Papa.'

'Well, I'm sure Aunt Sarah will be showing them some new recipes,' Mabel said. 'She loves to cook too. When this war is over I reckon we'll all get as round as Christmas puddings.' She chuckled, trying to lighten the mood, though she felt helpless to make Sophie happy.

'I wonder if the war will ever be over.' Sophie sighed. 'And even when it is, Mama worries about what we'll do. Our store in Clarendon has been closed down. She says no one will want to buy from us now that Papa has been in prison.'

'I'm sure that's not true.' Mabel reached across and patted Sophie's arm. 'No one at home believes your father is a spy. Everyone talks about how awful it is that people like him have been locked away. It's terrible. We all want you to come home and start your business again.'

Sophie shrugged. 'Mama is not so sure. She cries all the time and is afraid to go out in the streets. Grandmama says she should hold her head up and go about town as she wants, but Mama is too nervous. We hardly get out at all.'

'Then you'll come into town with Aunt Sarah and me tomorrow and we'll have a lovely day and try to forget the sad things that are happening. You will come, won't you? Your mama too. We'll all be together, so you'll be safe.'

'I don't know, Mabel. I'd like to. I hope Mama will agree. I doubt she'll come herself. Last time we went with Grandmama there was a march down the main street with people shouting and waving banners about. Mama was frightened. She's not used to crowds like that and she was sure something terrible was going to happen.'

'Percy says those marches are about conscription. There are as many people against the war as for it. We'll stay away from them so we don't get caught up. I'm sure your mama has nothing to fear.'

'I doubt we'd convince her of that. I'll be pleased enough if she agrees to me going with you. I'd like to get out for a while. It's always so sad here, and apart from cleaning house and mending clothes, I've so little to do. I certainly won't be able to spend any money.'

Mabel nodded. 'I know. I'm very grateful Father has agreed to my buying a new coat. It was only because of Mother's fussing over me being cold through winter. But you will help me choose it, won't you? We can have a cup of tea in one of the stores. Aunt Sarah will insist on that. Perhaps even a scone with it. She'll want to buy one for Percy, I'm sure.'

'Who is this Percy?' Sophie's face creased. 'You keep talking about him as if he's some kind of knight in shining armour. I thought you said he was the telephone repairman. Are you sure you can trust him?'

Mabel laughed. 'Of course I'm sure we can trust him. I met him at Aunt Sarah's while he was fixing her telephone. He's been a perfect gentleman and he's been very helpful with her moving into her new house. He's dropped in there for tea once or twice. He even came to dinner at our house one evening.' She swallowed and pushed away thoughts of her mother's interrogation of Percy.

'Really?' Sophie's eyes widened. 'That sounds serious. Do you like him? I mean, do you really care for him?' She leaned forward in her chair.

Mabel was surprised that she found it so hard to answer her friend's question. 'Well, I suppose I do. He's very interesting and kind and when I'm with him I feel …' She couldn't find the right word.

'You feel what?' Sophie prompted. 'Are you saying that you love this man?' Sophie's voice rose to a high pitch as she spoke.

Mabel sat back in her chair and let her eyes wander around the parlour walls, avoiding Sophie's expectant face. 'I'm not sure,' she eventually said. 'Maybe. I do feel special when I'm with him and I miss him when I haven't seen him for a week or so.' She shrugged and a smile crept across her face.

Mabel hadn't actually formed the words in her mind until now but as she let the feelings she had about Percy seep out of her heart, she realised that she was in love for the first time. The feeling was quite delicious, but frightening too. *I wonder if he thinks I'm only a poor, sick girl who needs protecting.* She desperately wanted Percy to see her as an independent, free-thinking adult–so much more than an asthmatic. She needed to believe it for herself.

'You do love him!' Sophie's cry broke into Mabel's inner world. 'Why, Mabel Smart, I do believe you're blushing. I'll have to go to town with you now, won't I? I'll have to meet this Percy Smith of yours, and see if I approve.'

Mabel sat up straight. 'You mustn't say anything, Sophie. Promise me you won't? I'd die of embarrassment if you said any such thing to Percy.'

'I promise I won't say anything. Of course I won't.' Sophie giggled.

Mabel was so pleased to see a smile on her friend's face that it was worth any embarrassment she might feel. Besides, she was as excited as Sophie about their trip to town. She had brought her best skirt and jacket and hoped to please Percy with her outfit. She might have spent more time wondering about how he felt towards her if her aunt hadn't entered the parlour at that moment to announce that their tea was ready.

'You'll have to finish your catch up later, girls. We have potato and cheese pies hot out of the oven and your mama says she's starving.' Sarah grinned at Sophie and gestured for the girls to follow her. 'And wait till you see the birthday cake we've made for you, Mabel. It's beautiful.'

Mabel could feel her heart beating as she rose from her chair. She didn't feel hungry at all. Her stomach churned with anticipation about tomorrow's outing. It was going to be the best birthday present of all.

***

Mabel threaded her arm through Sophie's and held tightly as they moved down the crowded street towards Victoria Square the next morning. She kept her eyes peeled on the path ahead, on the lookout for Percy. Every dark-haired man caught her eye and as they were approaching the main shopping corner, a small doubt entered her mind. *Perhaps he won't come. Maybe I've misjudged him. He's said all along that he wasn't comfortable coming into the Square because of the rallies.*

'There he is,' Sarah said, lifting her arm and waving.

Mabel followed her aunt's gaze. Percy stood on the corner, straining his neck and scanning the oncoming crowd. A smile spread across his face as he responded to Sarah's wave, raising his arm in the air. He began to move toward them.

'Ooh, he is dashing,' Sophie said beside Mabel.

Mabel nudged her. 'You promised.' She leaned into Sophie but kept her eyes on Percy.

As he reached them, he grasped Mabel's hand and she felt a tingle go up her arm. 'Hello, hello,' he said, grinning first at her and then Sarah. 'And you must be Sophie.' He nodded and reached out to shake Sophie's hand. She giggled and gazed up into his face.

Mabel felt tongue-tied and was relieved when Sarah spoke. 'It's very crowded, isn't it?'

'It is on the streets,' Percy said, 'but I think in the stores it will be quieter. Most people seem more interested in the rallies than shopping. Let's get inside. It will be warmer, too. The department store is just this way.' He gestured towards the right of them and began to shepherd them down the street.

Mabel felt his hand on the centre of her back; a gentle, protective gesture. A warm glow flowed through her body. She realised she'd been bracing herself against the cold wind, which had been blowing in their faces all the way down Main Street. It was good to turn the corner and get some relief from it, but even better was the sensation of safety that Percy's presence brought. She turned her face towards his and smiled her gratitude. His eyes found hers immediately and he winked. Her knees went to jelly and she thought for a moment she'd trip.

'Here we are,' he said, ushering her through the door to the department store. 'I'm sure you'll find the best range of things here.'

'Do they have a tea shop?' Sarah asked as she followed Mabel through the door.

'Yes, they do,' Percy said, still holding the door open. 'On the second floor.'

'Then let's start there.' Sarah turned back to him with a broad smile.

'I think it's your aunt who's in love with him,' Sophie whispered, leaning into Mabel's shoulder.

'Shh.' Mabel nudged Sophie again and furrowed her eyebrows. 'I won't forgive you if you embarrass me.'

Percy looked up as Sophie stifled a giggle. 'Upstairs it is then. Or we can take the lift.'

'Let's take the lift,' Sophie said. 'I've not been in one before. Mama doesn't trust them.'

When they were seated in the small tea shop, Sarah ordered tea and a plate of scones. 'With jam and cream, of course,' she added as the young girl took the order.

'I'm sorry, Ma'am, but we have no cream.' The young girl looked surprised that anyone would ask for such a luxury.

'But you do have jam?'

'Yes, Ma'am. We have strawberry preserve.'

'Good.' Sarah nodded, appearing satisfied.

'I haven't had time yet to wish you happy birthday for yesterday, Mabel,' Percy said, as the girl walked away. 'Have you and Sophie had a nice visit?'

'Thank you,' Mabel said, nodding and still struggling to find her voice with Percy. Since her realisation of her deep feelings for him, she could hardly think without her heart fluttering.

'They haven't stopped talking since we got off the coach yesterday.' Sarah rescued her. She pulled her scarf from around her neck and laid it over the back of the chair. 'It's so much warmer in here, isn't it?' She fanned her face for a moment.

'Just as well they haven't turned off the heating altogether,'

Percy said. 'It's bitter outside, but many of the shops have cut back on warming. Everyone's economising because of the war. I've even been wearing my coat inside the guest house.' He turned to Mabel. 'Are you looking forward to getting your new coat?'

'I am.' Mabel nodded, finding her voice. 'I hope they have a reasonable choice.' She flashed him a smile. 'The coach home leaves at four, so it will be cold by the time we get back.'

'It's a shame you don't have more time here,' he said. 'I could have shown you around a bit.'

His eyes were warm-chocolate brown and Mabel felt she was sinking into them. Time seemed to stand still and it wasn't until she heard Sophie's voice that she realised she and Percy had been gazing into each other's faces in silence for some while.

'Pardon?' Percy turned away from her and addressed Sophie.

The young waitress was laying out teacups, milk and sugar on the table in front of them. Sarah was rearranging them slightly, just as she would have at home. Mabel grinned at the familiar sight.

'Mabel tells me you come from Sydney,' Sophie said.

She seemed to be suppressing a giggle and Mabel tried to catch her eye. She didn't want Percy to feel he had to explain himself all over again.

Percy cleared his throat. 'Yes, I was working there for a short while before I came here.'

'But your home is there?' Sophie continued, her eyes still on him. 'And your family?' She seemed to be avoiding Mabel's attempts to signal her.

'A little north of Sydney,' Percy said, obviously uncomfortable.

'Here's the tea,' Mabel said with relief as the girl reappeared with a teapot. 'This will warm us up.' She reached across the table and pushed a teacup a little closer to Sophie, rattling it slightly as she did so and hoping that Sophie would be distracted enough to stop her questioning of Percy.

'Here come the scones,' Sarah said, as another girl approached with a plate. 'Very good.' She looked the scones over, clearly comparing them with her own and then raised her eyebrows at Mabel as if to indicate that they were only fair to middling, but would have to do.

Mable grinned and nodded, then reached for the jam pot. 'Percy, are you going to have one?'

'Of course.' He waited until the waitress had moved away. 'They don't look too bad. Not as good as yours, Mrs Goble, but not bad, all things considered.'

'Yes, we can't expect things to be perfect at a time like this.' Sarah took a scone and put it on her plate. 'But there are always blessings to be found, even in the darkest of times.' She smiled at Percy and then Mabel, raising her eyebrows in a manner that left no doubt about her delight at seeing the two together.

A chuckle erupted from Sophie, which she quickly turned to a light cough. 'Sorry,' she said, covering her mouth. 'I think my scone went down the wrong way.'

They began to drink their tea and nibble at their scones. Mabel found herself wishing it were just her and Percy at the table, so she could relax and enjoy his company without worrying what anyone else might say. She longed to know what troubled him, for she was sure that he was deeply unhappy about something that he couldn't talk about. Or wouldn't talk about with just anyone. But she didn't intend to be just anyone to Percy for much longer. She wanted to be someone he could trust with anything at all.

'So, are we ready to shop?' Sarah said a few minutes later when the plate of scones had disappeared. 'We don't want to hold Percy up for too long, do we? I'm sure he'll have to get back to work some time today.'

Percy finished his tea and turned to Sarah. 'It's fine, Mrs Goble,' he said. 'I have the whole morning off. I've agreed to work extra time next week. 'We work around the orders and complaints that come in, so I can easily make up time.'

'I see.' Sarah rose and tucked her scarf into her handbag. 'Then I'm sure Mabel will value your opinion about which coat she should choose. Won't you, dear?'

'I will.' Mabel fiddled with the front of her jacket, straightening out the collar and hoping Percy wouldn't see the flush that had risen up her throat and was now surely making her face shine like a beacon.

'Ladies' wear is the next floor up, I think,' Percy said. He pushed the chairs back into place around the table and followed Mabel to the lift.

After browsing for a while, Mabel chose a coat that had the approval of her aunt, Sophie and Percy. It was a deep blue colour, which looked very attractive with her dark hair, and was shaped neatly around her waist and hips, with a generous collar and large blue buttons down the front.

'You'll be warm as toast in that,' Sarah said. 'I'm sure Emma will be satisfied.'

Mabel completed the sale, explaining to the saleswoman that she would keep the coat on. As she moved away from the counter she turned to the others and did a final twirl. 'I feel very snug. Very ready for the cold outside.'

'You might like to wear this with it,' Percy said, fishing something out of his pocket and handing it to Mabel with a wry grin. 'Happy Birthday.'

Mabel looked up into his face, surprised and not knowing what to say.

'Goodness, how sweet of you.' Sarah again came to the rescue.

Mabel took the small package from his hand. 'You shouldn't have,' she said, fearing her words were muddled. She looked down and pulled away the wrapping to reveal a black box. When she opened it she gasped at the silver brooch sitting in a white satin cloth.

'It's beautiful,' she said, lost for more words.

'I thought it might go nicely with a new coat,' he said. 'It's a dove. They had one in the shape of a flower but I thought this one was more appropriate. Doves are for peace and I guess that's what we're all hoping for.' His words faltered a little and Mabel sensed his emotions were quite close to the surface.

'It's a lovely thought and a precious gift. I'll treasure it.' She gazed into his eyes and for a few moments she forgot where they were and who was around her.

'That's so romantic.' Sophie's voice broke into the silence.

Mabel turned to her friend and smiled. It seemed less important to be secretive about her feelings for Percy now that he had made his own so obvious. 'Would you pin it on my coat, Sophie?'

Sophie nodded and took the brooch from Mabel. As she pinned in onto the edge of the collar, Percy spoke again.

'Now, I'm hoping you will all let me shout you some lunch. I know a place where we can get a great vegetable pasty and maybe a hot chocolate.' He turned to Sarah. 'Or they have other things if you'd prefer,' he said.

'I'm sure that would be fine for lunch, Percy,' she said, 'but I really don't think you should be buying it for us. This was supposed to be your birthday treat as well, and I'm sure you need to save your pennies for … whatever your future holds.' A cheeky grin spread across her face.

'Not at all, Mrs Goble. I insist. It's a birthday treat just to have found friends to share with. The city can be a lonely place.'

Mabel's heart leapt. The thought of Percy alone in his guest house night after night made her feel bereft. She wanted to put her arm around him and tell him he needn't ever be alone, but stopped herself. *Goodness, whatever am I thinking? He'd consider me quite loose, I'm sure.*

'Very well.' Sarah nodded. 'No doubt I'll get the opportunity to repay the hospitality.' She winked at Mabel. 'What do you think, girls?'

Sophie wrinkled her nose and nudged Mabel. 'We'd love it, wouldn't we Mabel?'

Mabel's eyes hadn't left Percy's face. She let her smile do the talking and snuggled into her coat, glancing down at the brooch proudly.

'Follow me,' said Percy, as he headed for the lift again.

Outside they found the crowds had increased, people hurrying this way and that, shrinking into their coats against the cold wind. Mabel gasped as they turned the first corner and a gust of wind blasted her face. She gulped the air and sneezed loudly. Percy draped his arm around her shoulders and leaned into her.

'Are you all right?' he said, his voice being carried away by the wind. 'The wind has increased, I'm afraid.'

She hunched into her coat and nodded. 'I'll be fine,' she managed before another sneeze shook her.

'The café is just around this next corner.' He held her tighter and guided her along the street.

As they turned the corner they almost ran into a group of people huddled under the awning of the shops, singing. They were blocking the footpath and passers-by had to step out onto the street to avoid them.

'What are they singing about?' Sophie asked as they moved around the group, shielding their ears from the boom of a drum at the front of the singers.

'The usual, I suppose,' said Percy, as Sophie caught up to him and Mabel. 'It'll be a ditty written by the "go to war" mob, or the "stop the war" advocates. One or the other, and there's likely to be another group on the next corner singing the opposite. Here we are. Quick, let's get inside.'

Mabel felt herself being shepherded through a door. She could feel another sneeze coming on and pressed her hand over her mouth. *No, no, not now*. Her throat felt a little constricted and she breathed in deeply, praying the still air inside the café would free her airways. The sneeze didn't eventuate, but as she tried to breathe out, she felt her chest grab and she broke into a cold sweat. As she swayed, Percy put his other arm around her and led her to a chair.

'She's having trouble breathing.' She heard Sarah's voice as everything around her darkened.

Then there was only the tightness, the struggle to gasp for air, the sound of raised voices and the rising sense of panic. *This can't be happening. Not with Percy here. He'll never want to be with me now. It's so unfair.*

When she could see and hear properly again she was lying on a sofa in a strange room. Sarah was leaning over her, a glass in her hand.

'Sip this, dear. It'll help.' Mabel opened her mouth and let the mixture roll down her throat. She could taste ginger and something else she couldn't recognise.

'Where am I?' Mabel heard her voice as a rasp, barely audible.

'In the rooms behind the café, dear. The owners made this up for you. Have a bit more.' She put the glass to Mabel's lips.

After a few more moments, Mabel felt the fire in her chest subside. 'Where's Percy?' She was sure he'd be long gone, frightened off completely by the terrible sight of her fighting to breathe, looking hideous no doubt. Her hand went to her neck, seeking out the brooch on her collar, but there was no brooch, no collar. Her coat was gone. *Is this a horrible nightmare? Perhaps Percy isn't here at all.*

She searched her aunt's face. 'Where's Percy?'

'Stay calm, love. Percy's in the café with Sophie. You needed a little rest, is all.'

Mabel tried to push herself into a sitting position but found the effort too much. 'Oh bother,' she said as she dropped her head back onto the sofa. 'Why did this have to happen now? This ruins everything.' Tears sprang to her eyes. 'He'll think I'm so pathetic.'

'No, he won't. He's very worried about you; he cares very much. Now, rest a bit more, while I tell him you're on the mend.'

'How long have I been here?' Mabel had lost all sense of time as she always did when her attacks came.

'About half an hour,' Sarah said as she rose from the chair beside the sofa. 'I'll tell Sophie and Percy that you'll soon be all right. Promise me you'll stay put.'

Mabel nodded. She knew she couldn't move anyway. She sighed deeply. At least she could do that now without her chest catching. *Whatever will he think of me now?* She closed her eyes. A tear squeezed out from under both lids and rolled down her cheeks.

When a hand touched her arm her eyes flew open and she realised she'd dozed off. She turned her head and there was Percy, looking down at her, concern etched into his face.

'How are you feeling?' he whispered.

'I'll be fine … soon.'

'I'm so sorry,' he said. 'I shouldn't have taken you out in that wind, or with those crowds.' He touched her forehead softly and pushed hair from her face.

'It's not your fault,' she said. 'It happens sometimes. I'm so sorry it happened today, here, when everything was so … perfect.'

'So am I, but there will be other perfect times, I promise. All that matters now is that you recover and then I'm going to take you home.'

'What? No, you can't. I mean, you have to work.' Mabel's thoughts raced.

'I've already contacted my boss. He understands. I can

make up the time. I told him my dear friend is very ill and I must see her home.'

'I don't want you to be in trouble because of me, Percy. Please don't put yourself out. I already feel so foolish.' She tried to push herself up and this time, found she could sit with his help. 'Aunt Sarah and I can catch the coach as we'd planned.'

'I'll not hear of it,' he said firmly. 'I'm going to take care of you.'

She looked around and was relieved to see her coat draped over a chair close by, her beautiful new brooch shining from the collar. She smiled and nodded towards it. 'For a moment I thought I'd dreamed today.'

'No, you didn't dream it,' he said, patting her arm and giving it a light squeeze. 'And this hasn't spoiled anything.' He looked into her eyes. 'You must not think it makes any difference to how I feel.' He leaned closer. 'You do know how I feel, don't you?'

She took a deep breath and was again grateful that it didn't catch in her throat. She nodded. 'I think so,' she said, feeling the colour rush into her face.

They sat for moments in silence, both knowing no words were needed.

CHAPTER TEN

Baker's Gully, July 1915

Percy turned his carriage into the lane leading up to the Park Farm house with a sense of impending dread. Here he was, bringing Mabel home, pale and cold and needing to go to bed immediately. Perhaps a doctor would have to be called. He'd thought she might stay at her aunt's for the night and go home in a better state, but Mrs Goble had considered it a better idea to get Mabel home to her own room and the medicines her mother liked to give her.

'Emma would never forgive me if I kept her overnight in this state,' she'd said, 'and they'll likely want to call their own doctor.'

They'd wrapped an extra blanket around Mabel, on top of the one Percy had brought with his carriage, and also on top of her new coat, which she refused to take off even though there was the slight chance of rain on the way home. Percy was grateful that hadn't eventuated and even though his carriage was open to the wind, Mrs Goble had insisted it was better to get Mabel home rather than wait another hour or so for the afternoon coach. So all things considered, Percy was reasonably sure they'd done the best for Mabel. He prayed Mrs Smart would agree, but was still not looking forward to facing Mabel's parents again.

'Nearly there.' He turned to Mabel, who was almost covered with blankets. The small part of her face that he could see still looked

116

awfully pale and her lips had a bluish tinge. 'How are you feeling?'

'I'll be fine, Percy,' she said, although there was a definite tremor in her voice. 'A bit of a rest and I'll be good as new.'

She twisted slightly on the seat and smiled at him, her face resembling that of a porcelain doll. He wanted so badly to wrap her in his arms and make her well, but the front door of the house loomed in front of them and he knew he would have to give her into the care of her parents, at least for now.

When he knocked on the door Mabel's young sister, Isabel, opened it. She stood for a moment with her brow furrowed. Then, her eyes widened and her face broke into a smile.

'Hello, you're Mabel's friend, aren't you?'

'I am,' Percy said. 'I have Mabel in the carriage. If you could hold the door for me, I'll carry her in. She's not very well and I think she needs–'

'Isabel, who is it? Why are you standing at the door like somebody's maid?' Mrs Smart was suddenly behind her daughter. 'Oh,' she said when she saw Percy. 'It's the jockey … the telephone man.' Her face creased into a frown.

'It's Mabel, she's unwell. I've brought her home.' Percy indicated the carriage at the bottom of the steps and backed away from the door. 'I'll carry her in. She's quite weak.'

As he lifted Mabel from the seat of the carriage he could hear Emma calling for her husband in great distress. Isabel held the door open for him and as they went through, Mabel pushed the blankets from her head.

'Please put me down, Percy. I can walk. Let's not make more of this than needs be.'

As he carefully let her feet drop to the ground, Emma came scurrying back towards the front door with her husband behind her.

'I'm fine, Mother,' Mabel said, lifting one of the blankets from her shoulders.

Before she could say more, her mother took Mabel's face in both hands and exclaimed, 'My poor girl, look at you, pale as a sheet and cold as ice. Whatever were you thinking, young man, to have her out in this weather? Help me get her up to bed, Isabel and we'll call the doctor.' She put her arm around Mabel's shoulder, patting and clucking and shaking her head, taking deep breaths as if she herself were about to suffer an asthma attack.

'I think Isabel can manage to help Mabel to her room,' Albert said firmly. 'You sit down for a moment, Emma, and collect yourself.' There was no doubting that he meant to take charge.

Emma responded to the tone of his voice by pausing in her tracks and taking another deep breath.

'Very well, dear,' she said, although Percy could tell she was not happy to comply with her husband's wishes. 'Isabel, make sure she changes into something warm and suitable to rest in.' She raised her chin and patted Mabel on the back as Isabel continued to lead her sister towards the stairs.

Mabel looked over her shoulder at Percy. 'Thank you, Percy. I had a lovely day, really. I'm sorry it ended like this but I promise I will be well soon.' She raised a hand under the blanket, which was still draped around her, and waved at him.

Percy nodded and smiled, his heart aching at the thought of leaving her. While he was mulling over how best to explain the situation to her parents, Albert spoke to his wife again.

'Now, why don't you go and see that some hot tea is made, my dear? I'm sure Percy could do with something to drink and no doubt you'll need a cup for yourself. When Mabel is settled we'll have something sent up to her.'

Emma's shoulders went back and she appeared to be struggling to contain her agitation. 'Very well, dear,' she said, her mouth drawn into a tight line. She moved across the entry and disappeared into what Percy assumed was the kitchen.

'Now, come into the parlour, young man, and warm yourself by the fire. Perhaps you'd like something stronger to drink than tea?'

'No, thank you, Mr Smart, tea is fine. I'm sorry to have caused this upset.' He followed Albert into the parlour and stood in front of the large open fire on the back wall. The warmth made him realise just how cold he'd been on the trip home, and again his thoughts went to Mabel. *Perhaps I did the wrong thing, bringing her home. Perhaps she'd have been better to stay in Adelaide for the night.*

'I'm sure you didn't cause it, young man. I imagine it was quite disturbing for you to have to deal with Mabel's attack. I'm glad you were there to bring her home.' Albert's voice was calm and genuine and Percy felt relieved.

'I was glad to bring her home, Mr Smart, but it was hard to know what to do for the best.' Percy bent and rubbed his hands together in front of the flames.

'It happened in the city, I presume?'

Before Percy could answer, Emma came bustling into the room. 'I knew it was a bad idea for her to go into the city. I was sure something awful would happen. She's not used to those crowds and goodness knows what–' She stopped suddenly as if surprised that Percy was still there.

'Sit down, dear. I'm sure Percy will fill us in, but it's over now and Mabel will recover quite quickly as she usually does, so there's no need to get yourself all worked up.' Albert turned to Percy and, with a warm gesture, welcomed him to sit. 'Was it in the city, Percy?'

Percy moved to the chair and lowered himself into it. 'Yes, it came on quite suddenly. She was fine while we were having tea and shopping, and then–'

'Having tea and shopping?' Emma sat up in her chair, her

eyes wide. 'I thought she was going to the city with Sarah. What were you doing having tea and shopping with Mabel?' Her cheeks flushed with colour and she grabbed the arms of her chair.

Percy could see she was having trouble containing her annoyance, and that she was all too ready to blame him for what had happened.

'Emma, please.' Albert interrupted her. 'Go on, Percy.'

'I met Mabel and your sister in town, Mrs Smart.' Percy felt he needed to explain his presence with Mabel. 'When I knew she was going to be in town, I thought I could help keep them safe. With all the marches and rallies, sometimes it's very rowdy.' He looked to Emma, hoping for some sign of approval, but she simply rolled her eyes and turned to her husband as if to indicate that her worries had been justified.

'When we left the store I suggested we have a bit of lunch and, well, that's when it happened. There were a lot of people on the street, a band playing and singing and the wind was very cold, so I'm not sure what it was. Sophie and Mrs Goble–' He knew he'd said the wrong thing the minute it was out of his mouth. Seeing Sophie was the secret Mabel had asked him to keep. And the reason was very clear when he looked again at Emma and saw her expression.

'Sophie? You mean that German girl? She was there? Mabel was with her? You see, Albert. I knew it was a mistake to let her go. How did Sophie know that Mabel would be in the city, and for that matter, how did you know she was going?' Emma's glare moved from Percy to her husband and back again, but she didn't wait for either to answer. 'I tell you, Albert, letting Mabel go to Sarah's has been a big mistake. More goes on in my sister's house than I care to think about.' She waved her hand in front of her face and slumped back in her chair.

Percy was sure she'd fainted, until she sat upright a moment later and started again. 'No wonder Mabel had an attack. You know how het up she gets about that girl and her German father. And in amongst all those people! She might have been arrested or anything. Is that what you call helping, young man?' Her attention again focussed on Percy.

'I was at your sister's when they were talking about going shopping in the city,' Percy explained as calmly as he could. 'It was all quite harmless, I assure you. There was no danger of arrest or trouble for Mabel. I suspect it was the sudden cold wind, after being in the warm store, and then having to push through a noisy crowd. It might have been a little overwhelming for Mabel.'

'A little overwhelming?' Emma scoffed. 'Really, young man, you have no idea how fragile Mabel is.'

Percy sensed he was about to hear another tirade from Emma, but the kitchen maid appeared with the tea tray, and laid it on the table. Emma remained quietly fanning herself and straightening her skirt.

'Thank you, Beattie.' Albert smiled at the girl. 'That will be all. Mrs Smart will pour our tea.'

The girl nodded and left the room, after which Emma rose, though she seemed put out by her husband's direction, and began to pour tea.

'Let me help.' Percy pushed himself up from his chair, took a full cup from the tray and delivered it to Albert. The tension in the air was palpable. No one spoke for a few moments. Albert waited until Percy had taken his own cup of tea back to his chair and Emma had returned to her place with hers.

'Thank you, Percy. As I said before, you did not cause this upset, so you've no reason to feel at fault. I'm glad you were there. Things might have been worse, otherwise.'

'Things would have been better had she not gone at all,' Emma said, as if determined to have the last say, despite her husband's assessment of things. 'All this for a new coat, which I presume she didn't even get to buy.' She rolled her eyes and brought her cup to her lips with trembling hands.

Percy was about to inform her about the purchase of the coat when Isabel bounced into the room. 'Yes, she did, Mother. I've just been looking at it and it's lovely. She had it on under that blanket.' She dropped into a chair beside her mother and then turned to Percy. 'The brooch is beautiful, too, Percy. Such a lovely thought.' She grinned at him and screwed up her nose as if she delighted in announcing his gift.

She was a bright and happy girl and she reminded Percy of his sisters. *I wonder what Vera, Ida and Connie are doing?* Surprised by the thought, he realised he missed his family very much. Their faces appeared in his mind more and more these days, especially his mother and sisters. He ached to see them again.

'Brooch? What brooch?' Emma's sharp response shot through his thoughts.

'It's a small gift I bought Mabel for her birthday,' Percy said. 'When I knew she was going to shop for a coat I thought it would be a nice addition.' He gulped his tea and waited for the disapproval that was bound to come.

'You knew it was her birthday? I think you know altogether too much about our daughter, young man. That would be my sister again, no doubt. She has no sense of propriety at all.'

'Well, actually, Mabel told me herself,' Percy said, now quite piqued by Emma's attitude.

'Did she now? Then she's far too influenced by my sister and that's another reason her visits are much too frequent for my liking.'

'That's enough, Emma. Percy is our guest.' Albert's tone was sharp. He turned to Percy. 'Please forgive my wife, Percy. She gets very agitated when Mabel is unwell.'

'I understand,' said Percy, rising to return his tea cup to the table. 'Now, I really must be on my way. I'd like to get back to the roadhouse at Chandler's Hill before the rain comes. It looked a bit threatening as we were driving back.'

'Of course.' Albert rose and put his cup back on the tray. 'Thank you again for your kindness. I'm sure Mabel appreciated it.'

'I do hope she'll be well soon.' He looked back to Emma and nodded. 'Good evening and thank you for the tea.' She gave him a strained smile and nodded in return, clearly with no intention to rise and see him out.

'I wonder if I might call back in a day or so and see how Mabel is?' Percy addressed his request to Albert, but the response came back from Emma almost before he'd finished speaking.

'Certainly not.' Her tone was stinging and drew a look of disapproval from Albert. 'I mean, it takes Mabel a few days to recover fully,' she said with a softened voice. 'We wouldn't want her disturbed for a while.'

'Really, Mother, she's usually fine by the next day. You fuss too much.' Isabel's comment suggested she found her mother quite tiresome. 'I'm sure she'd like Percy to call on her again. She was very embarrassed to have spoiled their day out. I think Percy's been very dashing.'

Emma arched up. 'Really, Isabel, you ought to mind your own business. I'm Mabel's mother. I think I know what's best for her.' She rose from her chair. 'Now, I think we should let Percy be on his way.' Her tone indicated that the conversation was at an end.

Percy's stomach churned. He felt annoyed by Emma's attitude, both towards him and Mabel. She treated her daughter like a small child and he understood fully why Mabel escaped to her aunt's as often as possible. *Forming a dislike of Mabel's mother is not going to do my own cause any good*. The thought was pushing loudly at his mind, but without thinking any further about it, he turned to Albert.

'Actually, since I'm here, I may as well ask you now. I was wondering if you'd agree to my visiting Mabel. Not for a few days,' he added quickly when he heard Emma's intake of breath. 'But later. That is, I'd like your permission to call on her. My intentions are completely honourable, I assure you.'

Before Albert could answer, his wife was at his elbow. 'Young man, you hardly know our daughter and you certainly don't seem to understand her situation. Apart from her physical condition, which is far more fragile than you realise, she is already spoken for and certainly not open to being called on.' She said the last as if the idea was ludicrous, then threaded her arm through that of her husband and nudged him, clearly soliciting reinforcement for her sentiments.

'Spoken for?' Percy was taken aback. He searched Albert's face for confirmation.

Albert shook his head and patted his wife's hand. 'Now, dear, you're getting carried away again.'

Percy relaxed slightly at Albert's response. Still, he kept his focus on the man's face, hoping for a clearer refuting of the idea that Mabel was spoken for.

'My wife has hopes for Mabel's marriage with one of the landed families around here, Percy,' he said, his tone jovial. 'I'm not sure Mabel has the same ambition, but still it is the way of things here. Most of the families have been on this land for a hundred years or more and their children usually feel an obligation to remain part of the farming community and care for the land.'

'But I imagine your sons will carry on your work here and with so many large families on the land, surely all the children don't stay on the farms.' Percy's voice faltered. He felt out of his depth. He hadn't prepared himself to make a case for proposing marriage to Mabel. However, as the idea enlarged in his mind, he had every confidence he could support a wife and a family. In fact, the more he thought about it, the more certain he was that it was exactly what he wanted. How he would convince Mabel's parents of that was still beyond his grasp.

'You felt no such obligation to continue your father's work on his property if my memory serves me correctly.' Emma's voice broke into Percy's thoughts with a vengeance.

For a moment he was thrown. He had no answer for her accusation, for that was what it was. He was not in a frame of mind to remember exactly what he had said about his father. Again he wished he'd been completely truthful with Mabel and her family about his past, but now was certainly not the time to do that.

'I'm not quite sure what my future holds in regard to my father's land,' he said, keeping his tone even. 'But I assure you, Mrs Smart, I would only ever have Mabel's best interests at heart.'

'I think all this talk is a bit premature,' Albert said, to Percy's relief. 'Mabel will decide what's best for her in the end, with consideration of our advice, no doubt,' he added with a glance to his wife. 'So let's just take this a step at a time. We need to wait until she's well enough and ready to agree, or not, to Percy calling on her. For now, Percy, what's say we call it a day? I think we all have enough to think about for the moment.'

***

As Percy drove towards Chandler's Hill he knew he'd have his work cut out for him to convince Mabel's mother that he was in any way suitable for her daughter. But he had another problem that was pressing on him greatly: what to do about his father. He wondered if he should try to find his real father–who may be someone Emma Smart would approve of. But remembering that his family probably had no idea of his existence, Percy began to think he should just forget the idea.

Rain was falling lightly by the time Percy arrived at the roadhouse. He was wet, hungry and tired, but could neither eat nor sleep. He took out his mother's letter and reread it numerous times. Tears welled in his eyes as he thought about how worried she would be. He needed to tell her what he'd decided about his father, and yet he couldn't say for sure that he'd decided anything at all. His thoughts kept going back to Mabel. *How can I explain all this to Mabel, and then to her parents? Mrs Smart would never trust me with her daughter if she knew I was hiding so much of the truth about myself. And what about Mabel? Will the truth change how she thinks of me?*

He lay on his bed, wrestling with options, rehearsing them in his mind, anticipating reactions. When he rose early the following morning, he had no desire greater than to rush back to Baker's Gully and take Mabel in his arms and tell her the truth.

CHAPTER ELEVEN

Baker's Gully, August 1915

Mabel looked across the table at Richard Grimwood, decked out in his army uniform, perfectly pressed, every button shining. She could only assume from the conversation around the dinner table that before long he would be filthy and battered, if alive at all. His eyes told her that he was terrified. She glanced further along the table where her brother sat, listening with a grim face to the reports about the war. *Is David thinking of enlisting, too?* She shuddered at the thought. She was glad her younger brother, Frederick, was only fourteen, for he had more the temperament to consider fighting than David. His eyes were wide with apparent admiration as Mr Grimwood held court.

'The courage and spirit of the ANZACs have been hailed as the stuff of legends. It's hardly surprising that they show the kind of tenacity and endurance that's required in these situations. We breed our boys tough. Richard and Tom will do us proud, I'm sure.' He wiped his mouth with a napkin and tapped Tom on the shoulder. The boy beside him, his eldest son, nodded and grinned at his father, though Mabel thought the paleness of his face suggested he was as fearful of what was ahead of him as his younger brother.

'We'll try, Father,' Richard said. Mabel could hear the tremor in his voice.

'Of course you will, my boy. Damn shame that we've lost Major General Bridges. A fine field commander, I hear. Shot by a sniper just the day after he was knighted. Pity, but it's good to know there are young men ready to step into the breach left by those we've lost.'

'Please Edward,' Mrs Grimwood's voice also betrayed her fear. 'I can hardly think of our boys in that dreadful place at all. Please don't talk about the young men we've lost. It's unbearable.'

'Now, Lucy, dear, don't be hysterical. The battle at Gallipoli has been particularly ferocious according to the reports, thousands of men lost. The battle at the Nek this month was a fierce one for the Light Horse Brigade, and the assault at Lone Pine sounds equally dreadful. Still, for all that, the ANZACs are winning out. I'm sure once they advance from Gallipoli, the fighting will be easier. It's a difficult piece of coastline and they need to drive the Turks back.'

'I don't want to hear any more about it.' Lucy's tone was pleading. 'I want it to be all over so that Richard and Tom don't have to be in any battles.'

'We'd all like that, Lucy,' Emma said, leaning forward to catch her friend's eye. 'It's a dreadful business. I'm sure you're proud of your boys, but I'd be devastated if David was thinking about enlisting.' She turned to David and searched his face, as if seeking confirmation that he'd not changed his mind about joining the war.

He shrugged and shook his head. 'I've told you I'm not the fighting type, Mother. I'm sure I'd be useless.' David kept his eyes down and continued to eat.

Mabel was sure she could see her brother's hand shaking and her father had hardly said a word since they'd arrived. She knew he didn't agree with the war, but he would not be rude enough to argue with Mr Grimwood in his own house. The Grimwood girls and her own sisters were seated further down the huge table. They were fidgeting and exchanging quiet comments, probably about the latest fashions, Mabel assumed.

Everyone, except Mr Grimwood, seemed tense and on edge. All the talk of war, and this luncheon she'd been forced to attend, supposedly to say goodbye to Richard, was distressing for Mabel. *How Mother could possibly think this is a better way to spend my Sunday afternoon than visiting Aunt Sarah, is beyond me.*

'You're very quiet, Mabel,' her mother said, as if reading her thoughts. 'Are you feeling unwell?'

'Not at all, Mother.' She looked up briefly and nodded.

'Mabel's been very ill.' Emma turned to Lucy. 'She had a dreadful asthma attack, poor dear.'

Mabel heard her own sharp intake of breath. 'I've had a head cold, Mother. There's no need to make it sound like I'm close to death.'

'For the past few weeks you've had a head cold, but it did start with that dreadful attack in the city, didn't it?' Her tone was the one Mabel recognised as demanding agreement.

'I've been well for the past week, though, haven't I?' Mabel's shoulders went back determinedly. She refused to comply as she knew her mother wanted. She was tired of the fussing about her health.

All week Mabel had been planning to visit Aunt Sarah but her mother had resisted strongly, suggesting that she was too ill, that it was too cold, that Sarah hadn't been in contact, not even to see how Mabel was, so she was obviously busy with other things. All excuses to keep her from visiting her aunt and the possibility of seeing Percy.

It's so unfair to blame him for my asthma attack. Goodness knows what would have happened if he hadn't been there. And regardless, I intend to see Percy with or without her approval. It's time I stood up for myself. I'm tired of being treated like a child.

Signalling that she was not going to back down, she maintained eye contact with her mother. She knew Emma would not make a fuss in front of the Grimwoods.

'Thankfully, you were well enough to join us today,' Emma conceded. 'No doubt Richard is pleased to have you here to say goodbye.' She turned to Richard and her tone softened. 'I'm sure you'll be comforted to know that there are those at home here who will be praying for your safe return.' A smile spread across her face. She paused as if waiting for Richard to confirm her hopes. 'For you too, Tom, of course,' she added.

'Thank you, Mrs Smart.' Richard nodded.

He didn't even glance at Mabel. *I'm sure he's no more interested in me than I am in him. If Mother's waiting for me to give Richard a personal confirmation of my intention to wait for him, she'll be waiting a long time.* Mabel twisted in her chair and tuned in to what Isabel was saying to the Grimwood sisters.

'I heard he came home with only one leg and his head was all bandaged.'

There was a collective gasp from the sisters. 'Did you see him?' one asked.

'No, I heard some women talking about it after church. They said there are lots of men coming home with limbs missing.'

'Isabel, really,' Mabel hissed. 'Hasn't there been enough talk about the war?'

One of the Grimwood sisters raised her chin and rolled her eyes at Mabel. 'Father says the Huns need to learn that the rest of the world will not put up with their bullying.'

'But he just said it's the Turks they're chasing away now. I thought the Huns were the Germans,' the oldest sister said, her forehead creasing.

'Some people do call Germans Huns,' Mabel said, 'but that's not a nice term, and certainly not lady-like. Not all Germans are

130

bullies. I happen to know families who came from Germany and are perfectly decent people.'

'You girls aren't arguing, are you?'

Mabel was surprised to hear her father's voice. 'No, of course not, Father. I was telling Alice that I know some German people who are very nice. Well, they live here now, so they're not Germans at all any more, but I think it's unfair to suggest that all the German people are dreadful murderers.'

'Mabel.' Her mother gasped. 'That's no way to speak.'

'It's how a lot of people are speaking, isn't it? It's what many think. Why else would the authorities be locking them up, if they didn't think they were dangerous and dreadful?'

'It's not for the minds of young women to be speculating about the complexities of war, my dear.' Mr Grimwood frowned at her.

'It's a pity any of us have to speculate about it,' Albert said, his tone suggesting he'd had enough of this visit. He pushed back his chair, confirming Mabel's suspicion. 'Now, I think we should be making tracks. David and I have some work to finish up. Are you ready, dear?' He stood behind Emma's chair and touched her on the shoulder.

Mabel needed no encouragement to leave. She ignored the look of disappointment on her mother's face and motioned to her sisters. 'Clara, Isabel, we're leaving. Where are your coats?'

'I'll get them.' David rose from his chair, as anxious as Mabel to be on their way.

The girls exchanged goodbyes, as did Emma and Lucy.

'Thank you so much for the lovely lunch,' Emma said, gripping Lucy's hands in her own. 'I'm sorry to see Richard and Tom go, but as I said, we will be praying for them and for you all. I do hope the war will be over very soon and the boys will be back and getting on with their lives.' She turned to Richard. Mabel could see she was trying to catch his eye but he was focussed on talking with his brother.

'Father, please don't keep me from visiting Aunt Sarah,' Mabel pleaded with her father as soon as she could get him alone later that day.

'What are you talking about, dear? Of course I wouldn't keep you from Sarah. She's a lonely woman and you're great company for her.'

'But you do know Mother is trying to stop me visiting. She's afraid I'll see Percy there, I'm sure.'

'And will you?' His eyebrows rose.

'I suppose if he's there when I visit, I will. Aunt Sarah has taken a liking to him and he's very kind to her. Whenever he's working out this way, he drops in.' Mabel chuckled to hide the fact that her voice had caught in her throat. 'She says it's because he loves her scones, but I think the two of them have become quite fond of each other.' She hoped she wasn't colouring up as she spoke.

'Hmm.' Her father grinned. 'The two of them, you say? And what about you? Are you fond of him, too?'

Mabel took a deep breath. 'As a matter of fact, Father, I am. He's a good man. One I believe can be trusted. He's very interesting. We have lovely talks. I think he really likes me too.' She lowered her gaze, sure her cheeks were on fire.

'I've no doubt about that, love. He made that quite clear when he was here.'

'He did?' Mabel's eyes flew back to her father, regardless of her burning cheeks.

'Most certainly. In fact he asked my permission to call on you.'

'Here?'

'Of course, here. This is your home. Where else would he call on you?'

'Yes, of course.' Mabel felt flustered. 'And what did you say?' She held her breath.

'I said I'd consider it, but that it would be up to you who you'd like to have visit you, and ultimately who you'd like to court you.'

His words left Mabel speechless.

'I am assuming correctly that he was asking if he could court you, aren't I?' he prompted.

'I, well, I suppose if he asked to call on me that's what he meant. Oh, Father. I do like him very much. Would you agree to him courting me? I know you say it's up to me, but you'd have to approve and I'm sure Mother would not. It seems to me she doesn't like Percy, so I'm sure she'd be difficult about it.'

Mabel's words rushed out without a breath between and when she'd finished, she drew in a gulp of air. Her heart was pounding in her chest. For a moment she thought she might bring on another asthma attack, but knowing that would not do her cause any good at all, she slowed her breathing and relaxed her shoulders. 'You will talk to her about Percy, won't you? I know she thinks I'll marry someone like Richard Grimwood, but really, Father, I couldn't. Richard and I have nothing in common at all.'

'Except that his family and yours are farmers here in South Australia. Percy comes from Sydney and doesn't seem interested in taking up farming, or even raising horses like his father. How do you think he would support a family of his own?'

'He's very clever, Father. He's learning so much about telephones, so he could end up managing a post office. Aunt Sarah said he'd be good at that. He's also said he'd like to have a business of his own one day, perhaps a general store. He has lots of ideas.'

Albert grinned and touched her cheek. 'I'm sure he does, and though I doubt any of those ideas would delight your mother, I will talk with her about him.'

'Then you'll agree to his courting me?'

'He didn't actually use that word, dear, but I will agree to him calling on you. It warms my heart to see you so happy.'

'How can I get in touch with him?' Mabel asked her aunt the following Sunday after church. If I come home with you, can we call the post office and ask him to come out and do something to your telephone?'

Sarah chuckled. 'It's Sunday, remember? The post office is not open, but I could call in the morning and leave a message for him to telephone me. If you've sorted this out with your parents, then I don't see it being a problem if he comes to visit you at my place.' She straightened her hat and tucked strands of hair behind her ears. 'You have cleared this with your parents, haven't you? I'm in enough trouble with my sister without adding to it. She's barely been civil to me these past few weeks.'

'I'm not sure she'll be happy at all about my seeing Percy, but Father is agreeable, so I don't care. She's been very worried this week about Richard Grimwood going off to war. She's even reading the newspapers, hoping to see that the war has ended, I'm sure.'

'I doubt that's going to happen any time soon, I'm afraid.'

Mabel sighed. 'It's awful, but all the more reason for me to see Percy. I don't want him getting ideas about enlisting. I couldn't bear it. I'm going to tell Mother and Father that you've invited me over to stay the night. Is that all right? Then I can be there when you call in the morning and perhaps I can talk to Percy myself.' Mabel's heart fluttered at the thought. 'It's been weeks, and I'm sure he'd have felt discouraged by Mother when he took me home from Adelaide. She insists on blaming him for my asthma attack.'

'That's preposterous.' Sarah huffed and threaded her arm through Mabel's. 'Of course you can come for the night. I'd be glad of the company.' She chuckled. 'Even if your mind will be completely on Percy.'

Mabel squeezed her aunt's arm. 'Not completely. We can play cards tonight. We always enjoy that, don't we? Perhaps I can call Sophie this afternoon. I haven't spoken to her since we were in Adelaide either and I do worry about her. Her mother is suffering badly with all this internment business.'

'Yes, there's a lot going on, isn't there?' Sarah patted Mabel's hand. 'Lots to catch up on and plan for.' She nodded towards the steps of the church where Mabel's mother and father were standing talking with another couple. 'You'd best ask your parents, then.'

Mabel approached the steps and when she was close enough to hear her father speaking, she realised his tone was very serious. The man and woman standing with her parents looked solemn. Mabel could see her mother had the other woman's hands clasped in her own.

'We were terribly sorry to hear your news this morning,' Albert said. 'Such a terrible waste. He was so young and full of life.'

The couple nodded in unison and Mabel heard a sob erupt from the woman. Emma wrapped her arm around the woman's shaking shoulder. 'If there's anything we can do, please let us know.'

More nodding. The woman rested her head on Emma's shoulder and cried loudly. 'I still can't believe it,' she said between sobs. 'I keep expecting him to walk through the door. I didn't think we'd lose him, not forever. It's so awful.'

'It is,' Emma said, rubbing the woman's arm. 'Unthinkable. You poor dear. I don't know what to say.'

'We understand,' the man said. 'We've known others who've received the same news and there's nothing to be said. All our prayers for this war to come to an end seem to be futile, but we must hold onto hope that some of our young men will come home. We've another son over there. He's in the Light Horse Brigade. It's a miracle he survived this last slaughter at the Nek in Gallipoli. We can only pray now that he'll come home to us, but it might not be soon, unless he's wounded, and of course we don't want that either.'

The sobs from the woman in her mother's arms increased in volume and another couple joined the grieving circle. Mabel caught her father's eye and beckoned him.

When he backed away from the solemn circle and moved toward her she spoke quietly. 'I wanted to see if it's all right for me to go with Aunt Sarah, Father. She's invited me for the night.' Mabel glanced back to the bereaved parents and asked, 'Is it someone from the war?'

Her father nodded. 'Their son, I'm afraid. They got a telegram this week. He was killed at Lone Pine last week.'

'How terrible.' Mabel looked over the woman. She was wiping her eyes and talking to the other couple who'd joined them.

'You go with Sarah, dear. There's nothing we can do for the poor souls except offer some comfort.' He took her hand in his. 'Be careful, won't you? We don't want any more dramas.'

'I will, Father, and thank you.' She stood on her tiptoes and kissed him on the cheek before turning and walking back to where her aunt was waiting.

'So sad,' she said as she reached Sarah. 'Another young man killed. Will anything good come of the war, Aunt Sarah?'

'Hard to say, dear. I'm sure they're all fighting with the belief that there is a purpose for it all. It's difficult to understand, but all we can do is endure it and trust the good Lord brings something good out of it.'

***

'Percy, is that you?' Mabel held the phone tightly, excited to be hearing his voice. 'Thank you for ringing back.'

'Mabel? How are you? I was worried when I got your aunt's message. Are you all right?'

Mabel's heart missed a beat. 'I'm fine. I asked Aunt Sarah to phone this morning so that I could talk to you.' She waited, trying to gauge his response, and thought she heard a quick intake of breath.

'I see,' he said. 'I'm so glad to hear your voice. I've been thinking about you for weeks and wondering how you are. Your mother made it clear I wasn't to visit. It's been very hard to wait. Are you sure you're all right?'

'Of course. I did have a head cold again for the first couple of weeks after I saw you, not that it was your fault, not at all. It was just the cold weather. Anyway, I'm fine now and I was wondering … well, are you coming out this way any time soon?'

There was a long silence and Mabel's heart sunk. *Has he decided I'm too much trouble?*

'I'm checking my work log,' he finally said. 'I have one connection out that way at the end of the week, but I'd love to come sooner and visit you, if that's all right? I could take an afternoon. I've worked more hours these last few weeks than I should have. It's helped me not worry so much about you.'

'Really? You'd take an afternoon off?' Mabel could barely contain her joy.

'I could bring the carriage and we could go for a drive. Or we could visit at your house, or your aunt's house. Would your parents allow that?'

'I'm sure that would be wonderful. Father has told me that he agrees to your … visiting me.' She swallowed loudly. 'He said you asked him if you could come to the house.'

'I did. Are you saying he's agreed to let me come and see you sometimes?'

'He said it's up to me.' She grinned into the receiver. 'And I'd be very happy to have you call on me, if that's what you want.'

'Of course it's what I want. How about Wednesday afternoon

then? I'll come to your house and if the weather's pleasant we could go for a walk.'

'That's perfect.' Her heart was thumping in her chest and she was sure her cheeks were bright red. She was rather glad that he couldn't see her, but as soon as that thought crossed her mind, she knew it wasn't really true. Red cheeks or not, she was dying to see Percy face to face. 'I'll see you on Wednesday then.'

Mabel replaced the receiver and twirled around the parlour, her arms in the air. She was in love and it felt like the whole world was beautiful. She pushed thoughts of grieving parents and terrified young men and even Sophie's sorrows from her mind. There had to be time for happiness in this sad world and she was grateful some of that might be hers.

CHAPTER TWELVE

Bakers Gully, September 1915

'I'm so pleased it's a nice day,' Percy said as he led Mabel alongside the small brook running through Park Farm. From under the trees, which shaded the edge of the water, he could see the ploughed fields that spread out from the house. Cattle grazed in fenced paddocks and in the distance a tractor ambled across the landscape.

The affluence of the property registered with Percy. A wave of sadness washed over him. He imagined his mother and sisters in such a place as this, with a good income, plenty of wholesome food, the comforts of a generous home. *One day I'll make sure they have more than they've had to survive with.* The thought was not a new one, but one that had been pushed aside this past year as he'd struggled with his identity. He focussed back on the present and this girl beside him, hoping she would be the centre of any plans he had for the future.

'Your father has built up an impressive farm,' he said, smiling down at her.

'Yes, that'll be him or David on the tractor. He said at breakfast that they'd be working in the western fields today. They'll be pleased the wind has dropped and the rain has stayed away, at least until they get ready for planting.'

He nodded and took her arm, concerned she might lose her footing around the tree roots. 'I'm glad to see you looking so well. I've been beside myself wondering how you were these past few weeks.'

'I'm perfectly well now. I've come to accept that I'll have to deal with asthma, perhaps all my life, but I can manage it. I don't want you to think of me as a sickly child like my mother does. '

Percy sensed a growing determination in her, which added to her attractiveness. He took in the prettiness of her face, the warmth of her eyes, framed by soft braids of dark hair that hung over her shoulders and down across her chest. Without thinking he reached out and touched the scarf that was tied softly around the top of her head: a green band around the darkness.

'Of course I don't think of you like that,' he said as his finger trailed over her cheek.

She smiled and flushed pink. He wanted to draw her close and feel her softness against him. But he knew that first he would need to be completely honest with her. She deserved that, and whatever was the outcome of his revelation, he would have to deal with it.

As they moved on, the fabric of her sleeve felt soft on his hand and he was entranced by the swishing of her skirt around her shoes. 'That colour looks lovely on you,' he said.

'This old green thing.' She laughed. 'It's my warmest dress, so Mother insisted I wear it if going outside.'

'She worries about you a lot, doesn't she?'

'Far too much. I know it's because she cares for me, but it's time she realised I'm no longer a child. I'm ready to make my own decisions. I gave in about the dress this morning, but it's time for me to take a stand when it's important to me. You've helped me see that.' She leaned into his shoulder and looked up at him, her eyes searching his.

'Me? How so?' His heart lurched.

'You've been so brave, striking out on your own, deciding for yourself what you want to do in life in spite of those who think you should follow in your father's footsteps. You've moved a thousand miles from home and stood on your own two feet.'

She paused and her expression turned from one of admiration to concern. He realised his own face was likely registering the mixed emotions he was feeling. *If she knew the truth of my leaving home she wouldn't think me brave at all.*

Knowing he could put it off no longer, he took a deep breath and led her to a large fallen tree. 'Could we sit here on this log for a while? There's something I need to tell you.'

She looked a little disconcerted, but moved towards the tree and sat down. He gazed across the fields again for a few moments, unsure of how to begin. He could feel his heart thudding in his chest.

'I know your parents, particularly your mother, are concerned that I'm not a farmer. I'll likely never have a property like this.'

'Please don't concern yourself with that, Percy.' She laid her hand on his arm. 'I've told Father that I believe you can be completely trusted to provide for a family ... should you have one of your own.' Her last words came quickly. 'I mean, not everyone needs to be a farmer to be successful.'

'No, they don't, and I do believe I could provide well for a wife and children. I really want to talk with you about that, but first I need to be honest with you. I know your mother found it hard to understand why I wouldn't follow in my father's footsteps or take over his property.'

'But ...' she began.

'Please let me finish, Mabel. I'm not saying this very well. I'm afraid of what you'll think of me, to tell you the truth, but the fact is, I don't know who my father is.' He swallowed and took a deep breath.

She gazed at the ground for a moment, then twisted on the

log and looked into his eyes. 'I don't understand.' Her forehead creased and he could already feel the pain it would cause her to hear what he had to say.

He searched her eyes, desperately hoping for approval, for understanding. 'The man I've always known as my father is not my real father, not my birth father.' Her eyes widened. 'I only found that out a short while before I left home. You see, Jack, the man who married my mother and raised me, comes from a German background.' He saw her mouth tremble and was sure she was about to cry. It wrenched at his heart but he knew he had to go on.

'He was born here in Australia, in Grafton on the Northern Rivers, but his father and grandfather came to Australia from Germany in the 1850s. The family came to work here, to make a better life than was possible in Germany.'

He paused and took another deep breath, needing some response from her. She was silent. Her eyes went back to the ground. She clasped her hands together in her lap, her fingers twisting through each other. A magpie warbled above them. It was the only sound he was aware of except the thumping of his heart in his chest.

'But he's not your father?' she said, turning back to him, confusion distorting her face.

Percy shook his head. 'My mother told me the truth early this year when people of German origin began to be taken away and interned.'

'Like Sophie's father.' Mabel nodded.

'Yes. Some of my father's relatives are quite well known around the Clarence and she was afraid the authorities would start rounding us all up. She thought I should know that I'm not of German heritage. She was relieved to think I was going to Sydney to work, so I would be away from danger.'

When Mabel didn't say anything he went on. 'I did intend to seek work in the telephone business. I had planned to go to

Sydney, but when I left it was as much running away from what I couldn't face, as seeking my own life. I don't want you to think of me as terribly brave, Mabel. In fact, I'm ashamed of the way I've deceived you. I'm so sorry.'

His head dropped to his chest. Words caught in his throat. In that moment he was sure he'd lost Mabel and knew he deserved to.

There was a deep silence for a few moments before she turned to him and laid her hand back onto his arm. 'So who is your father?'

Percy swallowed and ran a hand through his hair. 'I'm not sure. I mean, Mum's not sure. No, that's not true. Goodness, this is hard.' He took her hand in his. 'She said he was an English jockey. He … he took advantage of her.'

Mabel gasped and pulled her hand away. She covered her mouth and drew back. 'How awful.' When her initial shock passed, she dropped her hands into her lap again and took a deep breath.

Percy thought she was holding back tears. 'Yes, it must have been terrible for her. I wasn't very sympathetic when she told me. I was too shocked, and well, angry, I suppose. I felt they'd kept the truth from me unfairly.'

She looked into his eyes. 'It must have been a very difficult thing for your mother to tell you, Percy. It's something any woman would want to keep from her son, I'm sure.'

A sense of shame welled up in him. 'I know I should have been more understanding of Mum. I wasn't thinking straight at the time. I was too shocked. The truth is, I've never felt really close to my father ... to Jack. I think some part of me deep down has always sensed there was something not right between us.' His thoughts wandered for a few moments as his memories of Jack, the struggle to feel understood by him, their different aspirations and values, paraded past the back of his mind.

'Don't misunderstand me,' he said, clasping her hands tightly.

'Jack's a good man. A tough one in some ways, but he loves his family and he's done his best to provide for Mum and his children. Mum says if it wasn't for him she doesn't know what she'd have done. Having a child out of wedlock … it must have been dreadful for her.' His words faded.

'Jack must be a good man, Percy. Did he know that your mother told you the truth?'

'Yes, he was there at the time, but he was against it. They'd kept it from me all these years, thinking it was the better thing to do. If it hadn't been for this war and the trouble it's brought for Germans here, I probably would never have known the truth. I'm sure it hurt Jack to think I'd reject him as my father after he'd taken me on as a youngster. It must have cost him to do that. Mum said he loved her and me, but still it would have been a big thing to accept an illegitimate child.'

He took a deep breath. 'I suppose that's what's hard to come to terms with. I was illegitimate. The more I've thought about it over the past months, the more I've felt like I don't know who I am or where I belong.' His shoulders slumped and he hung his head. Hearing his own words out loud reinforced thoughts he'd tried to chase away for so many nights.

Mabel touched his cheek and turned his face back to her. 'You are your own person, Percy. Your parents have obviously raised you to be a good man, a kind and clever one. The fact that your father isn't your birth father doesn't change that. It's not where you come from that's important. It's who you decide to be.'

He smiled and felt a rush of gratitude for her understanding. 'You think so?'

'Of course I think so. Your birth father can't have been a good man, so surely you're better off not to have been raised by him.'

He nodded. 'I'm sure that's what Mum thought. She tried to tell me, but I was too overcome to take it all in. I left soon after she told me and I've hardly been in touch since.'

'Oh, Percy, they must be beside themselves.' She frowned at him. 'That doesn't sound like the Percy I know at all.'

Her words jolted him and another wave of shame washed over him. 'You see. I'm not really as you've come to know me, then, am I?'

'Yes, I'm sure you are. That's why this is bothering you so much. You know in your heart it's not right to hurt your parents like this.'

He nodded and pushed his heel through the ground. *I could kick myself for the stupid way I've acted.* 'You're right. I do know that. I've had a letter from Mum. I know she loves me very much and she's a wonderful woman. It's true, I don't want to hurt her.'

'And your father?'

'Which one?'

'The one who raised you, of course. In my mind he is your real father. He deserves your consideration, don't you think?'

Percy grinned. 'You're being very understanding about all this. Aren't you shocked?'

She reached up and stroked his cheek. 'Yes, I'm very shocked, but I'm glad you told me. I want to know everything about you.'

'Even if my father … Jack, has only a few acres of a paltry farm and nothing to leave me? Not that I deserve anything from him at all.'

'I don't care about that. I told you, I've every confidence you would be a good provider, no matter what you do.'

'I'm not sure your parents will feel the same way, especially when they find out I've lied about my father.'

'So, this English jockey …' She huffed and waved her hand in the air. 'He's not someone you want to find, is he?'

He shrugged. 'I've considered it. He's not just a jockey. Apparently his father did have a big property near Sydney and raised thoroughbred horses. That part is true. He did take horses to the races in Grafton.' He grinned and squeezed her hands. 'It was also true that Jack was a great jockey. It was him who Mum skited about to me. He used to win the races at Grafton all the time. I imagine he beat this Englishman quite often.' Percy felt a flush of pride in Jack.

He was quiet for a moment. 'But no, the more I think about it, the less I want to find my birth father. You're right, I can't imagine ever respecting such a man. He must have been a selfish person and cruel. I can only pray I'm not like him.'

'You're nothing like that, Percy.' She edged a little closer to him on the log.

He put his arm around her shoulder and his stomach fluttered as she laid her head against him. 'I feel so much better,' he said. 'Except that I know I have to be truthful with your parents and I can't imagine how they'll respond. Your mother already disapproves of me.'

She turned her face towards him without lifting her head from his shoulder. 'Regardless of what Mother thinks of you, Percy, I think you're wonderful.'

'I'm so sorry I lied to you, Mabel. I was so confused about my past when I met you. I didn't know what to say when you asked me about my family.'

'I understand,' she said, patting his arm. 'I know you're an honest man in your heart, and you've been very brave to tell me now.'

Their eyes were locked for moments before he lowered his head to hers and kissed her lightly on the lips. 'Shall we walk some more, enjoy the sunshine before the afternoon chill sets in?'

She nodded and pulled away from him. As they rose from the log he took her hand in his and they wandered further along the creek in comfortable silence for minutes before he spoke again.

'So, how do you think I should go about telling your parents the truth?'

She turned and rested against him. His arms went around her

naturally and he soaked in the feel of her.

'I'm not sure,' she said. 'I don't know which part Mother will find the most distressing.'

'What do you mean?'

'Well, she's so worried about me having anything to do with Sophie because of the German internments. She thinks anyone who has those connections should be avoided. As far as the other goes, the fact that your mother was …'

'That I'm illegitimate, you mean?'

She nodded. 'Mother's a bit of a snob, as I'm sure you've gathered. Aunt Sarah says she's always been so. In fact, she won't even acknowledge things about her own family that she finds unsavoury.'

'Like what?'

Mabel pushed back from him and grinned. 'Like the fact that her father was a convict, that he was transported here and served time as a prisoner before he married Grandmother Golder.'

Percy was shocked. 'Really?'

'Yes, really. Aunt Sarah told me all about it. He was quite a rogue. Of course, he came good in the end and was very upright in the later part of his life. But not so when he was young.'

'Goodness. Who'd have thought?'

'Exactly. I was fascinated by the story, and after all, Mother has nothing to be ashamed of. Her father did the wrong thing as a young man and he was caught and punished for it. He did well later and provided for his family. Surely he's to be commended for that. I think it's better to know the truth about someone, but it seems Mother only wants to remember the good things about her father and won't hear the rest spoken of.'

'Is that why she and your aunt don't get along too well?'

'Partly. It's also because they are such different people. Mother disapproves of just about everything Aunt Sarah has done with her life.'

Percy sighed. 'All that doesn't give me much hope of your mother ever approving of me.'

She threaded her arm through his and leaned into him as they walked on. 'I told you, whether she approves or not, I'll make up my own mind in the end. But let's not rush in and put her off side altogether. I think we should tell Father about all of this first. I'm sure he'll be understanding. Then he can handle Mother. That's the best thing to do, I think.'

'If you reckon that's best, then I'm willing to do it that way. Perhaps I should have a talk with him alone. I'll tell him the whole truth, just as I've told you, and whatever he decides to do about it, I'll respect.'

'It'll be all right, Percy. I promise.'

***

When they returned from their walk Mabel's mother and father were in the drawing room having a cup of tea.

'Thank goodness you're back,' Emma said, rising from her chair. 'It's getting cold out there. Your father has been in for ages.'

'Only half an hour, dear.' Albert motioned for her to sit back down. He turned to Mabel. 'I think your walk has done you good, love. You've some colour back in your face.'

'That's from the cold wind.' Emma pursed her lips and settled back into her chair. 'Sit here and have a nice cup of tea. It'll warm you through. No doubt, Percy has to be on his way back to … wherever his roadhouse is. I'm sure he doesn't want to be out on the road after dark.'

'I'm sure he needs a warm drink before he goes.' Albert glanced at his wife and frowned, then turned to Percy. 'Why don't you both sit down? Emma can see that Beattie brings in some more cups and perhaps another couple of slices of that fruit cake. I do fancy some more myself but I'm afraid I've already eaten more than I should have today.' He patted his rounded belly and chuckled.

'Thank you, Father,' Mabel said, leading Percy to the table. 'I think that's a good idea. I don't want Percy going off without something in his stomach.'

Percy pulled out a chair for Mabel and then sat himself. He was aware of Emma's displeasure as she rose and headed for the kitchen. He winced as she pursed her lips and swept past the back of him. *Winning her over is not going to be easy.*

'I couldn't help but admire your fields, Mr Smart,' he said, focussing on Mabel's father, who was his only hope. 'You must be very proud of what you've built up here.'

Albert sat back in his chair. 'I have my father to thank for much of it, Percy. He came to Australia with nothing and worked a section of a farm owned by William Ferguson. We were all born in a little hut on that section. Later Father had some luck at the gold fields and was able to purchase land of his own. He built this house, but it started out as a wattle and daub cottage and a few outbuildings. Over the years he built onto it until it became the substantial home it is now.'

Percy looked around at the wooden panelled walls and rich furnishings and nodded. 'It's a lovely home.'

'Yes, it is, but even in that I was fortunate. I'm the youngest of my family. When my older brothers were ready to be independent, Father carved off parts of the property or gave them the means to start where they wanted. Two of my sisters married farmers in the area. I was just fifteen when he died and there was only my mother, one sister and one brother still living here then. Henry and Caroline both married a couple of years later, so I carried on with Mother and when she died in '91 the rest of the family decided I should keep the original section with the house.'

He paused as Emma came back into the room and settled

into her chair.

'Beattie will be in shortly,' she said tersely.

Percy sensed that she was very against her husband having given permission for him to court Mabel. His heart sank. 'You've made many improvements to the land since then, I imagine, Mr Smart,' he said, trying to distract himself from the tension Emma had brought back to the table.

Albert nodded. 'We have. David, and even young Frederick now, work really hard. They know it will all be theirs one day. The land is a tough taskmaster, not to be taken on lightly.'

'Yes, I've seen that. It's why I'd like to try my hand at other things.' Percy felt Emma's eyes on him, like spears piercing his skin.

'Percy would like to be a businessman, wouldn't you?' Mabel's sweet voice was a relief to the discomfort he was feeling.

He smiled across at her. 'I would, yes, if I can.'

'Hmph.' The barely audible huff came from Emma just as Beattie approached with a tray.

They sat quietly drinking and nibbling at cake for a few moments before Percy turned again to Albert. He could stand the tension no longer and if he didn't do what he'd determined to do quickly, he felt he might lose his nerve.

'If you've a few moments before I leave, I'd like to discuss something with you, Mr Smart.' He was sure his voice sounded like it had a crack in it. He shifted in his chair and cleared his throat.

'Of course, my boy.' Albert looked up at him from under bushy eyebrows, finished his tea and said, 'Why don't we go into my study?' He pushed back from the table.

Percy followed suit, relieved to get away from Emma, but increasingly nervous about the task ahead of him. By the time they reached the study and sat in the large leather chairs beside the desk, Percy could feel sweat running down his neck.

'You look flushed, Percy. Is the heating too much for you in here? I find it so sometimes. Emma insists on having it on full bore. She's afraid Mabel will get a cold.'

'It's fine for me, Mr Smart. I know Mrs Smart worries about Mabel.'

Albert nodded. 'So what did you want to talk to me about? No doubt Mabel told you that I've given my permission for you to call on her. I hope you don't put too much store in my wife's apparent concern about the situation. She tends to worry overly.'

Percy cleared his throat. 'Yes, I do see that … that she's concerned about the situation, I mean. That's why I wanted to talk to you. Well, not the only reason. I'd need to talk to you regardless. There are things about me that you should know, that you have a right to know, given my interest in Mabel.' He watched the older man's face as he spoke, noting the furrowing of his brow.

'I see.' Albert leaned back in his chair. 'Then you'd best go on.' He raked his fingers through his beard and then folded his arms across his broad chest. Despite the fairness Percy had so far sensed in Albert, he now felt like he was standing before a judge and needed to make a very good case for himself or he'd be out on his ear. Percy had no doubt Mabel's father would do whatever was necessary to protect his daughter from harm or disadvantage.

For the next ten minutes, which seemed to Percy like hours, he repeated what he'd told Mabel earlier. Although his inclination was to hang his head in shame as he spoke, he determined to hold it high, to face Albert directly, honestly and contritely, without appearing to be as weak as he felt. When he'd concluded, he leaned back in his chair and took a deep breath.

'That's the truth of it, Mr Smart. I'm so sorry I wasn't honest right from the start. I have a high value on honesty, which I suppose is why I was so shocked when my mother revealed the truth earlier this year. I've lived with a false understanding of my roots since I was a child.'

Albert held up his hands, as if to signal that Percy had said enough. Percy held his breath.

'I can see that it would have been difficult to reveal the truth when you first met Mabel, or us, for that matter. It's not the kind of thing a person wants to have spread all around.'

Percy nodded. He was unsure where Albert was headed. He thought it better to sit quietly and give the older man time to digest his revelation and make a considered response.

'I'll admit it's a bit of a shock.' Albert chewed his bottom lip. 'Not the facts of your birth. That's unfortunate, especially for your poor mother, though it seems she found a man who's to be admired.'

'Yes, sir. Jack is a good man. I'm afraid I haven't appreciated him enough.'

'If you didn't know that he'd taken you and your mother on in difficult circumstances, then it's understandable you might underestimate him. It seems you and he haven't had the strongest of relationship.'

'No, we haven't, sadly. I think that's always hurt Mum.'

'Then you might consider him differently now.' He ran his fingers through his beard again. 'And what about this other man? What do you think of him?'

Percy was surprised by the question. 'I've been trying to work that out, sir. At first I couldn't help wondering what he was like, whether I was like him, if I wanted to find him, see for myself what kind of man he was … is. But the truth is, I don't even know if he's still alive. I have no idea how I'd find him, and the more I think about it, the less I'm inclined to. He's never made any effort to find me as far as I understand. I think Mum would have told me if he had. I doubt he cares about me at all.'

As Percy spoke, the reality of what he was saying sunk into his heart. He'd be a fool to think of chasing a man who'd fathered him but had no interest in him.

Albert shrugged. 'It's hard to know if he's wondered about you, or if he's regretted his actions, felt remorseful. People do change, Percy, and I do believe there's good in everyone, even though the worst of them is often apparent too. Especially in their youth. We've all done things we regret, I'm sure.'

He tapped his hand on the arm of his chair and Percy wondered what was going through his mind. Was he thinking of his father-in-law? Or was he remembering his own youth? It seemed from his story that Albert's early years were spent working very hard to support his mother and build up his father's property. Percy couldn't imagine him having too many regrets.

'Don't you think so?' His voice jolted Percy from his rumination.

'Pardon?' Percy cleared his throat.

'I said, I believe there's some good in everyone and it might be worth giving this jockey the benefit of the doubt. He might have grown to be a respectable and decent man by now.'

'Are you suggesting I should try and find him?' Percy was shocked.

Albert shook his head. 'Not at all. I'm just saying that you shouldn't necessarily consider him an evil man. He's part of you. He may have some traits that you'd be proud to inherit. Perhaps your inclination for business, your adventurous spirit, for instance. I think you'd rest easier with what you know about your past if you could accept that people often grow into their better selves later in life. Holding on to resentment of any kind does none of us any good in my estimation.'

Percy sat quietly for a moment. 'Thank you, sir. That does help. I've struggled to think about being any part of the man he must have been when he was young.'

'And you might think better of your parents if you accepted that they did what they thought was best for you, both as a child and as you grew up. There might never have been a need for you to know about what happened to your mother, and what would have been the harm in you being innocent of it? It seems to me they're decent people who've done everything in your best interests.'

'I do see that, sir.' Percy grimaced. 'I know I've done them a disservice. I intend to correct that as soon as I can.'

'Good.' Albert slapped his hand on the arm of his chair and pushed himself forward.

Percy's heart sank. It seemed Albert might be indicating their conversation was over with no mention of Mabel. As Albert moved to the sideboard and took his pipe from a small tray, Percy's hopes rose again. He waited while Albert stoked the pipe and lit it, returning slowly to his chair. When he'd resettled himself and puffed fragrant smoke into the air around them, he looked across at Percy, his brow furrowed as if he were still deep in thought.

'Then all that remains is to consider what all this means for your relationship with my daughter.'

Percy swallowed. He was relieved the discussion was to continue, but afraid of where it would lead. 'Yes, sir,' he said, trying to prepare himself to give a good account of why he should be allowed to court Mabel. 'I do regret it coming to this. When I first met Mabel and she asked me about my family I was still so confused about it, I didn't know what to say. Things came out in a muddle.'

'Yes, I see that. And you wouldn't be telling her all of this, and certainly not me, unless you intend to be open and honest with us in the future.' His eyebrows arched and his expression left no doubt that his statement was a directive. 'I assume that means you have serious intentions towards Mabel.'

Percy sat forward and clasped his hands together. 'I do, sir. I have strong feelings for Mabel and I believe she returns my feelings. In spite of the fact that coming to Adelaide may appear like I am running away from my responsibilities, I feel it's been a Godsend for me to meet Mabel and I would do everything in my power to be the kind of man she deserves.'

Albert's face relaxed and he chuckled. 'I think you've proven that, Percy. I won't object to your continuing to see Mabel, but I'll be honest with you. I'm not totally sure yet that you're the right person to marry my daughter, so please take things slowly.' He almost rose again and then sat back in the chair before he spoke.

'Also, I'd appreciate it if you'd not say anything about all this in front of my wife for a while. She won't come to terms with it easily. Emma wants everything to be ideal for her daughters. I don't blame her for that, but reality is not always as she'd like it to be. Anyway that's my worry. Let's join the ladies again, shall we? We'll keep this between the two of us, and Mabel of course, for the time being.'

Percy pushed himself up from the chair. His knees felt like jelly and it took him a moment to get his balance. 'Thank you, Mr Smart. I do appreciate your generosity. I know I need to prove myself to you and I'll do whatever it takes to accomplish that.' He offered his hand and was grateful when the older man shook it warmly.

As they left the study and headed back to the drawing room, Percy felt his shoulders relax and the churning that he'd felt in his stomach for weeks began to subside.

CHAPTER THIRTEEN

Kangarilla, October 1915

Mabel and Percy wandered slowly towards Sarah's house. They'd had a lovely walk around the lanes of Kangarilla Village. The spring air was fresh, the sky pale blue with wisps of clouds. Mabel's heart was filled with anticipation. She sensed Percy was building up to asking her something special. He'd listened patiently as she'd chatted about her phone calls with Sophie, about her on-going agitation with her mother and the fun she was having with Aunt Sarah. There were moments when his attention had strayed and Mabel could see he was weighing things up in his mind.

'Is there something bothering you, Percy?' she asked, conscious they were close to her aunt's cottage.

He paused and turned to her, taking both her hands in his own. 'Not bothering me, no, but there is something I want to discuss with you.'

'Yes.' Her voice caught in her throat as she looked up at him.

'You know what I want to ask you, Mabel, don't you?'

'I think so, but I'd like to hear you say it.' She knew she sounded quite brazen, but she was desperate for him to voice what had been clear between them for months now.

He squeezed her fingers and smiled down at her. 'I love you, Mabel, and I want to marry you and spend the rest of my life with you.' He nodded. 'There, I've said it, but you knew that already, I'm sure.' He paused, his eyes locked on hers, brown pools of love she wanted to drown in. She held her breath and felt her heart beating in her chest as he leaned down and lightly touched her lips with his own.

'So what do you think?' He stood back from her, still holding her hands.

'I think that's the most wonderful thing I've ever heard.' She melted into him and let her head rest on his chest.

Wrapping his arms around her, he pulled her closer. 'So you're agreeing to marry me?'

'Of course I am. I've been waiting for you to ask.'

'So now we have to get your parents' permission.' He folded her arm through his and they moved on down the lane.

'Don't look so worried. Father will agree. Haven't you noticed how pleased he's been to see you the last couple of times you've visited me at home? He'll make Mother see reason. She'll go along with what he decides, eventually.' Mabel's stomach was doing flip flops. She couldn't wait to tell Aunt Sarah their news.

***

'Well, it's hardly a surprise to me.' Sarah beamed down at them as she served tea. 'So when are you planning this happy event?' She settled on a chair opposite them and pushed a plate of scones towards Percy.

'I have to convince Mabel's parents that I'm right for her first,' Percy said, piling jam onto a scone. 'I'd like to think we could marry early next year, but first I have to show them that I'm ready and able to support Mabel. I can hardly do that in my little room in the guest house, can I?'

Mabel hadn't considered where she and Percy might live or how things would be after their wedding. She was sure he would work that out perfectly well. Her mind ran to wedding dresses and having her sisters as bridesmaids. *I'm sure Isabel will be tickled pink, and Clara will make me a beautiful head piece.*

'Do you have any ideas of where you'd like to live?' Sarah said.

'I do have an idea,' Mabel heard Percy say.

She pushed images of her wedding dress aside and tuned back into the conversation.

Percy turned to her, his eyes lighting up. 'It came to me when you were talking about Sophie and her mother. It's clear Mrs Wagner is very unhappy. She must spend all day worrying about her husband. And Sophie's certainly miserable the way things are.'

'That's true.' Mabel nodded. 'But I don't see what that has to do with where we might live.'

'Didn't you tell me the bakery they owned is sitting idle at Clarendon?'

'Yes, but …' Mabel shrugged in her confusion.

'I've been thinking that it's a shame to have a business like that shut down, especially with all the shortages now with the war. No doubt people are missing their fresh bread and cakes and scones and the like.'

Mabel nodded. 'They are. Lots of people talk about it.'

'Then why couldn't we help Mrs Wagner to go back and start the business up again? I could organise to get the place ready for her and I'm good with figures and such. I could set up the business side if she wanted me to. I could rent a cottage somewhere close by and get it ready for us when we're married, and still do my telephone repair work. I'm travelling all around with that anyway and there's plenty of time between jobs. I'm sure Mr Johnstone at the post office would agree.'

Mabel's mind spun as Percy talked. She could see his excitement mounting as his ideas flowed.

'I think that's a wonderful idea,' Sarah said, leaning across the table. 'I'd be happy to help too. I'm not a bad hand at baking if I do say so myself, and I've time on my hands.'

Percy nodded and his smile broadened as he turned to Mabel. 'Do you think Mrs Wagner would consider the idea? Wouldn't it be good to see her have something of her life back, and something else to think about rather than worrying about her husband?'

'I'm sure it would be good for her, but I'm not sure she'll feel able to do it.' Mabel was still having trouble taking in the idea. 'I know Sophie would love to go back home. She's missing everyone. She'd help in the shop, too, of course. She was working in the kitchen with her mother before they left.'

'I think we could work that business back up in no time.' Percy rubbed his hands together. It would be good for everyone concerned. How about I find time to go and talk to Mrs Wagner one day this week?'

'So you're thinking this will help Emma and Albert to see that you're serious about supporting Mabel?' Sarah poured another cup of tea.

'I hope so,' Percy said. 'At least it would be a step in the right direction and it would surely be a good thing for Mrs Wagner.'

***

Mabel wondered whether to talk to her parents about Percy's idea. She had such admiration for him. Surely they would see how clever he was and how caring. She'd agreed to wait and allow him to ask their permission to set the wedding date, but perhaps she could pave the way by reporting something of his wonderful plan.

'What's going on in that head of yours?' Her father's voice broke into her thoughts. 'You've hardly touched your dinner.'

'Sorry, Father. I've been distracted with something Percy and I were talking about today.'

'You saw him again today?' Her mother's tone was terse. 'I thought he'd agreed to come here rather than sneaking to Sarah's place to see you.'

'He doesn't sneak to Aunt Sarah's. He likes to visit with her. I've said before, they're very fond of each other.' Mabel picked up her fork and loaded it with mashed potato. *Perhaps now is not a good time to sing his praises after all.*

'Besides,' her mother went on. 'I haven't had chance to tell you yet, but I've had word from my sister in Hackney. Poor Florence.' Tears sprang into Emma's eyes and she wiped them with her napkin.

'What is it, Mother?'

'Florence has seen two of her sons go off to this wretched war. Now she's had word that Jacob is missing in action, whatever that means.' She sucked back more tears.

'It means that he's possibly been injured somewhere on the battle front and not found yet,' Albert said, patting her hand.

'Or dead in a trench somewhere and not even recognisable.'

'That is possible, dear.' Albert went on, stroking her arm. 'But we needn't think the worst, yet.'

Emma turned back to Mabel. 'That on top of the telegram she received a month ago to say that Willis is being sent home because of injuries and something called trench foot.'

'That's …' Albert began.

'I don't want to know what it is,' Emma snapped. 'I'm just glad he's coming home.'

'That's so sad, Mother.' Mabel's heart clenched at the thought of her cousins going through such horror.

'I'd like to go and be with Florence for a little while, Mabel.' Emma looked up, her face deeply lined and flushed with sorrow. 'I need you to come with me.'

'What?' Mabel's mind raced. 'But, Mother, why? What can I do?'

'You can help me comfort my sister and assist in caring for

Willis for a bit. The younger boys are no help and her daughters all have families of their own.' Emma's tone had an edge and Mabel knew she'd have to argue hard to avoid complying with her mother. She was torn. Of course she wanted to help her aunt and cousin. She felt great pity for them. *If I didn't have so much on my mind ... if Percy hadn't suggested his plan and if he wasn't soon to ask for my hand in marriage ...* Thoughts flew around inside her head, but words wouldn't come. What argument could she possibly give that would justify ignoring her mother's plea?

She sighed and nodded. 'When were you thinking of going?'

'As soon as I can get ready,' Emma replied. 'Willis is apparently due home any time now. We can take the coach from Clarendon up to Adelaide one day this week. Harold will pick us up in his cart from there. It's not far from the city.'

'I see.' Mabel sat back and rung her hands together. 'All right, Mother, I'll get some things packed.'

'Thank you, Mabel,' her father said. 'I'd be very concerned if your mother had to go alone and Clara's tied up at the shop.'

'I know, Father. Of course I'll go and help.' *But please don't let it be for too long.*

***

Two weeks later Mabel dropped into a chair in her aunt's parlour, exhausted. The house was quiet at last. Uncle Harold and Aunt Florence had retired, their three young sons had been seen into bed and she had checked that Willis was as comfortable as could be, given the pain in his shoulder wound. He was healing as well as could be expected, the doctor had said today.

At least I'll have the bedroom to myself tonight, now that Mother has gone. Mabel was relieved that her uncle had taken Emma to Adelaide that morning, and put her on the coach back to Clarendon. She was sure Florence had had enough comfort from her sister to last her a while and Emma did not feel up to cooking or cleaning for Harold and the boys, so she'd decided she was most needed back at Park Farm. Of course, she'd also assumed that Mabel would stay on and help care for Willis. *A good reason to keep me away from Percy, I'm sure.*

Mabel had agreed to stay and help a little longer, though she could see that it was also better for her aunt to be kept busy. *Anything that keeps her from sitting and wondering if Jacob is dead or alive is surely a good thing.* Mabel felt deeply for her aunt. She couldn't begin to imagine what horror would be going through the poor woman's head when she thought about her son in that dreadful place.

Mabel wondered what Percy was doing, which was where her mind went as soon as she had a minute to think. No doubt Aunt Sarah would have let him know where she was, but she was longing to see him again. *Did he talk to Mrs Wagner about the bakery? When would he talk to her parents about their wedding plans? Is he missing me as much as I'm missing him?*

She picked up the newspaper on the side table and absently turned the pages until one headline jumped out at her. *Anti-war activist, Vida Goldstein, to speak in Adelaide.* Mabel scanned the article, which spoke of Miss Goldstein's work. *The Women's Peace Army, led by Vida Goldstein, which has been at the forefront of the struggle for women's rights, has been influential in obtaining jobs and fair working conditions for women and in helping soldiers' wives in the battle to keep their homes going.*

Miss Goldstein was against conscription, the article went on to say, and as Andrew Fisher had just resigned from the prime ministership and Morris Hughes had accepted the appointment, she was determined to challenge the new Prime Minister's pro-conscription stance. It seemed he'd already been promoting his ideas and fighting with many unionists about the issue. Miss

Goldstein was to give a speech at the town hall in Adelaide in three days' time.

Mabel was stirred with admiration. *How I'd love to hear her. And why not? Being so close to Adelaide here, surely I could go into the city on Friday. I could visit Sophie and find out how her mother has responded to Percy's idea.* A plan formed in Mabel's mind. *Perhaps I could see Percy! I'm sure Aunt Florence can manage without me for a day.* She folded the newspaper and laid it back on the side table. As she headed up the stairs to bed, her spirits lifted.

***

Three days later Mabel cleared her throat and knocked on the door to the guest house in Wakefield Street. A rakish woman with a scarf around her head opened the door and looked her up and down.

'Yes?'

'I'm a friend of Percy Smith's and I was wondering if he's home from work yet?'

'A friend of Percy's, you say?' The woman paused for a moment. 'I think I did hear him come in. He'll be upstairs in his room. He doesn't usually come down until tea time.'

'I'm sure if he knew I was here–'

'I don't allow female visitors to the bedroom.' She pursed her lips and sniffed. 'If you wait in the parlour I'll see if he wants to come down and talk to you.' Standing to one side the woman pointed to the door just inside the entrance. 'What's the name?'

'Mabel.'

The woman nodded briefly and headed up the stairs.

'Thank you,' Mabel said to the disappearing figure. She entered the small room and sat down in a lumpy lounge chair, which seemed almost to swallow her as she sank into the back of it. She pushed herself forward and perched on the front edge, straightening her skirt and tucking a few strands of hair back into the braids which circled her head.

'Mabel?' Percy's voice preceded him into the room. 'How on earth did you get here? Is something wrong?' He sat on the edge of the lounge beside her, clearly aware of its tendency to devour its occupants.

'No, nothing's wrong.' She smiled broadly, unable to hide her pleasure at the sight of him. 'I came in on the coach from Hackney. I'm sure Aunt Sarah has told you where I've been.'

'Yes, I spoke to her over a week ago. I've been wondering how you were going. How is your aunt?'

'She's doing as well as can be expected. I can't do a great deal more to help, now that Willis is beginning to heal. He's managing most things. The poor dears are still waiting for news of their other son. It's terrible, really, but I feel quite helpless.'

'I'm sure you've been wonderful. Isn't your mother there too?'

'She was until a few days ago when she decided she was more needed at home.' Mabel sniggered. 'Dear Mother. She was keen for me to stay, which I'm sure was really about keeping me away from you.'

'Yet, here you are.' He took her hands. 'I'm so glad to see you.' He leaned toward her and kissed her on the cheek. 'We'd best be careful. My landlady is very particular about what she calls "shenanigans" in her house. She's warned us over and over there's to be no lady visitors, and certainly none of the other kind of females in her house.' He chuckled.

'Yes, I did wonder if she was going to close the door in my face.' Mabel giggled and squeezed his fingers, enjoying the touch of him.

'So, tell me, did you come into town just to see me?'

'Actually, I came because I want to hear Vida Goldstein's talk at the town hall tonight and I wondered if you'd come with me.'

She dropped her eyes, wondering if Percy might disapprove.

'Vida Goldstein? Yes, I did hear something about that. She's talking against conscription, isn't she?'

She nodded. 'She's against the war altogether. She's very outspoken and she argues with the politicians about it too.'

'I've heard there have been a few scuffles between the new Prime Minister and some of the unionists,' Percy said. 'They're against conscription too. This woman is very brave for speaking out, but you know there's likely to be trouble there tonight. There's sure to be a group of the pro-conscription people protesting about her talk.'

'I know. That's why I thought you might come with me. I'm a bit nervous about going, but I do want to hear her, Percy. I think she's so courageous and what's more, she's right, isn't she? We have to stand up against the idea of making all young men go to war. What they are going through is terrible. Poor Willis can't mention it without shaking and crying, and he has dreadful nightmares. I doubt he'll ever be the same again.'

'Yes, I agree with the stance against conscription, and I certainly wouldn't let you go to the meeting alone. I'm glad you came here first.'

'I actually went to Sophie's first. I wanted to see if I could stay there the night, and her grandmother is happy for me to stay on the couch. I'll catch the coach back to Hackney in the morning.'

'Well, quite the adventurer, aren't you?' Percy chuckled and gave her a quick kiss on the forehead. 'Let's go out for a bit to eat before the meeting and I'll tell you all about the plans Mrs Wagner and I have made for her bakery in Clarendon. I'll let my landlady know I won't be in for tea.'

***

'I'm so proud of you, Percy.' Mabel sat in the small café seat, entranced by Percy's plans to move Mrs Wagner and Sophie back into the cottage behind the bakery and do whatever repairs were needed so she could start up the business again. 'I only had a few minutes with Sophie but she's very excited.'

'Your Aunt Sarah is really keen too. She's such a trouper. Between the two of them they'll cook up such treats that people will come for miles.' He bit into his pie and grinned as some sauce ran from the corner of his mouth. 'They'll make better pies than these, for sure. They're so mean with the meat. It's all gravy.'

'Everyone is trying to cut back, I suppose,' she said, breaking off a piece of crust. 'But Mrs Wagner does make a great potato pie.'

'Not better than yours, I'll bet.' He reached across the table and took her hand. 'I've missed you very much, Mabel. I hope we don't have to wait too much longer to speak to your parents about getting married.'

'I hope so too. I'll go home in a week or so, and perhaps we can make a time to do it then?'

He nodded, smiling as he took another bite of pie. 'Good. I've been asking about cottages to rent in the area. There are a few vacant ones. Some people from around there have had to move out with the internments and so many unemployed. The lines at soup kitchens and welfare houses are getting longer and longer around the city. We can only hope this madness ends soon, for everyone's sake.'

After they'd eaten, Mabel and Percy made their way towards the town hall where groups of people gathered. Some were gradually filing into the building. Others stood with placards and megaphones calling out to the attenders and waving their fists in the air.

'Cowards,' they yelled. 'Letting a woman tell you what to do! Where's your pride? Stand up and fight for your country like men.'

Mabel was appalled to see how many of the protesters were

women. 'How can they want their sons and husbands to go to their deaths?' She pressed into Percy's shoulder as they shuffled towards the door, caught in the crossfire of verbal assaults from both sides.

'I don't understand any of it, Mabel. Keep your head down and let's get inside as quick as we can.'

Inside they made their way down the aisle, taking empty seats as close to the front as they could.

When Miss Goldstein made her way to the podium, Mabel sat forward, enthralled.

'If the fullest freedom of speech and press is not given to the anti-conscriptionist, and conscription is forced upon the manhood of the country, there will be serious trouble. I ask those, whose duty it is to protect the people against tyranny and oppression, to fight as you have never fought before, for the people, and for those whose conscience directs them to oppose conscription, from which it has always been the proud boast of Britishers that they were free. The nation that stifles conscience, even in a time of war, proves that it believes that Might is the only Right. To say NO to conscription means the beginning of the end of militarism in Australia, and every other nation; the beginning of the reign of Right as the only Might there is or can be.'

Mabel grasped Percy's arm as the speech continued. Tears welled in her eyes when she thought of the people outside, still shouting in protest against the meeting.

'And you, women of Australia, are asked to say the same thing, and more, for as women you are faced with a greater responsibility in this matter than men. As the mothers of the race, it is your privilege to conserve life, and love and beauty, all of which are destroyed by war. You who give life, cannot, if you think deeply and without bias, vote to send any mother's son to kill, against his will, some other mother's son.*'

When Miss Goldstein stopped speaking everyone stood and clapped loudly, shouting 'yes, yes', before they began to make their way back down the aisle.

'Are you glad you came, Percy? Wasn't she wonderful?' Mabel had to shout in Percy's ear to make herself heard amongst the cheering crowd.

He nodded and put his arm around her shoulder as he edged forward, making a passage for her to move toward the door. 'I'm very glad, Mabel. She's amazing. I only hope her message reaches the ears of the politicians and they heed her words. I'm afraid some are pushing hard for a referendum and if that happens, the people will decide. It could go either way.'

'Do you really think the majority of people might vote in favour of conscription?' Mabel couldn't believe that possible.

'It's hard to say, but I pray I'm not forced to take up arms, Mabel. Come on, let's get out of here before a riot starts outside the building. I'll get you back to Sophie's house.'

As they walked back in the balmy air of the evening, Mabel clung to Percy's arm, and kept images of her wedding day foremost in her mind; the two of them, walking arm in arm, committing themselves to a future together, the sons and daughters she would give life to from their love. She would not allow the thought of Percy in a soldier's uniform to take root in her mind. Not now, not ever.

*Extracted from Australia's Women's Peace Army Manifesto by Vida Goldstein, 1916

CHAPTER FOURTEEN

Clarendon, October 1915

As Percy headed for Clarendon, he felt an excitement he hadn't experienced since he first started learning about telephones. A new challenge inspired him. His head brimmed with ideas, so the short trip from Chandler's Hill roadhouse was over before he knew it. He'd bought and borrowed the equipment he'd need: paint, whitewash, hammer and nails, gardening implements and a few other tools which one of his friends at the guest house in Adelaide had offered. He'd only seen the bakery from the outside, so apart from a new door handle, a coat of paint and a general clean-up in the back yard around the attached cottage, he couldn't tell what would need attention.

Sarah Goble was to meet him at the bakery and she'd promised to bring all the cleaning equipment they'd need for inside. As soon as it was liveable Mrs Wagner and Sophie would move back into the cottage and get the place ready for business. Sarah had already put the word out that the bakery would be opened before Christmas, so the local residents could expect to get their Christmas puddings, cakes and mince pies from Wagner's bakery as they'd been used to doing for many years before the war started. The good news had been received with excitement and was a welcome relief from the bad news of the war which constantly filled the newspapers and airwaves.

Sarah was waiting in her carriage when Percy pulled up. He waved and jumped from the bench seat, digging into his pocket for the keys Mrs Wagner had given him for the shop and the cottage.

'You've met Mabel's sister, Clara, haven't you, Percy?' Sarah nodded towards the young woman beside her on the seat as she began to climb down. 'She was keen to help.'

'Yes, we've met.' Percy flashed a smile. 'When I had dinner at your home. How are you, Clara? It's good of you to come and help.'

'I'm well thank you, Percy, and very happy to join in.' She slid to the footpath and shook Percy's hand. 'Many hands make light work as they say. Isabel wanted to come too, but Mother had other things for her to do today. I'm sure she'll come another time. We're all very excited about this venture. Having one of the businesses start up again in Clarendon is a sign of hope. I work at the milliners just down the road and lately you could shoot a gun down the street here through the week and not hit anyone.'

'Probably not a good turn of phrase at the moment, dear.' Sarah rolled her eyes. 'Which are the keys for the cottage, Percy? We'll take our things inside and get started.'

When the two women had unloaded and taken what they needed inside the cottage, Percy opened up the bakery and moved his tools in. He worked for a few hours, cleaning down walls and benches, ridding the shelves and corners of spiders and scrubbing the floor. He was reattaching the broken lock on the door when Clara appeared from the side lane to the house.

'You look done in, Percy. I've come to tell you we've got enough of a fire going under the stove to boil a kettle and Aunt Sarah's got tea and scones for us. You must be ready for a break.'

'That sounds super.' Percy dusted off his pants. 'She's thought of everything, hasn't she?'

'I'm sure you can't imagine Aunt Sarah not making provision

for tea and scones.' She laughed. 'And the cottage has come up really well. It's surprising what a good dust and clean can do. I'm sure Mrs Wagner and Sophie will be able to move back any time now. There's still water in the tank from the winter rains and plenty of wood out back for the fire. They'll need more for the bakery stoves, but I'm sure we can organise that.'

'I'm sure we can,' Percy said, clapping his hands together. 'Now that you've mentioned that tea and scones, I'm starving.'

'Mabel would have loved to be here, you know,' Clara said as they headed down the side lane. 'She'll be back from Hackney in a few days. She'll be excited to see what we've done.'

'It's just the beginning, so she'll be able to get involved when she's ready.' Percy's heart leapt at the thought of seeing Mabel again.

'You know Mother won't want her to get involved in cleaning. Just the thought of dust sends her into a tizz. She's afraid it will set off Mabel's asthma. There's nothing in our house that doesn't get thoroughly cleaned very regularly by Mother … at least supervised by her.'

'Of course,' Percy said, realising he'd have to keep that in mind when he and Mabel were married. 'What about in the bakery? I know she was keen to help out there once Mrs Wagner starts cooking again.'

'I'm sure Mabel will insist on helping but she'll have a fight on her hands. Mother thinks anything that floats in the air might start Mabel off, even flour, but we all know that Mabel sneaks into our kitchen whenever she can and helps Beattie with cooking. She loves it, and it's never caused a problem. With Mother, it's least said, least trouble.' She chuckled as she pushed open the cottage door.

'Yes, I see that's been the way of things,' Percy said, not sure it was going work in regard to his and Mabel's plans for the future.

'Here we are,' Sarah said, nodding towards the table, which was set with cups of tea, a plate of scones and a tub of jam.

Percy rubbed his hands together. 'Ah, Mrs Goble, you must have been up at the crack of dawn to make these before you came over here.'

'I'm always up at the crack of dawn, dear. Best time of the day.' She waited until he pulled out a chair and sat at the table, then handed him a cup of tea. 'I'm looking forward to being here at the shop early with Mrs Wagner. This has given me a whole new lease on life.' She grinned broadly and pushed the plate of scones his way.

After savouring his tea and scone for a few minutes, Percy looked up at Sarah. 'I'm not sure I've endeared myself to your sister with this idea. Clara tells me she won't be happy for Mabel to be involved.'

'I've told you before, Mabel will do what she wants, one way or another, but I wouldn't be too sure you haven't made a good impression with this project. Albert was very impressed when I told him about it last Sunday after church, and I'm sure Emma was too, though she wouldn't let it be seen.'

'Perhaps if she thinks it was your idea? After all, you made plenty of suggestions to get us started.'

'Oh, no, I made quite sure they knew it was your idea.' Sarah shook her head. 'It's the kind of thing that Albert considers admirable, and besides, any idea of mine would not be received well by Emma just as a matter of course. She's of the old school. She doesn't approve of women having ideas of their own and certainly not being in business.'

'Then she'll not be happy for Mrs Wagner to have the bakery back in business?'

'I've told her you'll be handling the business side of it. Don't worry so much about Emma's opinion, Percy. Her greatest concern is that her children are safe, well and suitably married. She'll soon see she need not worry about leaving Mabel in your hands.'

'It's true, Percy,' Clara said. 'Mother has much more to worry about with me. I'm happy to be a working girl. I'd love to have my own business and I've no intention of marrying any time soon. The woman who's running the milliner's shop now is only managing it for Aunt Sarah.' She grinned conspiratorially at her aunt, who nodded and rolled her eyes. 'It's our secret plan for me to run it eventually.' She clasped her hands together in front of her and her eyes lit up.

'To own it actually,' Sarah added, tapping Clara's hand across the table. 'Just as soon as you can manage the lease yourself.'

Clara nodded, her smile widening. 'The world is changing for women, Percy. New possibilities are opening up, and for all the terror of this war, it's going to help people see that women can do so much more than we ever thought possible.'

'It seems to me that your aunt has already achieved more than most would think possible for a woman.' Percy beamed across the table at Sarah.

'It's true,' Clara said, stroking her aunt's arm. 'But most women of Aunt Sarah's generation find it hard to imagine a life different from the one they've known. Mother certainly underestimates what we're capable of, especially Mabel, because she's had asthma to deal with, but it won't hold Mabel back from doing what she wants, you mark my words.'

'Well, your plans sound very exciting,' Percy said. 'I hope it all works out for you. And thank you for reassuring me about Mabel. I do see there's a lot of determination behind that sweet smile. I must remember not to underestimate her.'

He cast his eyes around the small kitchen. 'Looks clean as a whistle in here. You've done a great job this morning.'

'The bedrooms are all spick and span too. We'll scrub the laundry tubs this afternoon and we thought we'd leave the parlour to clean when Mrs Wagner comes next week. I'm sure she'll enjoy doing that with us. She'll want to put her photos back on the walls.'

'You're both very kind. It will be wonderful to see the poor woman back in her home and having something to take her mind off her troubles.' Percy bit into his third scone and pushed back from the table. 'I'm going to whitewash the walls inside the bakery and tomorrow I'll start painting the outside. It's not too bad, really, considering it's been unattended for nearly a year. A good wash down has made it quite presentable.'

'Perhaps David will come over tomorrow and repaint the sign out front. He's keen to make a contribution too.' Clara began stacking the cups.

'That would be great.' Percy headed back to the bakery, whistling as he walked down the lane. He stood outside for a moment before going in, gazing at the shopfront and imagining customers flooding through the door, the smell of fresh bread and cinnamon cakes coming to meet them.

I'll have a store of my own one day, maybe even two or three.

***

Percy woke on Monday morning, a little weary and with a few sore muscles, but elated at the thought of what he'd achieved over the weekend.

The postmaster greeted him as he entered the post office for work. 'Morning, Percy. I've a list of jobs here for this week.' He handed the list across the counter. 'A few new instalments and a couple of repairs. Mostly around the city. Oh, and there's a letter for you here, too.'

'Thank you, Mr Johnstone.' He scanned the list of jobs to see which were closest, then folded the sheet and put it in his pocket. As he went out the back to get his tools, he looked briefly at the letter, assuming it was from his mother. He would read it while he had morning tea. He was keen to hear her news. She'd written again since he'd replied to her first letter, thanking him for the money he was sending and filling him in on the news around Mororo. It seemed there'd not been any further internments, but the reports from those who were at Trial Bay were sad. Some of the men were holding up well, doing productive things and entertaining themselves as best they could. But others were fretting and sickly, had no heart for any of the activities that were offered, and desperately worried about their families.

Percy felt sorry for these men, but wondered if they'd be any better off among the constant rallies and protests, divisions over conscription, and the pressure to enlist. He was used to ignoring the hostility around him every day, but he was sure if it were generally known that his family had German origins, he'd be targeted severely by some.

The thought led him again to think about his father and his own origins. Lately it had seemed less important to him. He'd been greatly encouraged by Mr Smart to think better of Jack, who had chosen to father him and married his mother under difficult circumstances. It was something that deserved respect and he'd not shown Jack enough of that. He determined to make that right as soon as he could.

After a morning's work he found a quiet street, took out the sandwich he'd brought from the guest house and pulled the letter from his pocket. He was surprised to see, on closer examination, that it wasn't his mother's writing at all. As he began to read his sister's words, his heart sank.

Dear Percy,

Mum finally agreed to give me your address, so I could write to you. She's refused my doing so for the past few months. I thought it was important you know that Mum is very unwell. She's due to have a baby in December and she's been suffering badly throughout the pregnancy. I'm really worried about her and so is Dad. He agreed you should know. I can see he's sad that you are not here. I don't know the full story of why you left so suddenly. I'm sure it was more than a good job that called you away, barely saying goodbye. I have felt that something awful happened between you and Dad, and he's really feeling the brunt of it. Surely it would be better if you came home, at least for a visit, and sorted things out? I'm afraid that your being away is making Mum even sicker than she might otherwise be. She worries a lot about you.

You'll be pleased to know there is also good news—at least I think so. John Lange and I were married a month ago. We decided we couldn't wait until you came home, nor until the war ended, because it's looking like that's never going to happen—I mean with the war. Vera and Jack Wiblin are engaged, but they won't marry for a while because Vera feels she must stay home and help Mum now that she'll have a little one and she's so weak. At least we hope she'll have a little one. Mrs Wiblin, who's always helped Mum with births, says she's not sure the baby will be strong enough to survive, as Mum's so sick.

Mum didn't want me to tell you all this, but now I have and I'm not sorry. We all miss you, Percy. It's not the same around here without you. Please come home.

Your loving sister,

Ida

Percy could hardly breathe by the time he'd finished reading. His sandwich had gone soggy in his hand and his stomach was clenched tightly.

***

'What's up? You look like you've seen a ghost,' Mr Johnstone said when Percy returned his worksheet that afternoon.

'I've had bad news from home, I'm afraid.' Percy's voice caught in his throat.

'Not someone from the front, is it? We're sending out telegrams giving parents dreadful news about their boys every day now. It's more than a person can bear.'

Percy shook his head. 'No, it's my mother. She's sick … really sick. I'm going to have to go home.'

'I see.' The postmaster dragged his fingers through his beard. 'Will you come back?'

Percy paused. He hadn't thought beyond seeing his mother. 'Of course. The girl I'm going to marry is here. I'll be back as soon as I can, but I'll understand if you can't hold my job for me.'

'You're a good worker, Percy. Better than most. I don't want to lose you. Things have slowed up a lot with this war. Money's drying up. Everything's going on the war effort. It's not only those poor sods in the trenches that are dug in and stalled. It's like the whole country is in limbo.'

Percy nodded, his thoughts already with his family.

'That is to say that I can spare you for a bit,' the postmaster continued. 'You go and see your mother, lad. So many grieving mothers.' He tutted and shook his head slowly. 'It's a sad state of affairs.'

'Thank you, Mr Johnstone. I appreciate your understanding. I'll get going as soon as I can get a ticket onto a train. I daren't wait any longer.' He shook the postmaster's hand and hurried out back to unpack his cart.

As he packed that night, he wondered how best to get word to Mabel. He had to assure her he'd be back as soon as possible. He wrote a note to Sarah Goble explaining why he had to leave, asking her to tell Mabel about the letter he'd received and passing on his promise to return. The following morning he went to Mrs Wagner's home and told her what had happened.

'Of course you must go, Percy,' she said. 'Sophie and I will manage. We'll move back to our cottage in Clarendon and get started. Sarah is going to help. She's been wonderful. We'll give her your note and we'll be fine. When you come back we'll be cooking, you'll see.'

'I will be back, Mrs Wagner. I won't let you down, I promise.'

'You're a good boy, Percy. Your mama and papa must be very proud of you.'

'I'm not so sure of that, Mrs Wagner, but I hope to make them so.' He shook her hand warmly and gave Sophie a hug. 'You will tell Mabel that I'm sorry I had to go before she came back from Hackney, won't you, Sophie? I hate to do it, but I'm very worried about my mother.'

'She'll understand, Percy,' Sophie said. 'Just come back safely. I don't think Mabel could bear it if you didn't.'

'You tell Mabel there's going to be a wedding when I get back, and the sooner the better. Tell her to make plans.' He squeezed her hands and winked.

Later that afternoon he caught the train from Adelaide and headed back to New South Wales.

***

Percy slept on and off overnight and in the morning changed trains in Sydney for the trip to Grafton. He stayed the night there before taking the coach to Harwood, then walked the last few miles down the dirt track to Mororo. The closer he got to home, the more the landscape contrasted with the busy streets of Adelaide. The smell of dust rose up from under his feet. He'd almost forgotten how dry and scrubby the farmland was compared to the open, green fields around Clarendon.

Percy stopped dead in his tracks, panic rising in his throat. The small cottage he'd always called home was empty and abandoned. After searching the yards for signs of his family, he grabbed his bag, which he'd dropped on the front porch, and hurried towards the Lange's farm.

'Percy, Percy.' He heard his name being called as he approached the farm. It was Connie. His sister came hurtling down the track from a cottage on the corner of the Lange's property. She threw herself into his arms, causing him to drop his bag and almost topple over.

'I knew you'd come home, Percy. I'm so glad to see you.' She pushed back and looked him up and down, and then hugged him hard again, her face beaming, her eyes bright with unshed tears.

'But what are you doing here? Where are Mum and Dad? I went to the house and there was nothing there.'

'We've moved.' She cast her hand in the direction of the cottage at the end of the lane. 'We live here now. Mr Lange arranged it. It's better. We have a small piece of land across from the cottage and thirty milking cows. Mum saved money from the housekeeping and selling eggs … and from the money you sent home. She didn't tell Dad till it was all arranged, and Dad is working on the ferries over the Clarence because he's too old to do woodcutting now. He's in Harwood.'

'Hold on.' Percy held up his hands to stop Connie's rush of words. 'One thing at a time. None of this was in Ida's letter. It seems I've lots to catch up on, but first tell me how Mum is.' He took hold of her shoulders and looked into her face. 'She's all right, isn't she?'

Connie shook her head. 'Not really, but she says she will be once she's had the baby. She's in bed most of the time now. Ida told her that she'd written to you and she was sure you'd come home to see her. Ida and John got married and they're in the main house.' She pointed towards the Lange's homestead.

'Yes, she told me she'd married.'

'And Vera's engaged, and I want to get engaged to Freddie Lange but Dad says I'm too young and I have to wait until the war is over before he'll talk about any more weddings.'

'He's right, Connie. You're only fifteen. You've plenty of time. Now, let's get to the house. I want to see Mum.'

Percy was met with shouts of glee as he walked into the cottage and Rita, Dottie and Winnie clamoured to hug him. Over their heads he saw his youngest sister, Laura, standing back and eyeing him suspiciously.

'My, haven't you grown,' he said, smiling at her. 'You were such a little tot when I left.'

'She's nearly three,' Rita said, moving back to pick up her sister. 'I think she's forgotten you.'

Percy nodded, a flush of guilt washing over him. 'And Clarrie? How's he?'

'He's working at the Lange's. Dad says he's old enough to leave school, so he's helping on the farm and he helps milk our cows too, because Vera and Connie can't do it all, and Mum's too sick.'

'I see.' Percy shook his head. He felt overwhelmed with the changes that had happened for his family in the nine months he'd been away. *I should have been here to help them.* The second the thought passed through his mind an image of Mabel followed. He felt confused, tired and ashamed. 'Where's Mum?' he said, looking around at the doors that led off the front room.

Connie pointed to one. 'She's asleep, I think, but she won't mind if you wake her.'

Percy pushed open the door quietly and drew in a sharp breath as he gazed at his mother lying on the bed, still as death, pale as the sheet drawn up around her chest. The mound that would soon be his new brother or sister looked too small to hold a baby.

As he tiptoed towards the bed, her eyes fluttered open and when she turned her head slightly and saw him, they filled with tears.

'Percy.' Her voice was a whisper. 'Dear Percy.' She held out her hand. It seemed to take all her strength to do so and he quickly took hold of it before it dropped to the side of the bed.

He perched carefully beside her. 'Hello, Mum. It's so good to see you. I've been worried all the way home. I'm sorry … for everything. I should have been here. I shouldn't have left you. Please forgive me.'

He felt the weakness in her hand as she tried to squeeze his fingers. 'Shush now, son. There's nothing to forgive. You're here now and that's all that matters.' Her eyes closed again for a moment and then reopened. 'How did you find us? Ida said she'd forgotten to tell you we'd moved.'

'I knew the Langes would know where you were, and Connie saw me coming.'

'Ah, yes, Connie's been looking out for you every day. She was sure you'd come home. Your father will be back tomorrow. He'll be glad to see you.'

'I'll be glad to see him too, Mum.'

The smile that lit her face seemed to bring colour back into her cheeks. A tear rolled from one eye and he brushed it gently with his finger. 'I've lots to tell you, Mum, but you rest now and I'll get settled. I could do with a hot drink and some bread and jam.'

She nodded. 'You'll be hungry after your trip. Connie will see to it.' Her words came between short gasps of breath. 'Vera should be back soon. She's gone over to Anna's to get some fresh vegetables. Your father has started a garden, but as soon as this little one is out and on his way, I'll be well enough to get more vegetables in.' She patted his hand.

He waited until her eyelids had dropped closed and then left the room, his heart aching at her frailty. She'd always been wiry and a little too weary looking for his liking, but what he saw now frightened him.

CHAPTER FIFTEEN

Park Farm, South Australia, November 1915

Mabel leaned back into her chair. She'd been home from Hackney nearly two weeks, but she couldn't settle into anything and seemed to have lost her appetite altogether.

'You've hardly touched your dinner again, Mabel. Really, how are you going to maintain your health, if you don't eat properly? If I'd known that helping my sister look after Willis would have this effect on you, I'd never have suggested you go to Florence's home.'

'You didn't suggest I go there, Mother. You insisted.' Mabel pulled herself toward the table and picked up her fork. She looked down at the mound of mashed potato on her plate and her stomach turned over.

'Mabel.' Her father's tone held a warning about being disrespectful to her mother.

'If you'd heard the things Willis told me, you'd lose your appetite, too, Mother.' Mabel softened her voice. 'Poor boy, he– '

'I don't think we need to hear about the war at the dinner table, dear.' Emma laid down her knife and fork and turned to Albert. 'How do the crops look, dear?'

Albert grinned and patted Emma's hand. 'The crops are fine, dear.'

'I'd like to hear what Willis had to say about the war.'

David nodded for Mabel to go on. 'We only hear what the newspapers say ... heroic victories one day, slaughters the next. I read about the battles in August at Lone Pine and the Nek. Around 12,000 of our men were lost. It must have been terrible for Willis to have been there.'

'It was dreadful.' Mabel went on without looking at her mother. 'Those battles have been going on for months. Willis told me that one day in May there were so many dead soldiers between the enemy lines that a ceasefire was agreed to so that both sides could come out of the trenches and bury the bodies.'

'Albert, really, this is not a fit subject for Frederick to be hearing about.' Emma tapped her fork on the table and glared at Mabel.

Albert sat for a moment, chewing his lip before he spoke. 'I rather think it's not such a bad thing for a fourteen-year-old, dear. Who knows how long this war will go on? It's best if those who might think about signing up, know what it's really like.'

'Yes, I'm not a baby any more, Mother.' Frederick leaned across the table.

Emma gasped. 'You're not thinking any such thing, are you?' She looked aghast at Frederick.

'No, but I'm interested in how it was for cousin Willis. A lot of the boys talk about it at school. Some say they'll join up as soon as they're able and I've even heard it said that some fourteen-year-olds have enlisted by raising their age when they sign up.'

More gasping from Emma. 'That's dreadful. The authorities should be ashamed of themselves.'

'Can we hear about Willis?' David asked with a sigh.

Mabel nodded and cast her mind back to the night she sat up for hours listening to Willis because he couldn't sleep. 'He said this day in May would stay in his mind forever. Soldiers from both sides were picking up bodies and putting them into big open graves. He said the stench of death alone was enough to give him nightmares for the rest of his life. Most weren't recognisable. They were told to take the identity tags from around the men's necks and any papers from their pockets, so they would know who died.'

'I'm going to see if Beattie is ready to serve the sweets.' Emma pushed back from her chair and rose, swaying slightly as she got to her feet. She cast a withering glance at Albert and hurried from the room.

With all other eyes riveted to her, Mabel went on. 'I was trying not to cry when he told me the next part, but I couldn't stop tears running down my face. He said the Turks and Australians were passing each other all the time that day, sometimes even picking up the wrong bodies. When they realised it they would take the body to the right graves.'

The memory of Willis's words was so strong in her mind that Mabel almost gagged. She looked around the table at her brothers and sisters. Their eyes were glowing with threatening tears. 'I think the saddest thing was that Willis could describe one of the Turkish soldiers in great detail. They'd stood together, as many of the other soldiers did, and had a smoke, swapping cigarettes and sharing matches. Of course, with the different language they couldn't really talk, but they often managed to swap names. Willis said after that he didn't want to shoot the Turks any more. All the soldiers had started off hating them as the enemy, but on that day they realised the Turkish soldiers were simply young men, doing as they were told, and hating the killing as much as the Australians did.'

'That is so sad,' Clara said, sighing deeply. A long silence followed. Mabel was trying to keep her emotions in check.

'I assume Jacob was still there at that stage,' Albert said.

Mabel nodded. 'Yes, Willis said he and his brother kept an eye on each other and made sure they checked at the end of each battle to see that the other was still alive. But it was soon after that, when the fighting had resumed, that Willis was shot and taken off to a makeshift hospital. He never saw Jacob again and when he regained consciousness he kept asking about Jacob, but no-one could tell him anything. Willis says a lot of his nightmares are about seeing his brother shot and dying alone in the mud.'

'Sweets are on the way,' Emma announced as she came back into the room. 'I hope you're all still hungry.' She rolled her eyes at Mabel. 'Poor Beattie had to line up for ages to get us a packet of raisins. At least she got some extras for the Christmas pudding. Hopefully we'll be able to celebrate Christmas next month without all this talk of war.' She huffed as she sat down.

Mabel decided to go on, regardless of her mother's disapproval. 'Willis is feeling guilty about being sent home. He'd rather be there with his mates, and perhaps find his brother. His left arm is very damaged and the doctor isn't sure if he'll be able to use it properly again. Certainly not for firing a gun.'

'I should think he'd be grateful for that at least.' Emma straightened her chair next to Albert. 'Not going back to the war, I mean. Florence couldn't bear the thought of his being sent back. She has enough to worry about with Jacob still there in goodness knows what state.'

'She does,' Mabel said. 'But Willis says we ought to be proud of our boys over there. They're so brave. It's not like they thought it would be. Fighting for one's country sounds very noble, he said, but the reality is much harder than they were prepared for. Some have broken down altogether and can't cope, but most are courageous and determined to push back the Turks. That was their order and they'll do it till their last breath.'

'Of course they're to be admired, love.' Albert said. 'It's a pity they're at the mercy of decisions made by their superiors who aren't there to see how bad it is. It seems the troops are trapped on that peninsular with neither side willing to back up or surrender, and the dead piling up between them.'

He shook his head and looked up as Beattie entered the room with a tray of small dishes.

'Here's your custards,' she said, laying the tray on the end of the table. 'Only a few raisins in them, I'm sorry. It's the best I could do if you're to have any fruit in your Christmas pudding.'

Emma smiled. 'Thank you, Beattie. We'll manage.'

The pudding dishes were passed around and there was a hush at the table while they all ate.

'Have you heard from Percy?' Clara asked Mabel as she scooped the last of her custard from the bowl.

'Not yet,' Mabel said. It had been more than three weeks since he'd left and she'd been feeling more disappointed with each day that passed and no word from him. 'I'm sure he'll write as soon as he can. It's a small town where he lives. It's likely to be difficult getting mail out.' She felt her defences go up. 'His mother is very sick. He left word with Sophie before he went. I've no doubt he'll be doing everything he can to help.'

'As he should be,' Emma said, not looking up from her bowl. 'His mother and father must be relieved to have him home.' She took small spoonfuls of custard from her bowl as if to make it last as long as possible. 'It's the Northern Rivers of New South Wales, isn't it? That's where his family lives, I believe.' She raised her eyebrows at Mabel.

Mabel felt sure her mother was relieved not to have Percy in close proximity, and equally sure that her father had revealed Percy's real beginnings.

As if to confirm her conclusion, Albert cleared his throat in a way that indicated he was about to make a statement and they should all listen. 'The Northern Rivers is indeed where Percy's family lives.' He looked around the table and caught each eye. 'It seems there was a misunderstanding earlier about their home town.' He turned to Mabel. 'I've explained Percy's position to

186

your mother. We're both glad he's decided to spend some time with his mother and father, aren't we, dear?'

Mabel did not miss his implied warning to her mother not to say anything unnecessary about Percy's family.

'His mother is to have a baby in December,' Mabel said, 'and apparently she's very low with it.'

'I'd have thought she was a bit old to be having more babies.' Emma tutted and wiped her mouth with her napkin. 'Don't tell me Percy spoke to Sophie about such a thing. That hardly seems appropriate.'

Mabel didn't respond to her mother's first statement. 'When he received his sister's letter, he wanted to leave for home as soon as possible. He knew Sophie would let me know where he was.'

'But when and how have you seen Sophie to hear all this news?' Emma's eyes narrowed and she pinned Mabel with a disapproving glare.

'Actually, I went into the city from Aunt Florence's house and saw Sophie and her mother before I came home from Hackney.' Mabel thrust out her chin. 'It's only a short coach ride. I wanted to see how they were managing.'

'Did they tell you what a splendid job we've done on the bakery?' Clara said, a smile spreading across her face.

'They did.' Mabel ignored the disapproval on her mother's face. 'Sophie's moving back to Clarendon this week with her mother and sister. They're very excited and terribly grateful to Percy for all he did to get the place ready.'

'Percy isn't the only good Samaritan. David repainted the front sign and Isabel cleaned the back patio from top to bottom.' Clara nudged her brother. 'Aunt Sarah and I did our share, too. Remember?'

Mabel felt a flush of heat rise in her cheeks. 'I know Sophie and her mother really appreciate what you've all done. I can't wait to see it. I'm sure Percy will be thrilled when he gets back and sees the bakery up and running again.'

'What makes you so sure he's coming back?' Emma asked. All eyes turned to her.

A stabbing pain in Mabel's chest almost stopped her from speaking. 'Of course he'll be back, just as soon as his mother is on her feet.' She could barely control her annoyance at her mother.

'I'm just posing the likelihood that once he gets home and is reconciled with his family again, he might not be disposed to leave.' Emma brushed wisps of hair from her forehead.

'Why do you say "reconciled", Mother?' Clara asked.

'There was a misunderstanding between Percy and his parents before he left.' Albert spoke before Emma could. 'I'm sure Percy will sort it out. Besides, it's none of our business, so we'll just leave it at that, shall we?' At the last he turned to Emma and scowled.

'All right, Albert,' she said, 'But goodness, if the family can hear the dreadful details of the war, I don't see why they should be protected from the background of a young man who's eaten at our very table here and told us all manner of things that now turn out to be a *misunderstanding*.'

'Emma, I'm warning you.' Albert's scowl deepened.

'It doesn't matter, Father.' Mabel held out her hands as if to keep her mother and father apart. She turned to her brothers and sisters. 'Percy's father has a small farm, not a big property, as he implied the night he was here. He was trying to make a good impression, that's all. He was sad and confused because he left home on rather bad terms with his parents. He wants to make his own way in life and probably not as a farmer.' Her words came out as quickly as she could think of them. *That's sufficient truth for my brothers and sisters to know about Percy's past.*

'Anyway,' she went on more sedately. 'Whatever Percy's

background, I love him and I intend to marry him, so I hope you'll all accept him as part of our family.' She ignored the gasp that came from her mother and caught Clara's eye, raising her eyebrows and seeking some support.

'I think he's super,' Clara said without hesitation. 'I got to know him better while we worked at the bakery and it's clear he's a kind, generous man, who wants to help anyone he finds in need.' She nodded. 'So I don't see any reason for him not to be accepted into our family.'

'I agree,' said David. 'I've only spent a little time with him, but he seems to me to be a good bloke. I think you could trust him to be reliable and steady.'

Mabel turned to her younger brother and sister. 'Do you two agree?'

'Agree with what?' Frederick asked as he and Isabel looked up from what seemed to be a serious conversation at the other end of the table.

'That Percy's a good bloke,' David said.

The pair looked at each other and shrugged. 'Of course,' Isabel said. 'We like him, don't we, Frederick?' When her brother nodded his assent she continued. 'I think he's dashing. Is he coming back soon?'

'I don't know when he's coming back,' Mabel said. 'But I know he hasn't gone away for good.

'I can see you're all taken with him,' Emma said, 'but there's still the issue of his past–'

'His past is his business, Emma.' Albert spoke over the top of her. 'I don't believe anyone should be defined by their past. We all know of people who've had an unfortunate start in life, or who've made bad choices in their early days, but then turned their lives around and become fine human beings.' He tapped his pipe on the table and looked pointedly at Emma. 'Don't we, dear?'

Emma paled. 'I suppose we do.'

'And lots of people have things in their past that we prefer not to remember, don't they?' Mabel kept her eyes on her mother's face as she spoke. She knew she was being brazen but couldn't help herself. 'I agree with Father. It's the Christian thing to do to remember the best of people and not hold their past against them.'

She turned to her father and grinned. His expression suggested she'd said quite enough about that subject. But as her mother shrank down in her chair Mabel barely controlled the urge to continue. *What Percy did is not nearly as bad as Grandfather Golder, so Mother can hardly argue against him.*

While things seemed to be going her way she took another risk. 'By the way, I promised Sophie that I'd help serve in the bakery when it opens again. I'm sure they'll be busy leading up to Christmas.'

'I don't think that's a good idea, Mabel.' Her mother revived from her chastened expression and sat tall at the table again.

'There's no reason why not, Mother. I'm perfectly healthy at the moment and after doing so much at Aunt Florence's house, I'm having trouble filling my days here. I want to be more useful and I want to learn new things. It's the bakery or one of these groups of women who are doing something for the war effort.' She waited until her mother's face dropped and then winked at her father. 'Aunt Sarah will pick me up and bring me home. She's going to be helping Mrs Wagner cook.'

Emma let out a small whimper. 'That sister of mine has much to answer for. I only want what's best for you, Mabel. I want you to be happy … and safe. Surely it's what every mother wants.'

Mabel reached across the table and took her mother's hand. 'I know that's what you want, Mother, but you must trust that I know what makes me happy. With all the terrible things going on in the world, surely we can be grateful that I've found some purpose and some happiness.'

'You can hardly argue with that, my dear.' Albert stoked his pipe and drew on it loudly. 'I think there's a lot to commend Percy and I believe you'll see that for yourself, eventually.'

***

A clear blue sky heralded the first day of December. Mabel breathed in the warm air as she and Sarah headed for the bakery in Clarendon. Her chest felt free and her mind was brimming with images of Sophie's happy face, lines of people going into the bakery and a counter covered in fluffy pies and cakes.

'What a beautiful day,' she said. 'Thank you so much for picking me up, Aunt Sarah. I'm very excited about helping out in the bakery.'

'I'm surprised your mother agreed, I must say.' Sarah grinned.

'She's not really happy about it, but I think she's realising at last that I'm old enough to make my own decisions and quite capable of looking after myself. I'm almost twenty for heaven's sake.'

'Well, that would be a big step for Emma and I'm pleased to hear it. Does that mean she's accepted your feelings for Percy?'

'I think she's resigned to the fact.' Mabel nodded, but the mention of Percy caused her happy feelings to plummet. 'I'm a bit more worried about his feelings for me at the moment.'

'What do you mean? Have you heard from him?'

'No, I haven't and it concerns me, truth be known. He's been gone more than a month now. Either his mother is desperately ill and he can think of nothing else, or he's decided he'd prefer to stay there with his family than come back here to me.' Mabel's stomach churned at the thought of not seeing Percy again. It was unthinkable.

'I'm guessing it's the former, love. I can't imagine anything that would stop Percy coming back to marry you. No one could doubt the depth of his feeling for you.'

'Do you think so? I didn't just imagine it, did I?'

Sarah shook her head. 'No, you didn't imagine it, love. Give him a bit more time. I'm sure you'll hear from him soon.' She patted Mabel's knee. 'You'll have plenty to take your mind off your waiting today. There's a lovely surprise for you at the bakery.'

'There is?' Mabel pushed away her sadness. 'What is it?'

Sarah laughed. 'It wouldn't be a surprise if I told you, would it? Besides, Sophie wants to tell you about it herself.'

Mabel took a deep breath, again aware of the smells of summer around her. Grasses in the fields were high and dotted with yellow and pink wildflowers. Gum trees were blossoming and the sound of birds chirping was like music to her ears. She allowed the freshness of the environment to raise her hopes and her spirits.

'I saw Sophie a few weeks ago. She was very excited about going back to her home behind the bakery and thrilled with everything Percy organised. She said her mother's mood had lifted considerably and she can now see a future for the family. Is it more than all that, this surprise?'

'It is.' Sarah nodded and her smile spread across her face. 'But you'll have to wait until we get there.'

***

Mrs Wagner and Sarah leaned against the parlour wall and laughed while Mabel, Sophie and her young sister danced around the room, barely missing the large, floral-covered lounge chairs and the wooden coffee table in the middle of the room.

'It's all so beautiful,' Sophie said, grabbing a cushion from the lounge and hugging it to herself. 'I've dreamed of coming back but even in my dreams, it didn't look this pretty.'

'It's much as you left it, really,' Sarah said. 'We only cleaned and dusted. A bit of paint here and there makes everything look fresh.'

'I'm so happy.' Mrs Wagner sat in one of the lounge chairs and looked up at Mabel. 'Your young man has been incredible. You must be so proud. We would not have thought this possible if he hadn't suggested it. He convinced me I could do this and now here we are. I don't know how to repay him.'

Mabel shook her head. 'Your happiness is all the payment Percy will want. I'm sure he's looking forward to coming back and tasting some of your wonderful pies.'

'I hope so,' Mrs Wagner said. Her face was drawn and lined, and it wasn't hard to see she'd been under a lot of strain, but the change in her mood was also evident. Mabel could see her eyes were regaining the warm, friendly glow that had always been there before the war took her husband from her.

'This is wonderful,' Mrs Wagner went on, 'but there's still better news.' She clapped her hands together and Mabel thought the woman's face would burst with the smile that spread across it. 'Tell her, Sophie.' She nodded for her daughter to sit down and gestured for Mabel to do the same.

When the girls had sunk into the two seater lounge, Sophie turned to Mabel and took both her hands. 'The most wonderful thing,' she said, her eyes filling with tears.

'Tell me,' Mabel said. 'The suspense is killing me.'

'Papa is coming home.' The announcement shot from Sophie's mouth. 'He'll be here next week.'

Mabel was astounded. 'He is? Why that's wonderful, but how? Has the war ended?'

'We can only hope that will come soon,' Mrs Wagner said. 'But not yet.' She drew a piece of paper from her handbag and held it out for Mabel to see.

'It's in German, so you won't be able to read it, but it's a newsletter from the Camp. Some of the men have been putting it together since early in their internment. It was a project to help them fill their days, and it also kept everybody informed about whatever concerts or meetings were being held. They tried to report all the good news, like how well the gardens were growing, or how many of the men had learned to cook. Mainly light-hearted news like that.' She drew in a long breath and Mabel could see her eyes glistening with unshed tears.

Happy tears, at last. Mabel read the title on the top of the paper. 'Der Kamerad'.

'It means comrade, or friend, or workmate,' Sophie said. 'But it wasn't always good news.' Her face dropped. 'Papa didn't tell us until just recently, but after the first few months in the camp, a new commander was put in charge and he was very cruel. There was a lot of ill-treatment. Some men tried to escape and when they were captured, they were flogged.'

Mabel gasped. 'That's terrible.'

'Yes,' Sophie continued, 'so the men started to write about it in the newsletter. They recorded all the horrible things that were done to the interns.'

Mabel was confused. 'Is this why your Papa is coming home?'

Sophie patted her hand. 'Sort of. A visitor took one of these newsletters out of the camp a few months ago and gave it to the authorities on the mainland and there was an investigation.'

Mabel nodded. 'I'm glad to hear that.'

'The authorities verified what had been going on,' Mrs Wagner said, 'and the commander, a Captain Hawkes, was removed.'

'And better still,' Sophie said, 'the Department of Defence decided that the camp should close. It had the worst reputation of all the internment camps in Australia.'

'So all the men will go home?' Mabel asked.

'Not all, sadly,' Mrs Wagner went on. 'Some will be taken to New South Wales to a camp at Holesworthy. Men they are still suspicious of, I suppose.' She shrugged.

'But not Papa,' Sophie said, throwing her hands in the air. 'He's coming home next week. We can hardly believe it, but it's true. Isn't that the most wonderful news?' Her arms dropped to Mabel's shoulders and they hugged.

'Oh, it's such good news,' Mabel said, squeezing Sophie's waist.

'He'll still have to report once a week to the local police,' Mrs Wagner said, 'but that's a small price to pay for being home with us. And not only home now, thanks to Percy, but back at work here in the bakery. I've told him all about what you've all done for us.' She looked around the room and tears flooded her eyes. 'He says he'll be forever grateful.'

'That's such good news,' Mabel said. 'I'm going to write to Percy right away and tell him what's happened. I know he'll be thrilled.'

'You must tell him we still want him to be involved in the business, if he'd like that.' Mrs Wagner's face creased. 'He has such good ideas that he shared with me ... how to improve things and how to handle the business side of things. My husband would value his help, I know.'

Mabel nodded. 'I'll tell him that. I'm not sure what he'll want to do when he gets back.' Her stomach twisted. 'Or even when he'll be here. But I will tell him what you've said.' She turned to her aunt. 'I do wish he had a telephone, Aunt Sarah. How I would love to call him and talk to him. Just to hear his voice would be ...' She couldn't go on.

'Don't fret, love,' Sarah said. 'I'm sure you'll hear from him soon.'

Mabel nodded and took a deep breath. 'I imagine it might be a while before a small place like Mororo has a telephone service.'

'Right.' Sarah stood and clapped her hands. 'Now let's focus on the good news and set about cooking up a celebration. We have to make plans for what we'll cook for Christmas, too. It's less than a month away. The sooner we decide, the sooner we can get ourselves into one of those wretched queues and get the ingredients we need.'

CHAPTER SIXTEEN

Mororo, New South Wales, December 1915

Percy closed the bedroom door and headed back to the front room. His mother's condition seemed to be getting worse. The doctor said all her strength was going to the baby, which could come at any time, but until then, they had to let Fanny rest and pray for the best. Mrs Wiblin had come every day to check on how things were proceeding. She said hopeful things about the baby and about what a strong and determined woman Fanny was, but Percy sensed from the look on her face each time she left the bedroom that she was very worried.

'How is she?' Jack asked as Percy dropped into a lounge chair.

'The same. Always the same.' Percy shook his head. 'She's so frail.' He looked across at his father and noted the deepening lines in his face. His hair seemed greyer than before Percy had gone to Adelaide. *Or perhaps I didn't notice before that my father seems like an old man. Older than Mabel's father, though in fact he's ten years younger.* 'Do you think Mum is too old for this? She is over forty and she seems so weak. I'm worried.' He let his head sink into the back of the chair and sighed.

'It's a bit late to be wondering if she's too old for birthing. It's done now. We're all worried, but she's stronger than you think. None of her births have been easy. You likely didn't notice the others. Mrs Wiblin thought we might lose her three years ago when Laura was born.'

Percy's heart lurched. 'I didn't know that.' He sat upright. 'Then why …?' He stopped short. The last thing he wanted to do was to criticise Jack. He'd made up his mind to do quite the opposite but so far the opportunity for them to have a good talk hadn't arisen. 'We have to keep praying for the best, then. Surely it'll be over soon.'

'Mrs Wiblin says probably one day next week.'

Percy nodded. 'I've been meaning to say that I think you've done well moving to this place. I think the milking cows are a good idea and the land's better. I've dug a few extra vegetable patches and I can tell it's going to produce more than where we were.' He leaned forward, searching for more words. 'I think it's been good for the family.'

Jack's eyes roamed the room before settling on Percy. 'You can thank your mother for the move. It was her idea. She's the one with the money sense. She's always been better with figures than me. Must be where you get it.' He picked up his pipe from the side table and twisted it in his hands.

'But you're happy with the move, aren't you, Dad?' Percy saw his father's eyes fly open and realised it was the first time he'd called his father 'Dad' since he returned. He grinned across at him, feeling the time was right to say more. 'Actually, I've been waiting for a chance to talk to you, Dad.' He emphasised the term this time. 'I went off half-cocked when I left home. I was in shock. I said things I shouldn't have and they were unfair to you. I've been wanting to tell you how sorry I am.'

Jack nodded and there was a slight tremble in his chin.

'I've thought a lot about what you and Mum told me and I've realised how much you sacrificed for me and for her. You've been a good father. Tough,' he grinned again, 'but fair, and I know how hard you've worked to provide for us all.' He swallowed and took a deep breath.

'So you didn't go looking for your … for the man who …' Jack shook his head. 'I don't even know what to call him. There was a time when I would have hunted him down and made sure he got what he deserved, but that was a long time ago. I haven't thought about him for years … until these past few months.'

'There's no need to think about him now. I'm not interested in finding him or even knowing his name. He's done nothing for me … except hurt Mum. I have all the family I need right here.' Percy felt the shake in his voice. He resisted the urge to give his father a hug, knowing it would be awkward for Jack to receive.

Jack tapped his pipe into his palm and an awkward smile spread across his face. 'Your mother will be very relieved to know that. She's been worried sick that she'd lost you for good.' Jack's voice broke and he brought his pipe to his mouth. Percy had never seen his father so moved.

There was much more that Percy wanted to say, but at that moment Vera came through the front door.

'Whew, it's hot out there. Nearly six o'clock and it's still blazing.' She gave Jack a kiss on the forehead. 'How's Mum? Has anyone put on the stew for dinner? I had it half cooked before I went out this morning. Shall I make a cup of tea?'

Percy shook his head. 'Slow down, Sis. Mum is the same. She was sleeping a while ago, but I guess she might like a cup of tea now. Whatever we can get into her to strengthen her will be good. And no, we haven't put on the stew, but I'll do it now.' He chuckled.

'Sorry. I do go on. Mrs Wiblin was asking after Mum. She'll be over in the morning.'

'You spend more time there than here these days,' Jack said, stoking his pipe and still seeming to struggle with his emotions.

Percy stood and rubbed Jack's shoulder before he turned and

followed his sister into the kitchen. 'You're not over there all the time just to fill Mrs Wiblin in on Mum's condition, are you?' he said as she leaned over to light the stove.

She filled the kettle and pointed him to the pot of stew on the bench. 'You know Jacko Wiblin and I are getting married, Percy.' She grinned and her cheeks glowed. 'Hopefully early next year … as long as Mum is well enough, and the baby.' Her expression changed to one of concern. 'You do think she'll be all right, don't you? I couldn't bear it if–'

'None of that, Sis. Keep positive. I'm trusting Mum to come through this.' He took the lid from the stew pot and leaned over it. 'Mmm, smells good. I'll give it a stir and once that fire's under it we shouldn't have to wait too long for dinner. I'm hungry.'

'You should have thought about that a bit earlier and put it on, goose.' She tapped his backside lightly. 'What have you and Dad been talking about?'

'This and that. I told him I think this place has been a good move for the family.'

She nodded. 'I do too. I'm glad we're nearer the Lange's property. They're great friends to Mum, and it's good having Ida and John close too.' She eyed him seriously. 'You need to talk to Dad about you and Jacko planning to go into partnership. He can't be the last to know or he'll be hurt. Now, I'll go and check on Mum while the kettle is boiling, then I'll bring you two a cup of tea.'

Percy put the stew on the stove and gave it a stir, then went back to Jack. 'You're okay about the idea of Vera and Jacko Wiblin getting married, aren't you, Dad?' He settled himself in the chair opposite his father.

Jack nodded. 'Bound to happen sooner or later. They've been mooning about for months and now that Ida's made the break, I'm guessing it won't be long.'

'They'll make a good match, I reckon,' Percy said. 'In fact I had a talk to Jacko a few days ago. He's got some good ideas for farming and now that he's planning to have a family of his own, we thought we might work together on a few things.' Percy was tentative, not wanting to offend his father. 'I'd like to help out with our family, and Jacko and I reckon we can do that together.'

Jack's eyebrows rose. 'Oh, in what way?'

'Well, Jacko would like to get some land of his own. His father has enough mouths to feed and sons to pass on his place to. So we thought we could go into partnership and get some land. I've got a bit saved and so has he. We've talked to Fred Lange about leasing some of his land and putting cows on it, milking cows like you have, and we'd like to get a separator.'

'A what?'

'A cream separator. It means we could work up a cream and milk run between all of us for the area. It would be better for you than having to go into Harwood all the time. The farmers around here who have grazing cattle would buy from us and eventually we could get a truck instead of using a wagon and horses. The way things are going, trucks and cars will be everywhere. Much quicker to get around and better for making deliveries.'

Jack sucked on his pipe. 'You're way ahead of me. I'm fine with going to Harwood and working on the ferries. We still need more money than this place can generate and cutting down trees is all I've ever done. I'm relieved you're back to help out, though.'

Percy took a deep breath. 'I know, Dad. I'm not asking you to get involved in what Jacko and I are planning, if you don't want to. I just wanted you to know what I'm thinking for the future … for the family. Jacko's been talking to a fellow who's considering selling a milk run and we need to plan ahead. We'd all benefit from it.'

Jack shrugged. 'Down the track maybe. First things first. See how your mother is after Christmas. Once the baby's born she'll take a while to get strong again. It's hard for any of us to think beyond that.' He sighed deeply and laid his head back. 'I know how glad she is that you're back. Even milking the few cows we've got will be too much for her for quite a while.'

'Clarrie seems to be enjoying that,' Percy said. 'I watched him and Connie round the cows up this morning. They had them ready for milking in no time. Even Rita can do some milking. The kids are all growing up, Dad.'

'I guess they are, but Clarrie's only twelve and skinny as a newborn calf. It'll be a while before he's ready to take on too much.'

Percy let out a breath and shook his head. He wished Jack would take him more seriously, but didn't want to express any frustration with him. He spoke carefully. 'I was cutting down huge trees with you when I was twelve, remember? Clarrie wants to do his bit. He helped me put up some more fencing yesterday. He's knows what he's doing. You shouldn't underestimate him.'

'He's a good boy.' Jack nodded. 'But we need another man around here and for now, all I can think is what a help you're going to be. Keeping things going here has been a big worry for your mother and it'll be a great relief to her that you're here to take the load.'

Percy leaned forward and considered his words. 'Dad, I'll do what I can to help, and I'm happy to contribute financially, but ...' His thoughts were racing. He wondered if he should reconsider telling his father what was on his mind. The last thing he wanted was for there to be more conflict between them.

Jack frowned and laid his pipe down. 'But what?'

'I've some other plans too'

'Yeah, so you said, and I said they might have to wait a bit.'

At that moment there was a burst of voices as Clarrie and Rita came through the door with Dottie, Winnie and Laura at their heels. The room filled with their laughing and talking.

'Jobs are all done,' Clarrie said, clapping his hands on his thighs. 'Dottie milked her first cow and nearly fell off the stool when the cow swished her tail in her face. Just as well I was there to grab the bucket.'

'Good on you, Dottie,' Percy said as his young sister launched herself into his lap.

'It was fun.' She giggled and squirmed onto the chair beside him. 'I'm hungry. When's dinner?'

'Soon,' Vera said, coming in with a tray of cups. 'We'll have a hot drink and then you lot are going to have a bath before we eat. You all stink of cow manure.'

***

Percy headed for the general store in Mororo a couple of days later, after checking with Vera that they still handled the local mail. He had a letter to Mabel half written and wondered if she'd written to him. She'd been on his mind every day since he'd arrived home, but with his mother so unwell, he hadn't been able to concentrate on much else for long. He wanted to be able to assure Mabel that his mother was going to recover, to tell her that he and his father had made their peace. There were so many things he wanted to tell Mabel but moments alone had been hard to find and he was still fearful for his mother.

'Well, if it isn't Percy Smith,' he heard as he entered the general store.

He looked up at the man behind the counter. 'Hello, Mr Horden. How are you today?'

'Well as any of us, given the way things are.' The man leaned on the counter. 'Your mother will be pleased to have you back, I reckon. She said you were away working, but to tell you the truth, I wondered if you'd taken off to the front. Seems a lot of young ones have enlisted, even against their parents' wishes. I reckon they'll be sorry they did. From what we hear about what's happening over there, it's no picnic.'

'I can't imagine anyone thinking war would be anything but horrible, Mr Horden.'

The man nodded. 'That doesn't go down too well with some, does it? Lots of pressure for young men like you to take up arms, protect the homeland and all that. You don't feel obliged?'

Percy shook his head. 'It's a no win situation. I try to keep my head down.'

'Then there's those who are locked away at Trial Bay. Anyone you know?'

'Dad says some of the Fischers are there. I hear they're doing as well as can be expected.'

'Yeah, not as bad there as some places, it seems. They have some of the beach fenced off, so the boys can at least have a game on the sand or go for a swim. But I don't know how long that'll last. I heard there's some worry that Fritz might be lurking off shore in boats and come and try and rescue them.'

Percy huffed. 'Rescue? What, and take them to Germany? Can't see that anyone from around here would be interested in going to Germany.'

Maybe, but it seems there's some pretty elite German civilians out there. Some who've served as German consuls from Queensland, Tasmania and even Western Australia. They've lived in British territories in South East Asia. Some professionals and academics and businessmen, too. Fritz might want them back. Anyway, there's talk of cutting back on privileges in case the men get any ideas of escape.'

'Can't imagine they have too many privileges to cut back on.' Percy shook his head.

'I don't know. They grow their own vegetables and catch fish from the beach and they've got a restaurant going for those who've got money. I heard they've got an athletics club, education programs and they do concerts. Doesn't sound like a bad life to me. Most of us here are struggling to keep farms and stores going, while they sing and read books.'

'I doubt any of us would swap places, Mr Horden. They're locked away from their families. It seems to me they're doing the best they can to make use of the time, but it does sound like Trial Bay is a better place than the internment camp in South Australia.'

'South Australia? Is that where you've been?'

Percy nodded. 'I've been working at the post office there. Which reminds me, I came to see if there's any mail for us.'

Mr Horden shrugged and ran his fingers around his moustache, smoothing out the bristly grey hair. 'I'll check. The missus sorts the mail.' He turned and disappeared behind a curtained doorway.

'As a matter of fact there is one for you,' he said a few moments later as he pushed through the curtain and handed a letter to Percy. 'All the way from Adelaide. Someone special, is it?' He winked and a grin spread across his face.

'Sure is,' Percy said as he turned to go, anxious to read Mabel's news.

By the time he had walked home, he'd read Mabel's letter twice. He could see her sweet smile in his mind's eye. He resolved to finish his letter to her when he got home. *I wish there was a telephone here in Mororo so I could at least call Mabel's aunt, and perhaps even catch Mabel visiting there. How I'd love to hear her voice.* He was glad to hear that Sophie's father was coming home and hoped he approved of what Percy had done in the bakery. *Perhaps they won't need me at all now.*

When he walked in the front door he could hear moans coming from his parents' bedroom. His heart began to thump. He moved towards the room, but as he was about to enter, Vera rushed out.

'I'm going for Mrs Wiblin.' She pushed passed him. 'I think

the baby's coming.'

'Is it time?' he asked, grabbing her arm before she flew out the front door.

'Has to be. I don't think she can wait any longer. I've sent the kids outside with Clarrie. Connie's with Mum.'

'What can I do?' he called as the door closed behind her. There was no answer. He stood in the middle of the room, his heart banging in his chest. Jack was away working again. *Why does it seem he's never here when he's needed?* Percy shook his head. He knew he was being unfair.

If only I knew what a man's supposed to do at a time like this. A voice in the back of his mind suggested that men usually made themselves scarce and came back when it was all over. He took tentative steps towards the kitchen and thought about boiling some water. He wondered how he would be if it were his wife having a baby.

There was more moaning from the bedroom and he could hear Connie's voice soothing their mother. 'Please, God, don't let her die.' He heard his own voice as if it were coming from a long way away. He grabbed the kettle and filled it with water before stoking the fire under the stove. 'Hurry, Vera, please hurry.'

It seemed an eternity before Vera returned with Mrs Wiblin hobbling along behind her. They disappeared into the bedroom before he could finish saying, 'I've got water on the boil.'

As he sank down into a chair, Percy raised his eyes to the roof of the cottage. *You know how much she's loved and needed, God. Please save her.* He'd never thought too much about women having a hard time with childbirth, though apparently his mother had suffered with each of his siblings' births. *What was I thinking about all those years as the other kids came along? Not mothers and babies, obviously.* Now it seemed a much more relevant thing to consider. Mabel's face flashed before his eyes.

He would have liked to dwell on thoughts of Mabel and his plans for the future, but the distressing sounds coming from the bedroom distracted him. He paced the parlour for minutes before deciding to go outside and check on the other children. He had to occupy himself with something other than his fear for his mother.

***

Two days of handwringing, praying, crying, distracting the younger children, boiling water, pacing and worrying followed before Mrs Wiblin at last announced that the baby had been born. The poor woman had hardly left Fanny's bedside, dozing on and off in a chair beside the bed, between ordering cool cloths, fresh linen and chicken broth.

'It's over,' she said as she came out of the bedroom, closing the door behind her.

'Is Mum …?' Percy was almost afraid to ask.

Mrs Wiblin nodded. 'She's very weak, but I think she'll survive.' She shook her head and crumbled into a lounge chair. 'It was touch and go there for a while.'

Percy realised he'd been holding his breath and expelled air from his lungs. 'And the baby?'

'A little girl. Also very weak. I doubt you heard the faint cry she uttered. Poor little mite. She's had to fight every inch of the way. Time and the good Lord will tell us if she's to survive. For now we must focus on getting your mother back to enough strength to feed the dear pet, if she does.' Mrs Wiblin's eyes closed and Percy thought she'd drifted off to sleep.

He crept to the bedroom door. Pushing it open a fraction he could see Vera wiping their mother's forehead with a cloth. The sheet was drawn over her neatly. He could see the tiny bundle that was his new sister beside his mother's shoulder.

'Can I come in?' he whispered when Vera turned to the door.

She nodded. 'For a minute.'

As he moved to the bedside, he looked down at his mother's pale face. His eyes filled with tears. She appeared to be sleeping, but a moment later her eyelids fluttered and she looked up at him. A thin smile spread part way across her face.

'We did it, Percy.' Her hand reached towards him. It seemed to take every bit of whatever strength she had left and he quickly took her hand in his own.

'You're very brave, Mum. I'm sorry you've been through so much.'

Her head moved slightly from side to side. 'It's always worth it,' she whispered. She glanced at the bundle beside her. 'Pray for our little one, Percy. She's very weak.'

He nodded, his voice catching in his throat. 'I will.'

'That's enough.' Vera tapped his shoulder. 'She needs to sleep.'

As he made his way out of the room, Percy let out a long breath. *How would Mabel cope with such a strain on her? I'm amazed at how women find the strength to do this when they need to. Whatever battles men fight, I doubt they're any harder than what women go through for the lives of their babies.*

'Is she all right?' Connie's voice broke into his thoughts. 'You're as pale as a ghost.'

'She's so strong,' Percy said, squeezing his sister's arm. 'I have to give it to you women. You deserve more credit than you get for giving birth. I'm going to make a cup of tea.'

He heard his sister snigger as he headed for the kitchen. The battle was not over yet, but at least it seemed his mother was going to live. His shoulders relaxed for the first time in days and he felt the stirrings of hunger in his stomach.

***

'Alice,' Percy repeated. 'That's pretty.' He squeezed his mother's hand and grinned at his father.

Jack shrugged. He was on the other side of the bed, leaning back in a chair. He'd come home the night before, two days after the baby's birth, and taken the news in his stride. It was not the first time he'd missed the birth of one of his children.

'Whatever your mother wants.' He nodded at Fanny. 'Looks like the little one is going to make it.'

Fanny smiled and stroked the baby's cheek. 'She's a fighter. She's started to drink so that's a good sign. I'm not sure she'll be a strong child, but at my age I can hardly expect to be birthing strapping children. We'll take special care of her, won't we, Jack?'

'I'll try and get home more often,' he said. 'But with Percy here now, you're both in good hands.'

Percy's stomach lurched. 'Dad, Mum, there's something I've been meaning to tell you. It hasn't seemed the right time till now, but I don't see that I can put it off any longer.'

Fanny's eyes flew open and Percy sensed she was thinking the worst. 'It's not about the past, don't worry, Mum. And I'm not enlisting. You can rest easy about that. This is about the future.'

'I doubt your mother needs to hear your fancy plans for farming just yet, son,' Jack said.

Percy raked his hand through his hair. 'It's not about farming, Dad. Not really. It's about a girl I met in Adelaide.' He watched his mother's worried face soften and wrinkle into a smile.

'A girl?' She tried to push herself up a little in the bed.

Percy leaned over and helped her. 'Yes, Mum. Someone special. Her name is Mabel. We met … well, it's a long story, but the upshot is that I want to marry her.'

'Marry?' Jack sat up. 'It's a bit quick, isn't it? You were only gone a few months.'

'Nine months, Dad, and it doesn't seem quick at all. We hit it off right from the start.'

'So, tell us more,' Fanny said. 'What's she like? What's her family like?' Her cheeks flushed with colour. 'This is lovely news.'

'When are you thinking of marrying this girl?' A frown darkened Jack's face. 'You'll have to prepare things here first, won't you? I know you have plans for some land, but it takes time to get a house together and be ready to support a wife.'

Percy hid a smile. *I doubt Dad was all that prepared when he married Mum.* He braced himself for the difficult news he had to deliver.

'Actually, I wasn't thinking I would bring Mabel here right away.' He watched their faces drop and took a firmer grip on his mother's hand. 'I'd love for you to meet her, and you will, I promise, but I don't think she's ready to be this far away from her family yet. I doubt they'd cope with that. Especially her mother.'

Jack's frown deepened. 'Doesn't sound like a girl ready to be married to me.'

'She is, Dad.' Percy took a deep breath. 'She's a strong girl, but she has asthma attacks occasionally and though she doesn't make too much of it, her mother gets quite frantic. I'd like to be able to tell Mabel's parents that we'll stay around Adelaide for a bit, so that they can see she's going to manage married life.'

'I see,' Fanny said. 'That's very thoughtful of you, Percy. Is it what Mabel wants, too?'

'I don't know,' Percy said. 'We've not really discussed it, but I suspect it will make her parents more amenable to the idea of Mabel marrying and moving away from home if it's not too far to start with.'

'It sounds like the parents aren't keen on the idea of you marrying their daughter.' Jack's tone was sombre. 'Have you discussed it with them?'

'A little,' Percy said. 'At lease with Mr Smart. Mrs Smart

may not be so easily persuaded. She has other ideas for Mabel. She'd rather her daughter marry someone of means. One of the local farmer's sons.'

'Then she doesn't know you very well,' Fanny said, her eyes glowing. 'She couldn't get a better man for her daughter than you, Percy.'

'So are this Mabel's parent's people of means?' Jack scowled.

'They're quite well off, yes.' Percy said. 'Mabel's father inherited family land. He's done well for himself and I know he'll want to see Mabel is well cared for.'

'Sounds to me like you have a battle on your hands.' Jack shifted in his chair, then rose and started for the door. 'And you'll be leaving your mother to battle on here as well.'

'Jack, that's not fair.' Fanny said. 'You know we'll manage. We have the others to help.'

'You sure this girl is worth it?' Jack said, ignoring his wife's comment.

Percy nodded. 'I reckon you'd know what it is to take on a girl who's worth it, despite the challenges, Dad.'

Jack's hand was on the door handle when he looked back at Percy. He paused and his forehead furrowed before he nodded. A crease spread from the corners of his eyes to his hairline and Percy was sure he was holding back a grin. 'All right, son. I can't argue with that. A man's gotta do what a man's gotta do ... as long as it doesn't hurt your mother.' He opened the door and left Percy and Fanny alone.

Percy turned back to his mother. 'You'll love her, Mum. She's sweet-natured and very bright.'

'And pretty, I'm sure.' Fanny grinned. There was a murmur beside her and she drew the baby close and patted the rug. 'So when do you think you might be back?' Her voice was low and Percy noticed it trembled a little.

'As soon as possible, Mum. I've told Dad about plans I have for land here. Jacko Wiblin and I have discussed how he'd keep things going for me until I come back. I'd want to have something substantial to bring Mabel to, and I want to be able to help you and Dad out, too … and the girls, but I don't want Dad to think I'm taking over …'

'I understand, Percy.' Fanny gripped his hand. 'I know you'll do what is best, and we'll be just fine. You're not to worry about us.'

Percy let out a long breath, grateful for his mother's understanding. 'In the mean time I can work in Adelaide. I know I can support Mabel down there. We can get established and who knows, we might have a little one of our own to bring back with us by then.' He looked down at the swaddled baby and smiled, though the thought of Mabel giving birth still frightened him.

Fanny nodded. 'I think it's a good idea for you to be there a bit longer, Percy. Until this war is over, anyway. I'm still concerned with the way people go on about German families. There have been some nasty comments and even threats here at times. I'd rather you be safe and away from it all.'

'There are German families in South Australia too, and some of them have been interned. As a matter of fact I've been helping the family of one man who's been on Torrens Island in the camp there. But I've had a letter from Mabel to say he's just been released, so perhaps the war won't go on for much longer.'

'You've not had any trouble yourself, have you?' Fanny looked distressed.

'No, Mum. No one there knows I have any German connections.' He squeezed her hand. 'I had no reason to say anything when I went down there, but recently I did tell Mr Smart that my father was of German heritage.' He hoped his acknowledgement would please his mother. 'Mr Smart is a tolerant and kind man. I've no worries about being targeted in Adelaide.'

'That's good,' Fanny said. 'Then I think it's a good place for you to be, for now.' She shifted her head on the pillow. Her eyes were dark-ringed and heavy.

'I'm sorry this has been so hard for you, Mum.' He touched her forehead softly.

'You're not to worry about me, Percy. I will be fine. I have not been alone in this journey. The good Lord and I have had some long talks these past weeks. I can't remember having such talks since you were born.'

'Oh?'

She nodded. 'It wasn't so hard physically with you, but I was worried about how we would manage after you were born and what life would be like for you. I was very aware of being given the strength I needed then, and also the assurance that God would provide.' She smiled up at him. 'God gave me Jack and I've been very grateful.'

'I know, Mum, and so am I. I know I didn't act like that when you told me, but I've had lots of time to think–'

'You don't need to explain, Percy. I can see that you've accepted it now. Your father is not the easiest man, but we have a lot to thank him for, don't we?'

'We do.' Percy took her hands in his own.

'And now I'm trusting the future of this little one to the good Lord, too.' She glanced down at the baby and smiled. 'She's a gift, Percy. I'm not sure how long we'll have our little Alice. She's very frail and I doubt she'll be a well child, but for whatever time we have her, we'll treasure her.'

'But–'

'No buts, love. Whatever happens, we'll manage. You are not to concern yourself about her.' She squeezed Percy's hand. 'I'm happy for you, son. You go back and marry your Mabel.

When you get back home here it will be soon enough, and if you have a son or daughter to bring with you as well as a wife, then I'll be thrilled.'

***

'You won't go before Christmas, will you?' Tears rolled down Connie's face.

Percy hugged her. 'No, Sis, I won't go before Christmas. It's less than a week away now. I can't believe how it's snuck up on us.' He chuckled. 'I guess we've had a lot on our minds. But all's well now, so we can enjoy Christmas together and then I'll head back to Adelaide.'

She nodded, wiping her eyes on her sleeve. 'I'm happy for you, Percy. I can't wait to get married and you're a lot older than me, so I know you must be dying to have your wedding.'

Percy pushed back from the hug. 'Hold on there, Connie. I'm only eight years older than you and my wedding is not even planned yet.' He kissed the top of her forehead. 'But I doubt I'll be an old man before it happens. I'll be back before you know it, so no sad faces now.'

She snuggled into his chest. 'I'm dying to meet Mabel. Ida and Vera are, too. We expect a letter every month until you get back. We want to know everything. Promise you'll write?'

'I promise, and I'm sure Mabel will write too. She has two sisters, Isabel and Clara, and they're very close, so she'll miss them when she comes here. She'll want to be great friends with all of you.'

'I expect it'll be a bit much having eight sisters here.' Her laugh tinkled across the room.

'Perhaps it will. You'll have to be careful not to overwhelm her.'

Percy's image of Mabel surrounded by the laughter and constant chatter of his sisters caused him a moment's concern, but all that was off in the future. He still hadn't finished his letter to her, but now that he'd told his parents everything and was confident his mother was going to be well again, he resolved to get all his news to Mabel in the next post.

I hope she hasn't changed her mind while I've been away. The thought suddenly struck him. Her letter had been full of news about Sophie's family and also about the cousin that she'd helped to look after in Hackney. There'd been some news of continuing protests and rallies about the war. But she'd said little about herself, beyond hoping that all was well with his family and looking forward to hearing from him. *She must be wondering why I haven't written.* Suddenly it was of the utmost importance to tell Mabel that he was longing to be with her again, that he would be back as soon as possible to make plans for their future.

CHAPTER SEVENTEEN

Park Farm, December 1915

Mabel heard her mother's voice as if from a long way away. 'You've hardly touched your dinner, Mabel. You must eat.'

It was not the first time during the meal that her mother had interrupted her thoughts and fussed about how much she was eating. She glanced down at the plate of food in front of her.

'I'm not really hungry, Mother. I think I ate too much over Christmas.' Mabel forced herself to raise her eyes and look across the table. She tried to work up a smile that would convince her mother that she did not need to be harassed about eating.

'I hardly think so,' Emma said, dashing Mabel's hopes. 'You ate like a sparrow at Christmas dinner too. After all the trouble we went to in order to secure some decent food. It's because you've worn yourself out at that bakery. I knew it was a bad idea for you to be working so hard. Sarah should have known better than to encourage you.'

Mabel could tell her mother was going to give her the full lecture about her delicate health and the bad influence of Aunt Sarah and the worry of being around Germans. She tried to keep her tone respectful as she cut off the tirade.

'I'm not a bit ill, Mother. I enjoyed helping out at the bakery before Christmas. It was such fun. I was so happy to see

Sophie's family back together. Surely that can't have been bad for me. I've been home resting for the past two days and we've done nothing but eat and sit around.'

She watched her mother's brow knit as she spoke. 'Anyway,' she went on before Emma could interrupt. 'You must admit it was a delicious pudding that Mrs Wagner made us. She was so grateful for what we've done ... what Percy did.' She knew the last was a mistake.

Emma sat forward in her chair and patted her mouth with her napkin. 'You're not still mooning over that boy, are you? He's gone and you should be happy he's back with his family ... where he belongs.'

'Mother, that's not fair.' Clara's voice rang down the table before Mabel had a chance to respond. 'Percy deserves great praise for what he did for the Wagners and of course Mabel is missing him. We all do.'

Emma huffed. 'Really, you girls do go on. I'm sure the Wagners are quite capable of managing their own business. They did it for years before you and Percy got involved. It's his own parents he should be helping out, and it seems to me he's decided that for himself.'

'You don't know that, Mother.' Mabel's words caught in her throat. The thought of Percy not coming back to her was too much to bear. She couldn't imagine why she hadn't heard from him, but there had to be some explanation other than what her mother was saying and clearly hoping. She sniffed back tears.

'I know that mothers all over the country are longing to have their sons home, and not likely to let them go rushing off to far-away places the minute they set foot in the door.' Emma dabbed her eyes. 'Think of poor Lucy Grimwood. She's frantic about her boys. No news about Richard and Tom in that dreadful place. And still no word about your cousin, Jacob. These are the boys we should be worrying about.'

'I saw a man with only one leg in church on Christmas day,' Frederick said. 'He had crutches, but he nearly fell over when we were leaving the church. Bobby Linton said he had it blown off at Lone Pine.'

Emma gasped. 'What do you know of such things, Frederick? You boys shouldn't be talking about it at all. In fact, that man shouldn't have come to church like that. It reminds us all of what's happening. It's terrible.' Her voice trembled and rose in pitch. She drew shaking hands from the table onto her lap.

'Come now, Emma.' Albert tapped his fork on the table and turned from the conversation he was having with David at the end of the table. 'There's no call for you to get yourself all worked up.'

'We can't ignore what's happening at the front, Mother.' David's voice surprised Mabel. He didn't often get involved in trying to calm their mother.

'Seeing the results of the war might help some to decide against going,' David went on. 'It's a tragedy many will have to live with for the rest of their lives.'

'But the ANZACs got away, didn't they?' Frederick looked to Albert.

'There has been a retreat, son,' Albert said. 'Thankfully the offensive at Gallipoli has been abandoned. The ANZACs were evacuated a few days before Christmas. It was a clever move and saw 90,000 men get away under the cover of darkness with no further loss of life. However, after ten months in trenches on that peninsula with futile battle after battle, and the appalling loss of 8,500 Australians, not to mention the many thousands more who were injured, it's hard to celebrate it.'

'But our soldiers were very brave, weren't they?' Frederick looked disappointed by his father's assessment of the situation. 'Bobby said they're heroes.'

'The soldiers have indeed been very brave.' Albert nodded. 'There's no question of the courage of the ANZACs. However, that doesn't excuse the disaster that this has been, and apparently all to the shame of the British generals. In fact, one of our own journalists, Keith Murdoch, can be thanked for bringing the fiasco to the attention of our Prime Minister. As a result of Murdoch's report, at least one British general was dismissed.'

'So is that the end of it now?' Isabel asked. 'Will they all be coming home?'

'Not likely,' David said. 'Those who haven't lost legs or arms are being redeployed to the Western Front so they can keep the Germans out of France. The ones who've come home are like that poor chap at church, crippled, scarred for life. There's still talk of conscription, too. They need more boys to replace the ones they've destroyed.' He gripped his knife and fork as if desperate to hold onto his conviction that the proposition was monstrous.

'It doesn't bear thinking about.' Emma fanned herself with her napkin. 'How could Richard and Tom Grimwood not write and tell their mother what's happening to them?'

'Emma, you must be realistic,' Albert said. 'Some of the men will still be in makeshift hospitals, still fighting for their lives. The logistics of keeping track of the soldiers in that kind of war is beyond our comprehension.'

'And some will never be found,' David added. 'The fact is some will be buried in those trenches, unidentifiable. I hear of so many people getting notices that their sons are Missing in Action. Now that the troops have left Gallipoli, it's likely they'll never find them.'

Emma swayed in her chair. 'Please, Albert. You must stop the boys talking about this. It's enough to send a woman quite mad. We have to believe Richard and Tom will come home and when they do, they'll need our support and care.'

Clara leaned close to Mabel and squeezed her arm. 'At least

Percy's not over there. I'm sure you'll hear from him soon.'

'I hope so,' Mabel said. 'Surely nothing would have induced him to enlist.' She shuddered at the thought.

'Maybe his family wanted him to go,' Frederick said to Isabel, his voice almost a whisper, but not low enough for Mabel to miss.

'Please don't say that, Frederick.' Mabel pushed back in her chair and rose. She couldn't bear to think about it any longer. She looked across the table at her mother. 'I'm sorry to disappoint you, but whatever has happened to Percy, you should know that I'll not be waiting to hold Richard Grimwood's hand when he comes home, no matter how sad his situation is.'

She could hear her mother weeping as she left the dining room, but she would not be shamed into turning her thoughts to Richard Grimwood. Whatever reason Percy had for not contacting her, she was sure it was not a thoughtless act. There was a good reason and she prayed he had not been convinced by some pro-war activist that his duty was to fight for his country. As her fears swirled through her mind she ran towards her bedroom, letting the tears flow freely down her face.

***

As the long afternoon finally faded into dusk, Mabel heard a tap on her door. She'd spent the past few hours writing a letter to Percy. Perhaps he hadn't received the previous one she'd sent. The postal service might not be good in small towns. Maybe her letter had been misplaced or gone astray. None of which explained why she had not received a letter from him. Perhaps his went astray. Her mind went around and around, but it had helped to pen her thoughts again to him, to give him the latest news about the Wagners, and to tell him how much she was looking forward to seeing him again.

'Come in,' she said in response to the knock, praying it wasn't her mother. 'Isabel, hello. Did Mother send you? I'm perfectly all right, you know. I haven't had an asthma attack for months, so I don't know why she's fussing so. I've been enjoying the quiet here in my room.'

'Mother didn't send me.' Isabel held up her hands as if to ward of Mabel's words.

'I'm sorry.' Mabel patted the bed and gestured for her sister to sit down. 'I've just finished another letter to Percy. I'm wondering if he sent me one but it went astray.'

'Perhaps with all the extra mail at Christmas it's been held up.'

Mabel put her arm around Isabel's shoulder. 'You don't think he's forgotten me, do you?'

'Of course not. I'm sure he loves you very much.'

'Thank you, Isabel. You are a dear sister.'

'It must be hard for him to say goodbye to his family again and come back here. It's understandable he'd want to enjoy Christmas with them.'

Mabel chuckled. 'You've really grown up lately, haven't you?'

'I'll be eighteen soon, Mabel. I'm hardly a child.'

'Thank you for coming to cheer me up.'

'Actually, I didn't come to cheer you up. I came to warn you.'

'Warn me? What do you mean?'

'Well, I wasn't sure I should say anything, but I suspect Mother is looking out for your letter and I'm a bit worried she might not give it to you.' Isabel rolled her eyes and shrugged. 'I know that sounds terrible, but for the week leading up to Christmas I noticed that she hurried to pick up the mail from the front table after Beattie put it there. If I were anywhere near it she'd say, "I'll get them" before I could touch the letters. Then she'd flip through the envelopes as if checking who they were from. She was pretending otherwise, but she's not very subtle.'

'Do you think she was looking for a letter from Percy?'

Isabel nodded. 'I do. A couple of times I asked if there was something for you because I know how much you've been hoping for a letter.'

'And?' Mabel's stomach churned.

'She just shook her head and when she'd finished looking through the envelopes, she put the mail down without even opening it. She'd say, "It's only Christmas cards. I'll read them later" and then I'd check there wasn't one for you.'

'You don't think Mother would keep a letter from me, do you?'

'I'm not sure. When I mentioned that you'd be hoping for a letter from Percy, she said, "Even if there were one, it would only hurt her, and we don't want that, do we?" I'm sure she doesn't want you to be hurt by Percy not coming back, but she'd also be pleased herself if he didn't.'

Mabel sighed. 'I know she'd rather me wait for Richard Grimwood, but that's not going to happen.'

'I know, but Mother doesn't let go of an idea easily.'

'You're right, Isabel. Do you think she might already have hidden a letter from Percy?'

'I don't think so. I kept an eye on her when you were at the bakery. She wouldn't let me go and help, so I thought the least I could do was keep a watch out for you.'

They both giggled. 'Poor Mother.' Mabel shook her head. 'I know she wants what's best for me, but she doesn't understand that I've given my heart to Percy and I'm as determined to fight for him as all these young men are to fight for what they believe in.'

Isabel lay down on the bed and stared at the ceiling. 'How romantic. I do hope I fall in love like you have.'

'You will, sister dear. And when you do you'll know that nothing will stand in your way. Perhaps you'll fall in love with someone Mother approves of and you won't have any worries at all.' Mabel fell back on the pillow beside Isabel and they chuckled together.

***

222

The following morning Mabel sat on the front porch of the house with a cup of tea and the book she'd been reading. It was a bright, sunny day but not so hot as the previous days had been. She was enjoying the cool breeze, the chirping of birds in the nearby shrubs and also keeping one eye on the gate at the end of the driveway to the house.

'What are you doing out here, dear?' Emma's voice broke into the peace.

'I'm having a cup of tea and reading my book, Mother. Isn't it obvious?'

'Why can't you do that inside in the cool of the house? You'll get terribly overheated out here and who knows what seeds and dust are flying about.' Emma ran her hands through the back of Mabel's hair.

'Really, Mother, you do fuss. I haven't had any trouble with my asthma all summer. I'm perfectly happy here.' Mabel looked up at her and grinned. 'Besides,' she said, deciding to be completely open, 'I'm waiting for the mail. When I see the postman's cart, I intend to walk down to the gate and collect it.'

Emma's eyes flew open. 'Why on earth would you do that?'

'Because I expect a letter from Percy any day now and I'd hate for it to get mixed up with other mail and be misplaced.' She kept her gaze on her mother's face and narrowed her eyes.

Emma coughed and waved her handkerchief in front of her face. 'Really, Mabel, you do go on. Why should that happen?'

'Why indeed, Mother? I'm sure you'd rather I didn't see a letter from Percy, wouldn't you?'

Emma shifted around in front of Mabel and looked down the path to the gate. 'I would be concerned for you to get such a letter, dear, but only because I feel sure it will not say what you want to hear.'

Mabel remained quiet, intrigued as to her mother's reasoning.

Emma went on without facing Mabel. 'Your father told me

what Percy said about his past. Quite disturbing, all of it, and frankly I'm pleased he's gone back to sort it all out. That said, if he's as decent as you like to think, surely he'll realise he needs to stay with his family and take his responsibilities seriously.'

'So you think coming back here and marrying me would be irresponsible?'

Emma turned to her and smiled. 'Really, Mabel, marriage to Percy would be quite unsuitable. I'm hoping he comes to terms with the fact that he has little to offer you. He could never keep you in the manner you need. I can't see how he could take care of you. He has little idea—'

'Actually, Mother,' Mabel cut in. 'I think all of that is nonsense. Percy is very responsible and he has a clear idea of what is necessary for marriage. It may not be the same as what you and Father have … right away. But I trust Percy completely, and you might as well know that I have every intention of marrying him.'

'But …'

'No buts, Mother. I accept that you want what's best for me, but it's time for you to accept that I'm ready to make my own decisions. I know what I have to deal with in regard to my asthma, but I won't let it rule my life. I know what I want for my future now and I'd love for you to trust me to make good choices. You and Father have prepared me well for life, but now it's time for you to let me go.'

Emma's face paled as Mabel spoke and her bottom lip trembled. She turned away and gripped the railing around the porch.

'There's so much sadness in the world today, Mother. So much loss. Can't you be happy for me? Please?'

Emma was silent for moments and Mabel could see her beginning to sway.

Mabel sighed. 'Perhaps you should go inside, Mother. I think the heat is getting to you. We don't want you fainting.'

She was surprised but relieved when Emma turned back to her and touched her cheek lightly. 'I'll try, Mabel. I will try. I do love you.' As tears welled in her eyes she headed to the front door and disappeared inside.

***

Percy's letter arrived the following day. Mabel was waiting. As she walked slowly back from the front gate she tore the envelope open. With her heart beating in her chest, her stomach churning, she began to read.

Dearest Mabel, how I've missed you. I've wanted to write so many times, but am so concerned for my mother's health that I fear some days I will lose her. You'll be pleased, I'm sure, to know that my father and I are reconciled. We don't talk all that easily, but it's always been that way. I know at least I have assured him that I want no father but him. I've talked with him about my plans for the future and I have so many of those that my head is bursting with them.

Mabel took a deep breath. *Do his plans still include me? Was Mother right?* She was almost afraid to read on.

It's now two weeks on from the beginning of my letter, my dearest. I can't tell you how relieved I am to be able to say that Mum is doing quite well and I have a new baby sister, Alice. She's a very frail child, but will be much loved here. As for all my plans, I can't wait to talk to you about them in person, but uppermost is my plan to return to Adelaide and talk to your father about setting a wedding date. That is, if you'll still have me! I'll see you as soon as possible after Christmas, which my sisters insist I spend with them. I'm sure there will be family celebrations for your family too and I hope you enjoy them. I trust this letter is not too held up with Christmas mail. All my love, Percy.

Mabel could not wipe the smile from her face. Almost skipping through the front door, she dropped the other mail on the entry table and hurried into the house.

'Isabel, where are you?' she called as she went from room to room. Finding her sister in the kitchen, tasting Beattie's rock cakes, she waved the letter in the air.

'It's come, it's come.'

Isabel smiled with a mouth full of cake. 'From Percy?'

Mabel nodded. 'It is, and he's coming back. He should be here any day now. This was sent before Christmas. You were right. It must have been held up.'

'I'm so happy for you.' Isabel threw her arms around Mabel and they hugged, doing a little jig around the kitchen table.

'It must be very good news.' Beattie grinned at them.

'The best news, Beattie,' Mabel said. 'I think you should begin thinking about how we can get special treats for a wedding.'

Beattie's eyebrows rose and her eyes lit up. 'Well, well, and do your parents know about this wedding?'

'They will soon enough.' Mabel chuckled. 'But let's just keep it between us for now. I really should allow my future husband to ask Father formally for my hand, shouldn't I?' She held out her arm as if accepting the hand of another, and half curtsied.

'Isabel, I'm so happy I don't know what to do with myself.' The sisters hugged again. 'You will be my bridesmaid, won't you? Let's go and talk about our dresses. I don't think we'll have much time when Percy gets back. I don't intend to wait a minute longer than necessary.'

Isabel swooned and followed her from the kitchen.

'What are you two so happy about?' Their father's voice came from behind them as they started up the stairs.

Mabel turned and rushed into his arms. 'Father, I am happy. You will be happy for me, won't you? You will say "yes" when Percy asks you for my hand in marriage, won't you? You have seen how responsible and kind and generous he is, haven't you?'

Isabel laughed behind her. 'So much for waiting.'

'Goodness me.' Albert held her back from him and looked her up and down. 'What on earth has brought this on?' He glanced at her hand and saw the letter. 'I see. You've had word from Percy? He's coming back, I gather.'

Mabel nodded. Her eyes filled with happy tears. 'He's going to talk to you about a wedding date, Father. He has lots of plans and he'll tell us all about them when he gets here. You will listen, won't you? You will agree?'

'I don't even know what his plans are, dear, except it's obvious you're hoping wedding plans are part of them.' He laughed. 'When will he be here?'

'Soon. He said soon in the letter, but he wrote that before Christmas. I think he'll be here any day.' Mabel spun on her heels and clutched the letter to her breast.

'Well, I can hardly say no if he's as delirious with joy as you are about the prospects of marriage.'

She threw herself back into his arms and hugged him. 'Thank you, thank you, Father, I knew you'd agree. I must go to Aunt Sarah's tomorrow and tell her the news. She'll be almost as happy to see Percy again as I will be. You will tell Mother that everything's going to be fine, won't you? You will convince her to be agreeable. Percy has tried so hard to win her over.'

Albert nodded. 'I know he's tried, and he may well have to continue to try with her until such times as she's convinced he can adequately take care of you. That's what sons-in-law have to do.' He chucked her under the chin. 'All will be well, my dear. Let's take one step at a time, eh? Percy isn't even here yet.'

***

Two days later Mabel almost knocked Beattie over when the front door bell rang. She threw it open and flew into Percy's arms.

227

'I knew it would be you. I just knew it,' she cried, burying her head in his shoulder. 'I've missed you so. It's been the longest two months of my life.'

Percy laughed and stroked her back. 'It has for me, too, but it's over now.' He pushed her back and smiled into her face. 'You are such a lovely sight.' He pulled her close again and she melted into him, savouring the strength of his arms.

'Good afternoon, Percy.' Albert's voice came from the path leading up to the front door. He strode onto the porch and patted Percy on the back as Mabel reluctantly moved back from their embrace. 'You've been sorely missed, young man. I trust all is well with your family?'

Mabel knew her father's question held levels of inquiry. 'Percy has a new sister, Father, and his mother is much better. Isn't that right, Percy?'

Percy nodded. 'And things are much improved between my father and I,' Percy said, extending his hand to shake Albert's. 'We had a good talk and resolved things. I feel very relieved.'

Albert nodded, his face showing approval. A sense of relief flowed through Mabel.

'I hope there's not been too much bad news in regard to the war for your family and friends, Percy,' Albert continued. 'It seems not too many are spared some heartache.'

Percy nodded. 'We've been fortunate in that way, Mr Smart, and very thankful for it. Clearly the fighting is not over yet, though, nor arguments about conscription, so none of us knows what we'll have to face in the months ahead. There are tensions around Mororo, as in most places, about the internments, so my family remains uneasy about what might happen for our relatives. We can only pray that sanity is restored to our country before too long.'

'Agreed. We must all trust that God will see us through it, whatever happens.' Albert tapped Percy on the shoulder. 'Come on inside.' He gestured towards the open door. 'We'll get Beattie to make us a cup of tea. I'm sure she has some fruit cake left from Christmas. You missed quite a treat here, Christmas day, but I'm sure your family was glad to have you with them.'

'They were, Mr Smart. We had a good celebration. Not a lot of fancy food, but a lot to be thankful for.'

'I'm sure, son. I'm sure.' Albert led the way to the parlour and pulled out a chair for himself. 'Why don't we sit here? Mabel, would you ask Beattie about the tea, please? I think Percy and I have a few things to discuss. It's the first day of a new year and time to look forward to some blessings, don't you think so, young man?'

Mabel squeezed Percy's arm and left the room. She felt as if her heart had wings. After chatting with Beattie in the kitchen for a moment, she asked, 'Where's Mother?'

'I think she's still walking in the rose garden out back,' Beattie said, filling the kettle.

'Good,' said Mabel. 'I think you'd best make her a strong cup of tea for when she comes in, thanks, Beattie. She's going to need it.' She could hear the maid's giggle as she pushed through the kitchen door and headed back to the parlour and her husband-to-be.

EPILOGUE

Sydney Station, December 1919

There was a hiss of wheels as the train glided into Sydney station and stopped.

'Right, you lot,' Percy said, tapping Mabel on the knee. 'We have to change here for the northern train.' He lifted his two-year-old son from his lap as he stood, and placed him in Mabel's arms. 'Can you manage to get the children onto the platform, dear? I'll get the bags.'

A few minutes later, they were standing in front of the train schedule. 'There we are,' Percy said, pointing to the board. 'We have to go upstairs to another platform, but we have half an hour or so. No rush.'

As he smiled down at his daughter, he noticed her staring off to their right. When he followed her gaze, he saw a small group of men in uniform. Their haggard faces and downcast eyes struck him immediately.

'Are those men going to the war, Daddy?' Sylvia asked.

'No, dear, the war is over now. I suspect they're heading home.' *A year now since the fighting ended, but clearly it's not over for these poor devils.*

'Then why do they look so sad, Daddy? Grandpa said we won the war.'

'Yes, dear. We did win the war, but it's still sad for them to have been away from their families for so long. I imagine they're very tired. I'm sure they'll be happier when they get home.'

Percy noticed Mabel brushing hair back from Raymond's forehead and keeping her eyes averted from the soldiers. *No doubt, she's thinking about her cousins who never returned. All heroes, but at such cost!*

'Let's head upstairs, Mabel. We don't want to miss our train. Can you manage?'

Mabel nodded and hoisted Raymond higher on her hip. She reached for Sylvia's hand. 'Come on, sweetie. You mustn't stare.'

***

The next morning, Jacko Wiblin was waiting at the station at Maclean to meet them. Percy and Jacko talked all the way to Mororo in the cart about the progress of their business ventures and prospects for the future. It was all exciting for Percy. He was ready for new challenges.

'And your family?' Percy said as they approached the farm.

'Thriving,' Jacko said with a grin. 'Vera is blooming. Our Doreen is nearly three now and a real trick.'

'I'm already three,' Sylvia said from the back seat.

Percy laughed. 'Yes, and you don't miss a trick either, do you?'

'She hasn't stopped twisting and turning on this seat, trying to see everything we've passed.' Mabel chuckled. 'I don't know how she's heard what you men are talking about.'

'I saw a kangaroo,' Sylvia said. 'And lots of birds.'

'You sound just like our Doreen.' Jacko half turned on the front bench and winked at her. 'I'm sure you two will be great friends.'

'I can't believe three of my sisters are married and have children.' Percy shook his head. 'And two of them to Lange boys.'

'I'd be surprised if it's the last wedding between your family and theirs, actually,' Jacko said. 'All the kids are as thick as thieves.

There's been a lot of good support amongst the families around Mororo during the war years. We've had to rely on each other.'

Percy's heart sank. He knew Jacko meant no slight on him and was well aware he'd been sending money home these past four years. However, it was hard for Percy not to regret being away from his family for so long. He'd been torn, wanting to do the best by Mabel and longing to care for those he loved here in his home town. He breathed in deeply, letting the smells and sounds of the bush fill him. He was very glad to be home.

***

'What a great celebration Christmas is going to be this year,' Vera said, as she settled the children around the table at Fanny and Jack's home the next day. 'So much to be thankful for.'

She kissed Percy on the top of his head and squeezed Mabel's shoulders, after making sure they had pride of place in the centre of the family. 'This is our official welcome home to you two … I mean four,' she corrected herself, winking across the table at Sylvia, who was seated between two of her young cousins and clearly lapping up the attention.

There was a robust round of applause from the gathering.

'Thank you,' Percy said, smiling at his family before looking around at the array of food on the table. 'I can see you've all gone to a lot of trouble to prepare this. I can't imagine Christmas being grander. Mabel and I are thrilled to be here, aren't we, dear?' He put an arm around Mabel's shoulder.

'I'm quite overwhelmed, really,' she said. 'You've all been so welcoming.' Her voice cracked slightly and it was clear she couldn't go on.

'Were there lots of celebrations in South Australia last year when the war ended?' Connie asked as everyone began to eat.

Percy glanced at Mabel before he answered, reluctant to

encourage talk about the war now that they were home. He wanted Mabel to look forward, to put the sadness and loss behind her.

'Of course there was plenty of celebrating,' he said. 'Parties in the streets all around Adelaide, and in most towns people danced and sang for days. The soldiers have been welcomed home all year with great fanfare. There's no doubting the country's jubilation about the end of the fighting.'

He paused for a moment and took a bite of chicken, choosing his words carefully. 'However, so many families are still counting the cost that it's hard to think of the war without sadness. What with the commemorations for the fallen, rehabilitation for the returned, and then managing the outbreak of the flu epidemic, it's been difficult to look to the future, but hopefully we can begin to do that now.'

'It's certainly been frightful to see the young men who've returned here with terrible injuries. They'll never be the same again.' Fanny leaned into Percy's side and took his hand. She'd hardly walked past him all day without touching him on the shoulder or back, without stroking his cheek or her eyes filling up. He knew she was happy beyond words that he was home, and grateful he was in one piece.

He squeezed her fingers. 'Yes, Mum. The cost has been great.' He thought of the haggard souls of men he saw at the station yesterday. 'Our family has been very fortunate to have come through it with so little suffering.'

Fanny reached across Percy and patted Mabel's hand. 'I know your family has not been so blessed, dear. I'm so sorry for all your losses. It must be terribly hard to think about.'

Mabel nodded and her eyes filled. 'It is, Mrs Smith. Many of my mother and father's families have suffered greatly.'

'I read that there's an estimated 60,000 dead out of 230,000 Australians sent to the front, and around 166,000 wounded.' John Lange's voice came from the other end of the table. 'Sometimes

I wonder if the newspapers will ever stop reporting about the war. The Great War, they call it. Nothing like it in history. More countries involved than any previous war, and over 10 million perished. I don't know what's "great" about that.'

'And if the government had won the push for conscription, it would have been even worse,' Jack said.

Percy could see the familiar hard line of his father's jaw and wondered if the war had deepened the struggle that life seemed to be for Jack. Perhaps the hostility against the Germans had been a more painful thing for him to witness than any of them realised.

'I agree, Dad. I was relieved to see the vote on conscription defeated,' he said, catching his father's eye, wanting to reconnect with him as genuinely as possible. Their reunion this time had been surprisingly warm. Percy had no doubt that his father was pleased to have him home, and although he wondered if it was still more for his mother's sake than for Jack's, Percy was determined to work towards a better relationship with his father in the future.

'It has been dreadful for families like mine who saw so many go to fight, Mrs Smith,' Mabel said, her soft voice breaking into a moment of silence. 'But I've also been very sad for families like yours who've had to face internment, or the possibility of it.'

'Thank you, dear,' Fanny said. 'It has been a trial, though I don't think the suffering has been nearly as bad for us.' She leaned forward and smiled at Mabel. 'But please call me "Mum". I couldn't bear to be called Mrs Smith for the rest of our lives together.'

Mabel returned her mother-in-law's smile and her cheeks flushed. Percy put his arm around her shoulder. 'I'm sure Mabel will feel more comfortable with that, too, Mum.' He turned to Mabel. 'After all, Alice wouldn't know who you were referring to if you said "Mrs Smith", would she?' He chuckled as his youngest sister, just twelve months older than his daughter, climbed from her chair, tucked herself under Fanny's elbow and nestled into her chest.

***

Percy drew Mabel close and she snuggled into his shoulder as they settled into bed that night.

'I do love your family, Percy. They've been so good to me already.'

'How could they not be, my darling? I told you they'd adore you. I thought my sisters would never stop hugging you and asking a million questions. It's just as well we don't all live together. They'd wear you out.'

She sighed and looked up at him. 'We will have more children, won't we, Percy?'

'Of course we will, in time, dear. For now I want you to concentrate on getting strong and enjoying our new home. I know we've started small here in the cottage, but I intend to build you a wonderful home, with a verandah along the side and big windows, so the sun comes in, even in winter. And I'm going to get a motor car as soon as I can, and a telephone, and perhaps one of those new pianolas I've seen advertised. Everything your heart desires. I want you to have everything that will make you happy. So many things will be possible now that the war is over. We can look forward to a wonderful future.'

'Oh, Percy, what a dreamer you are. That all sounds lovely, and I'm sure you'll do it all, but you must know that all my heart desires is to be with you. I'm already very happy.' Her last words faded with drowsiness.

Percy watched the smile on her face relax as she sank into sleep. He kissed the top of her head and dropped back on his pillow, his mind filling with dreams of the future.